Andrea Newman is the

A Bouquet of Barbed Wire,

successful television scripts. She has also written numerous other television drama serials, including *A Sense of Guilt, Imogen's Face* and the forthcoming *An Evil Streak*. She divides her time between London and Sussex.

Also by Andrea Newman

An Evil Streak

Andrea Newman

WARNER BOOKS

A *Warner* Book

First published in 1977 by Michael Joseph Ltd
This edition published by Warner Books 1999

A CIP catalogue record for this book
is available from the British Library.

ISBN 0 7515 2951 6

Printed and bound in Great Britain by
Clays Ltd, St Ives plc

Warner Books
A Division of
Little, Brown and Company (UK)
Brettenham House
Lancaster Place
London WC2E 7EN

The author is indebted to Professor Nevill Coghill, from whose translation of Chaucer's *Troilus and Criseyde* (Penguin 1971) the epigraphs are taken.

Book 1

'I sing their pain as best I can'

One

That she had intended to die tidily in the bathroom was clear
enough from the amount of blood in the bath, but, being
completely unscientific, she had no idea how long the process
would take, and at some point, through either boredom or
panic, she had endeavoured to reach the sitting-room, leaving
a trail of blood to mark her slow progress along the corridor.
When I found her she was sprawled across my newly uphol-
stered brocade sofa, her leaking wrists still marginally out of
reach of the phone.

Two

But if you prefer to begin at the very beginning, I have no objection. When Beatrice asked me to be Gemma's godfather, I remember I made one of my feebler jokes (to cover my surprise and embarrassment, I think). I remarked in my flippant way that this would be the closest link God and I were ever likely to enjoy. Beatrice of course did not laugh, nor even favour me with a smile. She was shocked. She was always the kind of woman who shocked easily (a constant temptation to me) and more so, I suppose, since the death of her husband. To have a funeral and a christening within so short a space of time not unnaturally fixed her mind upon higher things. Eternity was, if not in her lips and eyes, certainly in the forefront of her thoughts, leaving no room for irreverence.

Holding the squalling infant wrapped in the family shawl, I pondered the words of the service, the life of rectitude to which the child was being condemned by proxy. I was responsible. Surely the works and pomps of Satan, whatever they were, would be more fun? The cries faded as the discomforts of virtue eased, and the red-faced, wrinkled creature looked at me with my dead brother's eyes.

Gemma was a posthumous child and even I, self-cast cynic that I am, could see the pathos in that. My brother Hugh was on his way home in 1945, having served his country with hardly a scratch, as they say, making us all believe that his was indeed a charmed life, when he carelessly stepped on a mine and blew himself up, together with several of the men serving under him. It was a messy accident that need never have occurred, and it took me some months to recompose his features in my mind — to stop picturing fragments of Hugh scattered all over the oft-quoted foreign field.

People tend to think, because I am flippant and cynical, that I have no feelings. That is untrue. I cared deeply for Hugh. I felt for him the kind of obsessive love that only jealousy can inspire, for he excelled in everything — looks, charm, sport, study and luck — and I was proud of my defeat. As he was younger than I, my progress through school and college preceded his, and my notable mediocrity provided him with, as it were, a plain carpet on which to perform and dazzle. I would even go so far as to say that his death was a greater loss to me than to his wife. But, as I am often reminded, I know nothing of marriage.

Beatrice's grief was genuine enough: they had not been married for sufficiently long to become either quarrelsome or bored. I simply did not regard her as a creature of much depth. No doubt she felt as much as she could and it was not her fault that her capacity for feeling was so limited. She was intensely practical, not given to flights of fancy, displays of emotion or any kind of introspective excess.

My brother Hugh had made the army his career and had seen ten years' service at the time of his death. Beatrice settled down with her child to a life of the middle-class poverty that some people call comfort, much in the way my mother had done with us in 1917 after our father was killed. It was unpleasant to see the pattern being repeated: the large house divided into flats and let to a succession of quiet, childless couples, for motherhood had not made Beatrice fonder of other people's children even at a distance, and certainly not in contact with her own property. Her pension was insufficient for her needs and the family assets, such as they were, shrank severely when my mother died and death duties had to be paid.

My mother had resisted all persuasion to make sensible provision well ahead of this event, seeming to believe it was less likely to occur with each year she survived. And, like many old people, she had not only clung to belief in her own immortality but also cherished her money as the only source of power remaining to her. She was not a greedy or a selfish woman but she wanted to give in her own good time. Useless to explain covenants, bequests, deeds of gift to her. She saw no urgency because she intended to live for ever. Meanwhile, money warmed her old age like a shawl.

She did, however, go so far as to make a will — a small concession to family pressure — and when this was read to us (the greatest possible secrecy having surrounded it during her lifetime) it provoked, as wills do, a family scene. Beatrice was horrified to discover that only half the estate came to her. The other half had been left to me. But since I was a bachelor and she had a child to support, it was obvious that she was entitled to two thirds and I to one. She argued this forcibly and I was compelled to agree; in fact it seemed prudent to agree before she concocted some even more specious argument and succeeded in proving that I was only entitled to a quarter or maybe a fifth. 'Surely you want to make proper provision for your own god-daughter,' she said, and I suddenly caught a whiff of the panic my mother must have felt. It was irrelevant to point out to Beatrice that the money was my mother's to dispose of as she wished and that we had even a moral duty to respect her wishes and abide by her decision. I genuinely believe I would have felt this if my mother had left me nothing but I could not hope to make Beatrice accept such a fanciful idea. I paid up. It was, after all, in Gemma's interest that I should do so.

Gemma was a beautiful child, and I speak as one who finds most children nauseating. I avoided her as far as possible until she reached the age of four, which is where, it seems to me, the humanising process begins. I wanted nothing to do with the moist and scruffy little animal preceding that stage, and I was rewarded for my patience. Gemma at four was enchanting. Nothing at all like her mother, fortunately (Beatrice is one of those rare and unlucky women who combine blonde hair and brown eyes with sallow skin and a large nose), but the image of dead Hugh, dark-haired and pale, with the same enormous cornflower-blue eyes, a colour so vivid as to be almost vulgar, surrounded by thick, dark lashes that looked as if they had been painted on. I was proud to be seen with her: I have always been much affected by beauty. Some people regard this as a vice or a weakness, but I do not. I took Gemma out once or twice a week, the more public the place the better, so that I could be envied and she admired; I bought her imaginative presents at Christmas and birthdays, considerably taxing my bachelor ingenuity, since I scorned to ask advice from Beatrice; but I never gave her money again after the affair of my mother's will. I considered I had given her enough.

Beatrice was pleased to see that I took my godfatherly duties so much to heart. 'She needs a man's influence,' she used to say. 'It's not good for a girl to grow up without a father.' Then she would stare at me suspiciously. (My family secretly fear that because I have never married I must be homosexual or a womaniser: they have not considered that I could be both, or neither.) It was unnerving and absurd, like being surveyed across a hedge by an anxious cow.

Occasionally, as a cure for insomnia, I would give my mind to the problem of why my brother Hugh, who could have had any girl whose path he happened to cross, should have chosen to marry Beatrice. I know, of course, that human nature, like God, moves in a mysterious way — it was this fact that first attracted me to a literary career — but the marriage of Hugh and Beatrice seemed more inexplicable than any other event I had ever observed. If I had been a believer in providence I should have said that they had been permitted to marry purely in order to produce Gemma. The achievement of Gemma and the brevity of the marriage would seem to bear me out. But I am not a believer in providence, inclining to the view that any supernatural agency there may be tends to the malicious rather than the benign, so let that pass. They married, Hugh died, and Gemma was born. I cannot think so ill of my brother as to believe that the marriage would have lasted had he lived.

Beatrice is a woman much given to moderation and I am a great believer in excess, so Gemma and I became conspirators from an early age. Most of my time with her was spent ensuring that she had more of everything than Beatrice considered good for her. If I took her out to tea I would ply her with cake and cream buns, éclairs and meringues, jelly and orange juice, until guilt overcame her natural greed. 'I mustn't have any more,' she would say eventually, her eyes round with longing. I would ask why not. 'Because Mummy'll be cross.' Then I would produce my ace. 'But Mummy won't know.' Poor Gemma wrestled with her conscience and generally lost.

'Now I don't want you making that child sick again,' said Beatrice before our next outing.

'Gemma's never sick,' I said righteously. 'Are you, Gemma?'

She shook her head, nervous and excited at being caught in the adult crossfire.

'Well, last time you took her out she couldn't eat her supper and she was nearly green when I put her to bed,' said Beatrice, snapping her thin mouth trap shut.

'What nonsense,' I said. Gemma trembled: no one else ever spoke to her mother like that.

It was the same when Beatrice went out in the evening. As Gemma grew older I took to spending occasional weekends with her and Beatrice in the country. It was pleasant for me to get out of London sometimes and Beatrice would take advantage of my presence to visit various people she claimed were friends, leaving me alone with Gemma. The game then was for me to persuade Gemma to stay up beyond the prescribed bedtime hour. I usually succeeded, and a delightful atmosphere of wickedness would build up during the evening. 'Just one more round,' I would say if we were playing cards, and watch the ensuing struggle with her conscience as Gemma's eyes crept guiltily to the advancing clock. On the most spectacular occasions she would be flying up the stairs in her nightdress as Beatrice scraped her key in the lock at midnight.

'What time did that child get to sleep?' Beatrice demanded at breakfast. 'She could hardly get up for church this morning and she had great dark circles under her eyes.'

I shrugged innocently. 'I put her to bed when you told me but I've no idea when she went to sleep. Do you want me to spy on her?'

She stared at me. 'What extraordinary words you use.'

'It's my profession,' I said smugly.

'You don't let her read in bed, do you?' she accused me. 'She'll only strain her eyes.'

'Read in bed?' I echoed, shocked. 'Of course not.' And remembered the golden days of Gemma's childhood when I had read her Grimm and Hans Andersen, the little mermaid dancing as if on knives for her love, the girl spinning till her

14

fingers bled and she dipped the spinning-wheel in the well and lost it, the horse's head fixed above the gate, the dwarf putting a ring of hair on the girl's finger, and later, something about being flayed alive. Those were our favourites, when Beatrice imagined we were still with Little Grey Rabbit. I watched Gemma turn pale as I read; I would stop and wait till she begged me to go on. Eventually Beatrice's voice would peal up the stairs: 'That's enough now, you two,' and I would drag myself away, downstairs to a good dinner with a dull woman. In the morning, accusation. 'Whatever did you read to that child? She had nightmares.'

'Did you give her cheese for supper?' I enquired.

Beatrice sighed; she was building a great reputation for martyrdom. 'Really, Alex, it's too bad. You come down here and get her over-excited and I have to cope with the results. You've no idea how hard it is to bring up a child alone. You really mustn't undermine everything I do.'

'Perhaps, if you feel like that, you'd rather I didn't come at all.' My injured voice. I was surprised that it worked: I daily expected Beatrice to put a complete ban on my visits. But that, I suppose, was too extreme an action for her temperament, and besides she had a curious sense of family loyalty. I was the only male relative left on whom she could depend, and of course I was Gemma's godfather. A rift was unthinkable, and would have reflected on her judgment. I used to fear that she might remarry, which would have reduced my influence considerably, but luckily her natural endowments made this unlikely, and as time went by, my position became completely secure.

Three

Gemma at fourteen started to become interesting. Hitherto, she had been an attractive plaything, with all the charm of a puppy or kitten. But there is, necessarily, a limited amount of subversion that can be practised on a child. My scope was restricted by her age. Oddly enough, it was Beatrice who alerted me to the first crisis. We had met for lunch on one of her rare shopping expeditions to town. I could not see the necessity for shopping, since nothing she bought could possibly enhance her appearance, but she seemed to consider these periodic efforts essential.

She behaved strangely through lunch, not listening to the anecdotes I had prepared to amuse her. She was absent-minded, vague, unlike herself. I studied her face, while I talked and she failed to listen, and thought how rapidly she was ageing. The make-up she used, though it probably qualified as discreet, settled itself in the folds of her face, the frown creases on her forehead, the wrinkles round her eyes, the streaks of dissatisfaction that ran from nose to mouth. She ate too much and took no exercise, so a double chin was emerging, apart from the comfortable spread of her figure under her clothes; and her lipstick, too dark to be flattering, leaked into the sharp, fine cracks she had etched in her mouth by pursing her lips too often in disapproval. She was too young to be running to seed in this way, but it was happening nevertheless. I was glad that my brother Hugh was not there to see it.

'I've got to talk to you about Gemma,' she said abruptly. 'I'm very worried about her. She's met this boy. Well, he goes to the local boys' school but he's always hanging about the gates, waiting for her. He walks her home and they stand around talking for hours. I think she likes him.' She looked at me despairingly. 'I don't know what to do.'

'Need you do anything?' I was soothing. 'It's natural, isn't it? She's bound to start getting interested in boys sooner or later.'

'Well, I thought later rather than sooner,' said Beatrice sharply. She was really worried. 'He's quite unsuitable. Peter Hughes. His father runs a bicycle shop in the village. I don't want Gemma associating with people like that.'

'Unless she's planning to become a child bride, does it really matter whom she associates with?' The words struck me as quaint, more suited to a description of criminal activity than adolescent friendship.

'Of course it matters,' said Beatrice. 'There's no knowing where these things will lead if they're not checked. I am solely responsible for her, after all. If any harm should come to her, it would be my fault. People are very merciless about parents these days. Whatever happens, it's always the parents' fault.'

'But why should anything happen, Beatrice?' I asked. 'And what sort of happening do you have in mind?'

To my amazement she flushed: A blonde, sallow woman, prematurely faded, with dull red cheeks, is an extraordinarily unattractive sight. I fixed my gaze on a distant pot-plant, green and inoffensive.

'You must know what I mean,' she said.

I let her flounder for a few seconds. 'A romantic entanglement,' I said finally. 'Romeo and Juliet. Well, she's the right age. Stolen kisses behind the shrubbery. Would that be so terrible?'

'I wish you'd be serious,' said poor Beatrice. 'She's far too young for any nonsense like that. I don't want her being mauled by common boys from the village.'

'Would it help if his father was a lord?' I enquired.

'If she makes herself cheap, she'll get a bad reputation,' said Beatrice. 'And you know what that means. All she's got are her looks and her good name. She's not a clever girl, I'm afraid. Last term's report was most discouraging.'

'You sound as if you're trying to sell her to the highest bidder,' I said. 'Isn't it a little early for such desperate measures?'

'She's not a clever child,' Beatrice repeated. 'I've got to be practical. She's very average at school, she's got no special talent. I can't see her having a brilliant career at anything.'

'Therefore she must make a brilliant marriage,' I said. 'Is that what you mean?'

'Well, why not?' She eyed me sternly. 'She'd be very happy if she met the right young man.'

'But not a boy from the bicycle shop. Of course not, I quite see that. Are you afraid his adolescent passion will overcome him? Do you see him flinging Gemma across the seat of his cycle and pedalling off into the distance? Does he perhaps run the junior branch of the Surrey White Slave Trade?'

'You're impossible,' said Beatrice. But she managed to smile.

'What do you want me to do?' I had been flippant long enough.

She looked quite grateful for my change of tone. 'Talk to her,' she said. 'Could you? Explain to her that boys don't respect girls who make themselves cheap. She'll accept it, coming from you.'

'You mean it's not true?'

'I mean she thinks you're a man of the world.' She did not explain what she herself thought I was. 'If *I* tell her, I'm only her mother, trying to spoil her fun. We've already had arguments about what time she comes in. She wants to go to dances in the village and mix with all kinds of people. She complains that some of the other girls have more pocket money to spend. I tell her they have fathers to support them.'

As always with Beatrice I felt uneasy at the mention of money. 'Yes, I do see that a rich husband is the answer,' I said, 'as soon as she reaches the age of consent. Do you think we could falsify her birth certificate, just to be on the safe side?'

'If I didn't know you so well,' said Beatrice, 'I'd be really angry.'

Four

'Mummy's being ridiculous,' said Gemma crossly, curled up in the big armchair. 'Everybody in my form has a boyfriend. I can't be the only one who hasn't, I'd feel so silly.'

'Does that mean any boy would do?' I said. 'Or is Peter special?'

He wasn't, of course. I saw that at once. Her face puckered up with the effort of unaccustomed diplomacy.

'He's all right,' she said slowly. 'He's very nice. I like him.'

'All right,' I said. 'I believe you.'

'Well, you *know*.' She appealed to me, with a gesture of the hands that I found particularly attractive, flexing her spatulate fingers with eloquent helplessness. 'I've got to have someone to go out with, haven't I? I mean I can't not have a partner for the school dance, I'd feel *awful*. Everyone else has got somebody to go with.'

'Yes indeed,' I said. 'It would be dreadful to be a pariah at your age.'

She pouted. 'You're laughing at me. What does that word mean?'

'A social outcast.'

'I thought it was a dog.'

'It can be. Why did you pretend you didn't know what it meant?'

'I don't, not really. It just makes me think of dogs.'

'A dog of low caste in a Hindu village,' I elaborated helpfully.

'Poor dog.'

'I expect it gets used to it. Maybe it doesn't even know.'

'I bet it does. I expect people keep kicking it and throwing stones at it. Are they beastly to dogs in India?'

'I've really no idea.'

'I bet they are,' she said gloomily.

I felt we had exhausted the dog, entertaining as it had been. I had, after all, a duty to Beatrice. 'Gemma,' I said tentatively. 'This boy, what's his name——'

'Peter.'

'Peter. Is he . . . fond of you, do you think?'

She eyed me warily. 'You've been talking to Mummy.'

'Not exactly. She's been talking to me. It's not the same thing.'

'No. Well, tell her he's all right. He doesn't . . . *do* anything.' She flushed. 'That's what she's worried about, isn't it?'

I hesitated. 'Something like that.' I thought we were on dangerous ground and I did not want to stem the flow of adolescent confidences.

'Well, he doesn't.'

She sounded so grumpy that I felt expected, even compelled, to ask, 'Do you wish he would?'

The flush deepened but she showed no sign of wanting to put an end to the conversation. 'Other people's boyfriends do.'

'Do they?' I said. 'Or do they just say they do?'

'I don't know.' She looked grateful. 'That's what I keep wondering. I mean, I don't believe everything I'm told.'

'No,' I said gravely. 'Of course not.'

'But I think it's true. Some of it, anyway. I don't think Janet would tell me lies.'

'Is she your best friend?'

'Yes. She might exaggerate a bit but I think most of it's true. Anyway, Peter's not a bit like her boyfriend. Do you think he really likes me?'

'At least as much as you like him.'

'Oh!'

'Well, he may need a partner for the school dance too.'

'Yes. I hadn't thought of that. So he doesn't really fancy me at all, that's why he hasn't even kissed me.' She stared at her skirt and blushed, looking so young, confused and irresistible that it was all I could do not to kiss her myself.

'Of course he fancies you,' I said. 'He's just being respectful. Your mother would be proud of him.'

'Well, it's a bit boring. I feel terribly out of it when everyone else is talking about what they did at the weekend. I'll have to start making things up soon.' She was totally serious. 'I can't talk to Janet at all at the moment, I'd feel so silly if she knew. I can't talk to anyone.'

'You can talk to me,' I said.

'Can I?' She seemed actually grateful. 'Can I really? You don't mind? You don't think I'm silly?'

'No.'

'And you don't think I'm a dead loss. I mean, you don't think every boy I meet's going to be like Peter?'

'No,' I said. 'I certainly don't.'

She relaxed a little. 'That's all right then. Only — we're doing *Romeo and Juliet* this term and I had to read that speech, you know, the one about the fiery-footed steeds and all that . . .'

'I know the one.'

She looked up, pausing dramatically: such eyes, that a man could have drowned in, or a boy, even such an insensitive retarded lout as Peter obviously was.

'Did you know I'm the same age as Juliet?'

The naivety and self-importance of the young never cease to astonish me. 'Yes. A few weeks younger, actually.'

She lowered her eyes again and I had to content myself with admiring the lashes. 'I wish something would happen.'

Five

Very little did happen, though, for several years: Beatrice saw
to that. Gemma was kept at school for as long as possible, then
transferred to some other establishment where she learnt to
cook, type and arrange flowers. She was not sent abroad:
Beatrice could not accept that any surveillance, however
expensive, would be as effective as her own, and she had
traditionally British fears about the unbridled appetites of
continental men. English appetites, though presumably under
better control, were further diluted by numbers and a deliber-
ate policy of confusion. Gemma's young men — I abandoned
all attempts to memorise their names after the luckless Peter
Hughes had been dismissed — were alternately welcomed and
spurned. 'Mummy's in one of her moods,' became an essential
statement in Gemma's life. Although my sympathies lay
naturally with Gemma, I had to admire — as an artist — the
skill with which Beatrice over-encouraged the young men (till
Gemma grew sick of them) or subtly allowed them to make
fools of themselves, or let them softly perish through cold
neglect. She also developed headaches and various mysterious
ailments, despite which she nobly tried 'to do my best for you,
darling,' so that Gemma, whether coming home reluctantly
early from a dance or sourly submitting to an uncongenial
dinner party, was forced to admit that her mother had only her
welfare at heart and would make any sacrifice to give her
pleasure. Therefore she could not accept these sacrifices and
offered her own instead.

Beatrice was aided, of course, by the fact that none of the
young men provided exactly what Gemma was looking for,
and whatever qualities they did possess were generally lost in
the crowd that Beatrice encouraged under the pretext of giving Gemma 'a good time'. Safety in numbers is a sound

though old-fashioned policy, but I have never seen it pursued with greater verve. Poor Gemma, of course, wanted only to fall in love, but like an animal trying in vain to make a nest, was never allowed to settle long enough to build anything but the most flimsy structure.

We talked, she and I, at intervals, and always with a feeling of trust and intimacy, although often in a vague and elliptical way. Knowing that I was the only person in whom she chose to confide completely (there was a touch of rivalry between her and Janet) was a heady sensation. Listening to her words, seeing the play of emotion on her face, I sometimes felt she was more truly mine than if I had penetrated her. She was still a virgin, I was sure of that. The young men changed constantly; the miracle remained unaccomplished. I ran over her complaints in my mind.

—'He's very attractive and he makes me laugh, but we never talk about anything important.'

—'He's so intellectual—why doesn't he kiss me more often?'

—'He's awfully nice, just like a brother. I wish I fancied him.'

—'I don't feel comfortable with him at all. I keep waiting for him to pounce.'

Affection made me dishonest and, much as I might have lied to a terminal cancer patient about their chances of recovery, I tried to convince her that she would one day find all the qualities she sought in one person — despite all the evidence around her to the contrary. Love, or the desire for love, is after all very like a fatal illness. She latched eagerly onto my reassurances. 'Do you really think I will? Oh, I do hope so. It's not a bit the way I imagined it.' Poor child, she was nourished on romantic literature. 'Give it time; be patient,' I tried to say, but these are the qualities that youth thinks it can least afford. She was almost nineteen. Five years of half-measures, of endless popularity and continual disappointment: that must have been far more searing than my jaundiced middle age. If you expect little or nothing, you are seldom let down, but poor Gemma was young and therefore expected everything.

Six

Christopher Clark: the very name has a fine solid English ring to it. Lacking the affectation of a final 'e', it suggests the courage of its own convictions. Insert the prefix 'Dr' and you have a pillar of society, the dependable middle-class professional man, dedicated to doing good and making money, and seeing no contradiction between the two. No wonder Beatrice was excited.

'Such a nice young man . . . a doctor, you know . . . only thirty . . . and he seems really interested in Gemma.' These essential points were reiterated breathlessly, monotonously, incoherently to me throughout weeks of increasing hysteria. Beatrice had sighted land; she had struck oil; her ship had come in. I realise of course that I mix my metaphors, a practice I normally deplore; but for once only mixed metaphors will serve to convey the flurry of Beatrice's conversation. After a lifetime of wading through shells containing nothing but boring old oysters, she had at last discovered a pearl.

I was reluctant at first to examine this pearl, preferring to indulge my own fantasy. I imagined a hearty young man (Gemma had met him at the tennis club), fair and florid in the traditional English way, inclined to sweat but terribly good in a crisis. Gemma herself did not talk about him: not having heard the wedding bells resounding in Beatrice's ears, she imagined she had merely found a good partner for the mixed doubles tournament. There was, of course, great competition in the village for such an eligible young man, newly arrived in the district to join an expanding practice, but, luckily for Beatrice, Gemma's beauty, her affability and her more than adequate backhand made her a clear winner.

Christopher Clark: I could not have been more wrong about him. A thin young man, taller than I expected when he rose from his chair to greet me; dark-haired, sallow-skinned, almost gaunt in the face as if from fatigue or starvation; looking older than his years, then (a sudden smile lighting up the hollows) looking younger and full of that rare commodity, genuine charm; shaking hands firmly, asking how I was and actually seeming to care. I thought of his patients being greeted by this apparition in the surgery: surely at least half their psychosomatic ailments would disappear on sight.

We waited for Gemma (he was taking her out to dinner to celebrate their victory on the court) and he asked me politely about my journey down, my whereabouts in London, my profession, and the pleasures of weekending in the country, all as if my answers were of the greatest possible concern to him. He chatted amiably about himself in return, but without revealing very much. Perhaps there was not much to reveal.

Gemma was late: a bad sign, I thought. Beatrice called up the stairs to her and plied us with more drinks. I accepted; Christopher Clark declined, as a driver. I applauded his will-power.

'Oh, it's not difficult,' he said deprecatingly. 'I never do drink very much. What I'd really like now is a cigarette but unfortunately I've given them up.'

He spoke as if this had been an accident or an arbitrary decision imposed from above, rather than a matter of his own personal choice. I admired his prudence but I did not warm to him. It is the misfortune of prudence to be admirable rather than attractive. I even began to wonder if Gemma had not in fact found herself rather a dull dog, as they say. Then we heard her step on the stair and the dull dog pricked up its ears and started to wag its tail. I caught a look of complacency on Beatrice's face before she disguised it. Gemma came in, looking and smelling delicious and acting offhand, with the sort of confidence a woman only has when she knows she is about to be unconditionally admired. 'Hullo, Chris, sorry to keep you waiting,' announced carelessly, flung over her shoulder as she turned to me: 'When did *you* get here? Oh, how lovely to see you,' and hugging me, though more for his benefit than mine, I felt.

I did not allow myself to be distracted by Gemma: I made a fuss of her as a loving uncle should but kept my eyes on her escort. His face was flushed; he had knocked over his empty glass (and not even noticed) when he stood up to greet Gemma. Suddenly he seemed too tall, and his hands and feet too large. Now he turned to Beatrice. 'We won't be late back. I'll take great care of her.' Already they were partners in conspiracy. Gemma seemed unconcerned, flitting round the room, cramming nuts and olives into her mouth and sipping Beatrice's sherry. 'Gemma, darling, you can have a drink of your own if you want one,' Beatrice remonstrated lovingly, playing the affectionate mother to Dr Clark's attentive suitor.

'No, no, then we'll be late for dinner and that will never do,' said wicked Gemma, enjoying her power. 'Chris will be cross. Hey, that's rather good. Chris–cross.' She giggled.

'Gemma, that's not fair,' said Beatrice. 'You're much too indulgent with her, Dr Clark.' I heard her revelling in the prefix. Gemma swooped down on us both with goodbye kisses; Dr Clark shook hands. They were gone. Beatrice sat back with a sigh and allowed a smile of self-congratulation to spread over her large face. I poured myself another drink. Before she could ask me what I thought, I said, 'Oh yes, he's in love with her all right.'

Seven

For the first time in her life Gemma became secretive. I knew of course that she and Dr Clark were frequently together but I knew it only because of Beatrice's squeaks of approval, to which I was subjected almost daily on the telephone. Gemma herself said nothing and I felt it would be a confession of weakness to ask. I had never been excluded from her confidence before: I did not know how to handle it. The pain of it surprised me, I who had thought myself at last immune to such humiliations. To have it proved to me that there was still even a fraction of my heart that could be so vulnerable was alarming, to say the least. I feared the loss of control: over Gemma and over myself.

So I could hardly have been more surprised when a few weeks later Dr Clark rang up. He sounded nervous. 'I'm sorry to presume on a brief acquaintance,' he said. 'I got your number from the phone book.'

I was immediately cheered. 'Oh yes,' I said. 'Why not?' He could easily have obtained the information from Gemma or Beatrice: that he had not done so suggested conspiracy, which is always attractive.

'The fact is ——' he said, and hesitated. I didn't help him. 'Well, I want your advice.'

I invited him to lunch at my club, where he appeared ill at ease. After very little small talk he said abruptly, 'You see, the thing is, I want to marry Gemma but I don't know how she feels about me.'

'Well, neither do I,' I said unhelpfully.

'She hasn't talked to you then?' he asked, with an eager acceptance of doom.

'If she has,' I said, 'you can hardly expect me to betray her confidence — now can you?'

'No, of course not.' He played with the food on his plate; he

27

looked more than ever gaunt and shadowed, totally vulnerable. I began to enjoy our conversation. 'I just thought . . . as she thinks so much of you, as your opinion is obviously very important to her . . .'

'Yes?' I was gratified. If Gemma had not talked to me of him, at least it appeared that she had talked to him of me.

'Well, I thought you could give me some idea, I mean if I should speak to her . . . if you think I stand a chance.'

'I can't imagine why you haven't asked her already,' I said, taking pity on him, although in fact the reason was perfectly obvious: love had completely eroded whatever self-confidence he normally possessed. I was interested to observe such an old-fashioned phenomenon at close range: Dr Clark, it struck me, might well have been the hero of a Victorian novel. 'Don't you realise that every mother with a marriageable daughter has been after you from the moment you set foot in the village?'

He smiled. As usual his face lightened, making him seem positively attractive. If Gemma was not in love with him, it could only be because he was so obviously in love with her. 'I wouldn't have noticed,' he said. 'As soon as I saw Gemma ——' He paused, and I wondered what extravagance he was about to commit. 'Well, I suppose it seems ridiculous to you, you can't possibly see her as I do, but to me . . . well, she's everything.'

The usual inadequate hyperbole. I was lost for a moment, witnessing absolute love. Other people's emotions never fail to absorb me. The intensity with which they feel creates my belief in their value as human beings. Unlike me, they have not yet opted out, not yet discovered that human feelings are treacherous and doomed to end sooner or later in boredom or pain. I longed to pitch Dr Clark into this maelstrom of suffering, to see if he would swim or sink: he was obviously yearning for a guiding hand to shove him over the edge. I longed also to involve Gemma in something beyond her control: then surely she would confide in me again. Or was she silent because he had become less manageable and more special? Was she threatening me with a sudden need for privacy?

'So why haven't you asked her?' I said.

28

'Because she might refuse,' he said simply. 'As long as I wait, I can still hope. I really can't ask her without some encouragement, there's too much at stake.'

I considered this man, in his prime, sought-after like an estate agent's favourite district, highly qualified, holding lives melodramatically in his hands when occasion demanded, completely demoralised by a girl I had seen grotesquely bandy in nappies, but who had now grown bewitching enough to torment us both.

'Do you want me to put in a word for you?' I asked, thinking the cliché was all he deserved. And yet I envied him: it wasn't all contempt. He at least stood a chance.

His face lit up flatteringly. 'Would you? Would you really do that?'

'For what it's worth,' I said. 'But I think you overrate my influence.'

'Oh no,' he said curiously. 'I don't think that.'

I was alerted to some danger I could not define. Perhaps I had underestimated Dr Clark. 'Besides,' I went on as if he had not spoken, 'what if too much encouragement had the opposite effect? Gemma's always led a very sheltered life, you know. Her mother's seen to that. Now her mother obviously approves of you. Don't you think the time may have come for Gemma to rebel?'

He looked concerned. 'You mean if her mother didn't approve I might stand more chance?'

'Right in one, Dr Clark,' I said. 'So why should I add my voice to the chorus of approval and ruin your chances altogether?'

I could see that he did not enjoy my levity, but he was obliged, in the circumstances, to go on being civil to me. I saw myself rather as a malingering hypochondriac, tiresomely claiming too much of his time and attention but too profitable to be shaken off.

'What do you suggest then?' He still managed to be charming, even deferential, but I thought it was fairly clear that we disliked one another.

'If I were you I should seduce her.' I leaned back to observe the effect of this suggestion and thought I discerned shock.

'That is, of course, if you haven't already done so,' I added, certain that he had not.

'I'm afraid I don't quite follow you.' I had strained his courtesy to the limit: he was offended, both by the suggestion itself and by my intrusion into his privacy. I had trodden on sacred ground.

'As a seducer,' I went on, feeling the old-fashioned term was appropriate, 'you would represent to Gemma something she knows would shock her mother.'

He said quickly, 'But her mother wouldn't know.'

'All the better. Gemma would be in possession of a secret — the delicious knowledge of behaving in a way her mother would consider wicked, while still being regarded as innocent. What could be more delightful? After all, there's no way you can make yourself less eligible in Beatrice's eyes. But there is a way you can appear more exciting to Gemma. At the moment, you are merely adoring, devoted, respectful. She probably knows you want to marry her, so she has the upper hand. But if you seduce her — without proposing — she'll be confused. Dazzled with pleasure — one hopes —' I added maliciously, 'yet prey to anxiety. Remember she's an old-fashioned girl. The wind of change hasn't blown very far into Surrey yet. She'll be afraid of pregnancy, afraid of losing you. All the romantic novels she's ever read will be there in the back of her mind to help you. A vision of herself dishonoured. Seduced and abandoned, like a popular heroine. Has she lost your respect? That dread word. Will another girl steal you away? What are your intentions? Has she ruined her future prospects? She'll have sleepless nights. A proposal then and she'll fall into your arms, weeping with gratitude.'

He stared at me. 'You're talking about the middle ages,' he said inaccurately.

'I'm talking about Gemma. She's been conditioned. By her mother, her background, her reading, her temperament. There are plenty of girls like her, no matter what the papers say.'

He instantly dismissed the heretical suggestion that Gemma might not be unique. 'But it's Gemma I love. I want to marry her.'

'I know,' I said. 'And I'm telling you how to do it.'

30

Eight

Gemma's wedding: the small church banked high with flowers; the smell of incense (Beatrice of course was High Anglican); the quavering voice of the vicar, an elderly friend of the family, as he put forward the unlikely proposition that Christopher Clark should worship his bride with his body; the matron of honour Janet, the only friend from school (Gemma had never made friends easily), now hugely pregnant and about to leave for Canada with her husband, clutching her own and Gemma's bouquet to her stomach like a wreath for her unborn child; the mad organist playing just a shade too fast for the choir; Beatrice's snuffling tears of joy behind me as I declared beyond all reason that I gave this woman to be married to this man.

They both spoke softly, seriously, their small clear voices audible yet tenderly faint. We were witnessing such a private ceremonial that we were almost intruders. The triumphal music afterwards (Widor, as I recall) made optimistic mockery of marriage as most of the congregation knew it, suggesting unalloyed bliss. Outside, some idiot with a camera clicked and clicked, making us line and regroup like soldiers in any combination from one to dozens, flashing our self-conscious smiles. At the reception, anaesthetised by champagne, I made some ridiculous speech about standing *in loco parentis* and Beatrice started to cry again. Christopher replied with something brisk and grateful, the couple circulated, cake that nobody wanted to eat was cut, and a lot of people got drunk.

I could not see her clearly, my little one, in her swirl of white, with her smile for which no adequate praise had been invented, but I know she glided around the room and gave everyone a few precious moments of her time. Some hours must have passed, I suppose, but it seemed very soon that she

31

was drifting away from me, unfamiliar in a new blue suit, still smiling but looking slightly puzzled by her own happiness, her own actions. There was a lot of noise and flowers were thrown and foolish people did things with shoes to the departing car and confetti fell like multi-coloured summer snow. The goodbye kisses were meaningless, only the ever-increasing distance between us was real, and I had lost her. 'Thank God,' said Beatrice by my side. 'Thank God, thank God,' until I wanted to kill her, until it would have given me the purest pleasure to squeeze and squeeze her neck until her face turned black and her eyes and tongue bulged out. I do not know what happens in these cases but I imagine it must be something satisfyingly repulsive. 'Thank God, she'll be safe with him,' she breathed, as the car disappeared out of sight.

When I got home, I wept.

Nine

She had said to me, 'I suppose I must be in love with him.'
Wandering round my room, pale as a lover from mythology
or folklore, not quite hearing what I said because a luminous
veil of self-absorption hung between us. 'I've never felt like
this before,' she said, and looked at me, mutely imploring
indulgence.

It was so obvious: her whole system had undergone a severe
shock. Well-brought-up girls take these things very seriously.
The normal course of events, to be enjoyed, shrugged off and
giggled over by others less respectable, to them is world-
shattering.

I said untruthfully, 'Gemma, I don't want to pry. But you
can have a love affair, you know, your first or your hundredth,
and it doesn't have to mean you're in love.'

She coloured embarrassingly. I waited. 'I can't ——' she
began, and stopped. 'No, I really do love him,' she said.

I poured her a drink, and one for myself. At least it gave me
time to think. I said, 'Gemma, my love, listen to me. It can
happen to any of us. At any age. It even happened to me once
or twice. Can you believe that? It's a fever, a disease. Delicious,
engrossing, intoxicating, but it passes.'

'No,' she said, her eyes above the glass challenging me to
prove her love was not eternal.

'You're nineteen,' I said futilely. 'Don't you realise how
often this can happen in your life?'

We stared at each other, completely sundered for the first
time. 'I'm going to marry him,' she said.

I had known of course from the beginning that this was
what we were discussing. I had done my work too well. Hoist
with my own petard, I think is the expression, beloved of
English schoolmasters, for elucidation in lessons on figures of

speech; I believe I even included it in my own classic textbook, the one that still pays the rates.

'I'm not trying to stop you marrying him,' I said dishonestly. 'But I am trying to stop you feeling that you must. Enjoy it, make the most of it, but wait till you're rational again. Then if you still want to marry him — perhaps. But in a year, six months, you may not even want to know him. If you meet someone else you may find you've been drinking beer. The next one might be champagne.'

'You don't understand,' she said, the classic words dividing youth from age.

I was so frightened (though ashamed of my fear) that I did not attempt to argue. 'I want to,' I said.

There was a long silence. She drank her drink and looked around the room. She had given up smoking under his influence but I could see her twitching as she missed the accustomed prop. 'I can't do without him,' she said slowly. 'Before' — and the colour flooded her face again — 'I think I took him for granted almost. You know — he was just someone who took me out. It was nice. I could tell he was keen on me. I felt . . . powerful. But now . . .' She lapsed into long retrospective silence so erotic that it seemed to colour the room. 'Now it's different.'

'I know,' I said. 'I know.' I felt myself becoming inadequate. 'But it's a drug. Believe me, Gemma. A drug.'

'Maybe that's what I want,' she said defiantly.

I got up. My drink was not finished but I put some more ice in it for punctuation. My head had never been clearer but I could see defeat grinning at me from a corner. I had been too clever for my own good and I had underestimated both Gemma's appetite and Dr Clark's ability.

'You don't have to marry your first love,' I said. 'Can't you see, this whole experience just gives you an idea of your own potential. You've no idea what you might be able to achieve in the future.'

She looked at me, shock turning to actual distaste. I saw it clearly; I had never seen it before. 'You mean,' she said slowly, 'you want me to go on like this for the rest of my life? One affair after another? Is that what you want?' She was so angry she had ceased to blush and the love-lorn pallor had returned. She had never looked more attractive: I wanted to scoop her up into my arms.

Why not? was what I longed to say. Instead I said, 'I want you to be happy.' The truth, and yet how inadequate when what I meant was: I want you to suffer, survive, enjoy, despair, expand and die. I want you to live. That's what I want for you.

She said coldly, 'That's fine then. Because I'll be happy with Chris.' Then suddenly she relaxed and a look of rapture passed over her face. 'Mummy'd be so shocked if she knew.'

Ten

It was about this time that I became involved with Oswald and Miranda. A petty, inadequate revenge, and one doomed to misfire, both by damaging me and failing to touch the person for whom it was intended. No: I am being too partisan. Strange how even at this distance old prejudice seeps through. It was simple compensation, if I am to be accurate. Not meant to hurt Gemma. Merely the last fling of an ageing, rejected lover. Not meant to hurt anyone, in fact, least of all myself. But my aim was unsteady.

They both had other names, of course. I renamed them after they came under my spell. I could still in those days exercise a kind of magic, if I cared to put my mind to it. And I did care. Only life was too empty for me to be excessively particular in my choice.

Oswald had a normal, healthy, attractive name that suited him admirably. He was a lively, athletic boy with an enquiring mind and the sort of enthusiasm that is the prerogative of the young. He radiated energy and curiosity. So I downgraded him: I envied his facility to charm and conquer. Miranda was a different matter. Pale and subdued in manner but with extraordinary hair, the yellowish-red colour of leaves that fall early, before the end of August. So she was upgraded, romanticised, removed from her ordinary little name. I like to pretend I cannot even remember what they were called before I set my mark upon them. I wanted to uplift her, to put her high above him, out of his reach. And him I wanted to degrade, to place far beneath her. Myself at the centre, I would have easy access to both.

They sat at my feet, sometimes even literally, sprawled on the carpet, rolling their ridiculous unhygienic joints which I shared to bridge the generation gap. They had been thrown

36

out of their lodgings for this curious modern habit, which made it easy for me to offer them shelter — easy but reckless. They were not in love, I swear they were not in love, then, as I looked at them, but they were entangled. Yet out of this entanglement came at first not strength but weakness. Separately I could not touch them; together they were vulnerable. Sometimes I used to wonder if they had in fact banded together for the sole unconscious purpose of being destroyed.

I had the feeling that my interest in them made their relationship exist: I provided a hot-house climate in which it could flourish. They talked about themselves incessantly, as only the young seem able to do, never bored, finding their own emotions perpetually of absorbing fascination. Miranda's pale grey-green eyes, startling in her freckled face, would glaze over with intensity as she analysed her feelings for Oswald; he would glow with absurd vivacity as he talked about her. They were like brother and sister: only my presence provided them with an incestuous bridge of words.

Eleven

'It's a lovely little boy,' Beatrice shrieked at me down the telephone. I glanced at my watch: it was half past four in the morning.

'Is she all right?' I asked carefully.

'Eight pounds two ounces,' yelled Beatrice as I spoke. 'Isn't that splendid? Oh, I'm so happy, I can't believe it. I'm a grandmother. Christopher's here, we're drinking champagne. I've been crying. Aren't I a fool?'

'She's all right then,' I said.

'What? Oh, Gemma. Yes, of course she's all right, what d'you mean? Oh, I don't know how to——'

'Let me speak to him.'

Silence, tinged with indignation. 'Who? Christopher?'

'You said he was with you.'

Another pause. 'Yes, of course he is. We're celebrating.'

'Then let me speak to him.'

There was some muffled muttering and then he came on the line.

'Alex. Sorry to wake you up, but we thought you'd want to be the first to know.'

'You mean the third.'

'What? Oh, yes.' He actually laughed.

'Is Gemma all right? Medically speaking, I mean.'

'Yes, of course. She had a bit of a rough time but she's fine now and the baby——'

'I don't want to know about the baby,' I said. 'Not yet. I want to know about Gemma. Give me your professional opinion. What sort of rough time did she have?'

There was a short silence. When he spoke again his voice had iced over.

'Well, it was a forceps delivery, which was a bit of bad luck for her, but she's perfectly all right. Very tired but very happy.'

He dispensed his knowledge so casually. The telephone was clammy in my hand. I reached for a cigarette and lit it with difficulty.

'Stitches?'

He seemed surprised at the question. 'Well, yes, she had an episiotomy but that's fairly routine——'

'Not always,' I said.

'I don't think you quite understand——'

'On the contrary, I know all about it.' I had spent Gemma's pregnancy reading medical textbooks. 'It can be avoided.'

There was a sharp pause. Then: 'I really don't think we need go into all these details of my wife's delivery. I can assure you she had the best of attention, in case you're suggesting otherwise. Grayson is a first-rate chap, a personal friend of mine——'

I put down the phone.

Twelve

Gemma's post-puerperal depression lasted a long time. In hospital she was euphoric, or, as Christopher had put it, 'very tired but very happy'. She talked incessantly, like someone high on drugs or alcohol, extolling the baby and her own new exalted frame of mind. Motherhood had changed her, she said. She elaborated on this at great length but the gist of it was that she felt transformed by the elemental nature of the experience. Something like that. It all made me feel faintly sick, and possibly envious too. Christopher sometimes intruded on my hospital visits and sat there looking smug, though he forbore to use the actual words 'I told you so'. Beatrice would also turn up, gushing as she unwrapped flowers, grapes and woolly animals, so I was seldom alone with Gemma.

I gave her a silver bracelet, inscribed with the date of the child's arrival, and studied her face. It was certainly true that motherhood had changed her, though not entirely in the way she meant. She looked subtly different, as if all her features had been taken apart during her ordeal, and though reassembled in the same order had somehow lost their former symmetry. There was a look of strain, of uncertainty, even of surprise at her own survival. She looked as though she had been very ill, or away on a long journey. She did not look, in a word, herself. It was like watching one of those films in which a secret agent is the double of the heroine and is forced to impersonate her. They are identical, even played by the same actress, and yet you know that something is wrong.

When she got home with the child, an event to which she had been looking forward intensely, the euphoria gave way to continual fits of weeping. Beatrice tried to jolly her along; Dr Clark assured me it was all perfectly normal, a word to which I took great exception. Influenza may be normal too, or in certain countries smallpox or cholera, but that seems no reason not to take it seriously and extend some compassion to the sufferer. I was the only person who appeared to sympathise with Gemma: Dr Clark complained that this sympathy was misplaced because it only made her worse. 'It's quite a natural reaction,' he said. 'It happens to lots of women. They look forward to the whole thing so much that when it's over they get a feeling of anticlimax. Maybe like publishing a book?' he added feebly, to appeal to me. 'And apart from that, they're physically very tired and rundown and their hormones——'

I interrupted him savagely. 'I really don't want to hear about Gemma's hormones, thank you all the same. Nor do I particularly care how many millions of other wretched women have the same reaction. It's Gemma we're talking about and Gemma we're supposed to be caring for. One person. An individual. Not a load of statistics in the *Lancet*. Your wife. My niece. Your daughter,' I added, rounding on Beatrice.

She flushed angrily. 'Really, Alex, there's no need to get so heated.'

'It seems to me,' I said, 'that there is every need.'

'You may find it satisfying,' said Dr Clark, icily calm, 'but the fact remains that it does no good and may even do positive harm. Gemma is going through an uncomfortable but perfectly normal reaction to the experience of childbirth. Giving her all this excess sympathy is simply self-indulgence on your part and likely to make her feel a freak. If you really care for her as much as you claim, you'd make some effort to control yourself in her best interests.'

'I notice you have no difficulty in controlling yourself,' I said.

He stared at me and finally could not resist the provocation. 'What's that supposed to mean?'

I lit a cigarette, partly to prolong the moment of confrontation and partly to offend him. He loathed people smoking in his presence.

'I notice a considerable change in your attitude to Gemma,' I said. 'Over the past year, that is. I can remember a time when you were metaphorically on your knees, desperate to marry her. Once she was actually your wife and certainly after she became pregnant, you allowed yourself to be positively casual, even complacent about her.'

We looked at one another, straight in the eyes, two enemies on a battlefield. There was no pretence left. Beatrice was breathing heavily, shocked but afraid to speak.

'That simply isn't true,' he said at length, calm as ever. 'But even if it were, I have no need to explain myself to you. Gemma and I, as it happens, have a perfect understanding. You remind me very much of a man who can't believe in anything he doesn't see. No wonder you have no religion. Well, not everyone cares to parade their feelings in public. The deepest feelings, in fact, are naturally private. You have no idea of our relationship because it is no concern of yours. Why should we show it to you? So kindly don't speak to me of things you don't understand.'

'I'd rather not speak to you at all,' I said without pre-meditation.

He smiled, and I realised the extent of my error. 'That's easily arranged,' he said. 'I simply shan't invite you to my home again. Gemma is of course free to visit you as often as she wishes. I imagine that arrangement will suit us all very well.'

Beatrice, to my amazement, burst into noisy tears.

Thirteen

'Chris has been marvellous,' Gemma said. 'I really don't know how he put up with me. I was so awful.'

I smiled politely.

'Oh, I know,' she said. 'I know. I'm so sorry you had that stupid row. But it will blow over, really it will.'

'Probably.' I was secretly hoping it would not, enjoying the stolen-fruit aspect of Gemma's visits to me. Sometimes Beatrice was willing to babysit; on other occasions Gemma was obliged to bring the child with her and I had to endure his snuffling presence, the carry-cot on my bed, the discreet nappy-changing in the bathroom, the frequent bouts of screaming hysteria. Gemma's patience amazed me: she seemed so loving with him, so unperturbed.

'I'm working on him,' she said now.

She meant Christopher, of course.

'Please don't,' I said. 'At least not on my account. I'm perfectly happy with things the way they are.'

'But it's so silly,' Gemma said. She frowned: it was clear that we were marginally spoiling her happiness. Two people who loved her must necessarily love each other; it was part of her simple code. 'He'll come round,' she said with confidence.

'And suppose I don't?' I said to tease her, although in a way I meant it.

'Oh, but you will,' she said. 'Won't you? For me? When you're ready, I mean.' And she gave me one of her irresistible smiles, nearly the old Gemma again, the carefree enchantress I remembered.

'I suppose so,' I said, beguiled.

She leaned back in her chair, making herself thoroughly comfortable. 'You see,' she said, 'you don't really understand Chris. He can't show his feelings in public, so naturally you think he's being tough and cold when you see him. But he's only being self-contained. When we're alone he's lovely to me. Really.'

I let it go. She was, after all, only two years married, still intoxicated by her presumed complete knowledge of another human being.

'It was my fault really,' she went on, pouring out generosity and also power. 'I shouldn't have been so neurotic. I really went to pieces — that's why you both got so upset. I think it was the awful responsibility of it that struck me, once I got home. When Chris was out and if I rang up Mummy and she wasn't there, I felt completely alone with Jonathan. It was terrifying. Like a nuclear disaster. As if there was no one else alive except me and Jonathan, so I was entirely responsible for him. If I did anything wrong he might die. That's why I just couldn't stop crying.'

'I know,' I said. But I didn't, and I grudged her the experience.

'Anyway, it's all right now,' she said happily. 'I can cope. It's easy. Honestly, I look back sometimes and I really wonder what all the fuss was about.'

'You look very well,' I said with tactful truth.

'Oh, I feel marvellous. Really, it was so ridiculous cracking up like that. Poor Chris. He had a dreadful time.'

'It will help him to understand his patients.'

'Miaou.' She grinned at me cheerfully. 'You *are* naughty. He's really so nice and you just won't give him a chance. Can't you be friends for my sake?'

'Give it time, Gemma.'

'Oh, all right. But it really is awkward for me. I want to invite you to dinner. It's not the same without you. Chris's friends are awfully dull.' She stopped, flushing slightly, having caught herself out in a disloyalty. 'No, that's not true, they're nice, but they're too clever for me. I can't think of anything to say to them.'

'So you need your idiot uncle to play buffoon,' I suggested.

'Something like that.' She smiled, clearly not in a mood to let me get away with anything. 'No, you know what I mean.

You and I could be frivolous and they could talk shop. It would balance out.'

'Yes, Christopher does seem a trifle serious,' I said, greatly daring. 'As far as I remember.'

'Well, he's got a very responsible job.' She eyed me sternly. 'You can't expect him to be . . . well, like us.'

The word sang in my heart. We were a unit again, two against the world, alien and irresponsible. Even dangerously provocative, with a bit of luck. A law unto ourselves. Yes? Oh Gemma, are you coming back to me? Are you sliding within my orbit again, my love, my child, my creation?

'The only thing is . . .' She frowned. 'Oh, I probably shouldn't ask.'

'Ask.'

'Well, I was just wondering. Are those two students still with you?'

'Oswald and Miranda?' I said unnecessarily. 'Yes.'

'Hm.' She considered this, turning her glass in her hand, suddenly, I felt, in need of a forbidden cigarette. I lit one, to exacerbate her need.

'I wish you'd get rid of them,' she said. 'I mean, isn't it awfully unethical, fraternising like that? Having them in your home, isn't it a bit dangerous?'

I rejoiced I had got her on the raw at last. 'Not really,' I said. 'It depends on your point of view. They need somewhere to live. Why shouldn't I take them in? I'm too old to be cautious.'

'I don't know,' she said honestly. 'It just seems unhealthy somehow.'

Her intuition amazed me. 'Really, Gemma, now *you're* being ridiculous.'

She considered this; she always tried to be fair. 'I can't help it,' she said at length. 'I just don't like them.'

Fourteen

Oswald and Miranda left me about the time of Gemma's second pregnancy, although the two events were in no way connected. They were in love, they said. They required to be alone. They found my presence suffocating and intrusive. They considered I was poisoning their love. They compared me to a vampire sinking its fangs into their necks and sucking forth blood. They lacked privacy: I had seduced them into my home by offering them free accommodation which I knew they were in no position to refuse. I had therefore taken advantage of them by giving them what they most needed; in return I expected their lives; I demanded their innermost thoughts to feed my diseased imagination; I was exploiting them as human beings, like someone keeping animals in a cage and requiring them to mate for his own amusement. I was evil, and they were lucky to escape from me, yet they still found it in their hearts to pity me because they had so much more than I.

All that in a letter which I have kept but do not care to reproduce verbatim, as I find its hysterical tone offensive. Written by Oswald but signed by them both, the product, no doubt, of one of their pot-smoking orgies which I had missed while visiting Beatrice. A letter left harmlessly lying on the kitchen table with the keys to the flat, but which, after studying the venom it contained, I was surprised not to find pinned to my pillow with a mediaeval dagger. They lacked the courage to face me, of course, and so ran away in the night when I was not there.

Fifteen

The child clung to Gemma's left breast, which was grotesquely swollen with milk and traced with blue veins like a road map; she cradled its elongated head in her hand and encouraged it to suck, although it did not seem to need much encouragement. 'Aren't I lucky she's a girl?' she said fondly.

I had not considered this before but now that she mentioned it, it did strike me as vaguely familiar, so presumably everyone else, such as Beatrice and Christopher, had already told me so, only I had not been listening. 'Yes,' I said, trying to sound a note of real enthusiasm. 'Very lucky.'

She had not asked me if I minded the breastfeeding. With the first child, there had been a certain reticence; now, total maternal confidence had taken over. How could I be offended by something she found so natural? Not that there would have been much point in her asking: had I told her, she would only have been hurt. But I felt I was an involuntary intruder on a private ceremony, and besides, I did not care, aesthetically, to see Gemma's breasts in that condition. I tried to look away, but there was something obscurely fascinating about such intimate exposure; I pondered the strange fact that in a few months Gemma's breasts would be back to normal, a state in which I could appreciate them, and I should never be permitted to see them again.

'One of each,' she went on, 'what marvellous luck. When you're only allowed two, I mean. Oh, I pretended I didn't mind, all the time I was pregnant I kept telling myself and everyone else it really didn't matter a bit, in fact two boys might even be easier in the long run — but oh, the relief when they said she was a girl. And I couldn't think of any boys' names this time — that was a bad sign, wasn't it?'

She smiled at me, completely unaware that I had absorbed

only one remark. '*Are* you only allowed two?' I asked. 'Why?'

'Oh.' She looked away, then back at the child. 'Chris has got a thing about population. He thinks we should all keep it down. I suppose he wants to set a good example to his patients. Oh, he's right, of course.'

'Of course.'

'I mean I agree with him, really.'

'Really?'

'Well, nearly.' She gave me a guilty smile.

'Would you like to have more?'

'It's not that exactly, I mean it's not as definite as that, it's just the feeling that I can't. That I mustn't.'

'Yes, I do see. Any prohibition increases temptation.'

'I suppose so.' She had clearly not considered the matter in these terms. 'No, it's not just that.' She stroked the baby's bald head; it clutched at her breast with its crinkled hand. 'She was so easy to have, so much easier than Jon, and she's so much more placid already than he ever was. I don't know, maybe it's me, maybe I'm just more confident with her, I know what to do this time, I'm relaxed. That's why it seems such a pity, giving up something as soon as you learn how to do it well.'

'Like never dancing Giselle again once you've got it right.'

'Yes. What made you say that?'

'You wanted to be a ballerina when you were a child.'

'So I did. I'd almost forgotten. Why do you remember more about me than I do?'

'Perhaps I'm more interested in you than you are.' And than Christopher is, I thought.

She laughed. 'You can't be. I'm not very interesting.'

'There you are, that proves it.'

'Oh, *you*. Why can't I ever outwit you?'

'Probably because I am old and full of low cunning.'

'You're not old. But full of low cunning, well, maybe you are. I don't know.' She smiled at me.

Hard to describe and impossible to exaggerate how much these conversations meant to me. Moments of tender, inconsequential intimacy such as I had once feared we might never have again. At the same time, not panic exactly, but that

48

warning voice: now that she is back, after her long excursion, make sure that you keep her close to you. Don't let her escape again.

'There's another thing, though,' she said.

'Yes?'

'About children, I mean. Once you've had them, if you're not going to have any more, *then* what do you do?'

'I don't know. Bring them up, I suppose.'

She sighed. 'Yes, of course. I was just being silly.'

Sixteen

We were all hideously reconciled at the christening. I say all, because during the estrangement Beatrice had shown signs of discomfort, as well she might, at being forced to straddle such a tricky social fence: loyal to me in private but still *persona grata* at Christopher's boring dinner parties. Now, in church, we were forced to reassemble as one family. I had often pondered the mystery of Christian forgiveness but had not before experienced the element of compulsion that went with it. I was there to be forgiven, whether I liked it or not. Oh, nothing overtly tasteless, of course; it was all very British. Christopher coming up to me, a strong handclasp, to be manly, and a pat on the shoulder, to be condescending. 'Good to see you, Alex; glad you could make it,' was all he said. In other words we were to pretend we had never insulted each other. A splendid tradition. I even allowed myself to wonder frivolously if at least one of Gemma's motives for having the baby had been to bring about this rapprochement. A pity it had to take place in church, though, since I am never at my best on alien ground. A pity, too, that it seemed the function of my family to drag me willy-nilly nearer, my God, to Thee. No doubt they would do a first-rate job on my funeral, too, when the day arrived. Christopher might even deliver an oration for the dear departed, suggesting a life misguided rather than misspent, and Beatrice would murmur what a pity it was I had never married, I had been like a father to Gemma, you know, such a shame I never had children of my own, it might have made all the difference.

We assembled afterwards at the Clark residence, the first time I had been admitted under its sacred roof for several years. Gemma gleefully pointed out various domestic improvements to me: she had turned into quite the talented little . . . homemaker is I think the word for it. I admired her efforts; Beatrice fussed round us, helping her with sherry and small things to eat; Christopher and a gaggle of medical cronies discussed professional matters in loud voices. Gemma and I concentrated on each other and Jonathan: he was not a particularly engaging little boy but even so I could see he was profoundly disturbed by the new baby, so I thought he deserved some attention. What Gemma and I called jealousy, Christopher referred to as sibling rivalry, which was of course normal (his favourite word). Beatrice in her turn said his nose was out of joint and chucked him under the chin. The new baby began to scream its dislike for the entire occasion and was put away early for the night.

'The joys of family life,' I remarked as I drove Beatrice home. She wanted me to stay the night but I was pretending an early appointment in town.

'Oh, you.' She laughed; she was a little drunk. 'Why do you always want people to think you're cynical?'

I said nothing. How like Beatrice, I thought, to make believe that unpleasant facts are not unpleasant after all but merely false.

'What makes you think I'm not cynical?' I said at length, as she seemed to expect an answer.

'I know you.' This extraordinary statement left me entirely speechless. 'You've got a soft heart underneath. Look at all you've done for me and Gemma. I'll never forget how you gave us that money when Mother died.'

She was like a highwayman praising the generosity of his victims after they had handed over their valuables at gunpoint.

'And today,' she went on, 'it was so nice to see you and Christopher together again.' Suddenly she made a most peculiar noise and I realised she was actually crying.

'Beatrice,' I said, 'whatever's the matter?'

The noise was repeated, a cross between a sick cow moaning and water running out of the bath. 'I'm so happy.'

'That's good,' I said. 'I'm very glad.' The sherry had obviously been stronger than I thought.

Beatrice took out her handkerchief and trumpeted into it. 'It's been such a lovely day . . . that dear little baby . . . and you being there . . . and Gemma's so happy with Christopher . . . oh'— another great howl— 'I do wish poor Hugh had lived to see it.'

As I was equally glad he had not, I kept silent, blessing the lethal landmine. Typical, I thought, of Beatrice to turn maudlin at the end of such a tense and beastly day when we were alone and there was no one who would take her off my hands. I parked carefully and helped her into the house, where she insisted on cooking me dinner. As I thought this might sober her up, I let her get on with it. The meal was superb as ever but the conversation a high price to pay: Beatrice reminisced endlessly about relatives dead and alive whom I had long since forgotten. She wanted me to stay the night and make an early start if I must, but luckily the problem was solved for me when she fell asleep in front of the television set. She snored, and she had put on a lot of weight. I stood looking at her for a moment, marvelling that Gemma had ever emerged from those ungainly loins— then I crept away, into the night. On my way home I drove unnecessarily past Gemma's house. There was a light in her bedroom, although it was only half past ten: I wondered if she and Christopher were making love. I decided not: Christopher looked to me like a man who preferred a decent covering of darkness for his erotic pleasures. More likely reading the *British Medical Journal* — perhaps a piece on new birth control methods — and for Gemma . . . a magazine on mothercraft.

Seventeen

Picture the scene: Christopher carving at the head of the table (yes, he really does preserve traditions like this), Beatrice on his right getting more than her fair share of meat, Gemma opposite him looking thoughtful, and me on her right, or Christopher's left if you prefer, facing Beatrice and offering up silent thanks that the children have at last been put to bed. The subject: one of those sex scandals beloved of the British press. It may have involved a politician or a doctor or a duchess, I don't remember; in fact we probably had conversations about all three at one time or another and I am amalgamating and compressing them into one quintessential evening. What I extracted was this.

Christopher: 'I'm sorry, Gemma, I can't agree with you. It doesn't depend on circumstances, it's a matter of principle.'

He actually pronounced those words; I am not inventing. I would certainly not put words in his mouth, nor indeed go anywhere near his mouth for any purpose whatsoever if it could be avoided.

Gemma said, 'But it's people's *feelings* we're talking about. You can't just condemn them without knowing all the facts and you can't know all the facts just from reading a newspaper.'

Beatrice tried to make peace. 'Perhaps Christopher meant that people in such responsible positions can't afford to have human weaknesses like the rest of us.'

To my surprise, Christopher turned on her. 'On the contrary, I'd say the same about anyone, whatever position they held. The effects are more serious, of course, in this particular case, but the principle's the same, whoever's involved. I know it's fashionable nowadays to talk about the permissive society so maybe I'm old-fashioned.'

I choked on my glass of wine to camouflage laughter. He looked at me suspiciously but could prove nothing.

'I see the casualties of the so-called permissive society far too often to think there's anything amusing about it,' he said crisply.

'If you're talking about young people, then of course I agree with you,' Gemma said. 'But these are adults. You've got to make some allowances for them having strong feelings and not always being able to control them. These things happen.'

'Certainly these things happen,' said Christopher, carving with surgical precision, 'but they needn't, and with a little more *self*-control, they wouldn't.'

'Don't you think' — I could no longer resist joining in — 'don't you think perhaps discretion is what we need more of, rather than self-control?'

He handed me my plate. 'In what way?'

'I was thinking of the eleventh commandment . . . Thou shalt not be found out.'

Beatrice started to smile, then, catching Christopher's glance, flicked the smile off abruptly like a light switch.

'Is that really what you believe?' Christopher asked me contemptuously.

I ate some meat to give myself time to think. He had certainly given me the worst pieces, with a lot of fat and gristle. 'Well, you must admit,' I said, 'that if the whole affair had remained a secret no one would have been hurt. In fact, I often wonder — if no one knows about something, can it truly be said to have happened?'

'Forgive me, Alex, but in my view that's metaphysical rubbish. Adultery is always a serious matter, whether it's secret or not, and if you abuse a position of trust as well, that only makes matters worse. It means you have no integrity.'

Gemma said quite sharply, 'Isn't integrity a matter of being true to yourself?'

'I don't think so, not entirely.' He was still perfectly calm. Calm but inflexible. 'We all have social responsibilities, we don't live in a vacuum.'

Well, I supposed I should be grateful that he had not actually said, 'No man is an island.' In fact I was somewhat surprised: he had looked all set to let loose another stupendous cliché upon us. And to think that I had once — however briefly — found him charming. A moment of puppyhood, no doubt, right at the beginning, when he was still trying to please, before he was sure he could capture Gemma and mould her to his taste.

Gemma said, 'Yes, all right, I agree with that, but nobody's perfect and I just think we should all be more charitable when people make mistakes. You know — like hating the sin but loving the sinner.' She must have thought she was being cunning, invoking religion.

Christopher permitted himself a smile. 'Well, now at least you've used the right word.'

Beatrice said uncertainly, 'The meat's delicious, Gemma. Done to a turn.'

In fact it was overdone. Cooking had never been Gemma's strong point.

'Is it? Good,' said Gemma absently. 'I'm sorry, Chris, but I can't help thinking how much those people must have suffered, whether it came out in public or not. I mean, all those letters and phone calls and trying to commit suicide — imagine what somebody goes through to get in a state like that. You can't just condemn them, however wrong they are. You've got to sympathise.'

'That's where we differ,' said Christopher, helping himself to more gravy. 'I don't have to sympathise at all.'

Just straws in the wind, no doubt, but I treasured them nevertheless.

Eighteen

And the beginning? A soufflé one day in September, I suppose. My diary says simply: 'Gemma here, lunch, 12.30', and below that, writ small, indeed by a hand cramped with irritation and too many hours with a dustpan and brush: 'Ring agency'.

Gemma was early. I was so accustomed to her being late that I was still on the telephone when she rang my doorbell and I had to interrupt my conversation to let her in. I left the agency lady assuring me that she would do her best for me, no one could do more, and returned, having welcomed Gemma, to hear that if all else failed she would send me an out-of-work actor by the end of the week. That hardly seemed satisfactory, but I could tell from the sound of her voice that she had reached the end of her patience, and besides, I badly wanted a gin and tonic, so I thanked her and hung up.

'You look cross,' said Gemma teasingly. 'Aren't you pleased to see me? Shall I go away?'

I smiled and started the drinks ritual. 'I'm delighted to see you, my dear Gemma, but less than delighted at the prospect of cleaning my flat by hand for another three days. Ice?'

'Two, please.' Gemma treated ice like sugar, alternately stirring it and crunching it up. I watched her with my usual pleasure as she licked the finger that had played with the ice. 'Have they found you someone else then? Definitely?'

'Hardly that. They're threatening me with a paid-up member of Equity, no less.'

'Oh well,' said Gemma, deep into gin and tonic. 'She may be pretty.'

'She happens to be a he.'

'Well. Why not?' She actually blushed: I found it one of her many charms that she still could.

'It's all a vicious rumour,' I said. 'Concentrate on facts. It's a fact that not only has Mrs Thing left me but the vacuum cleaner has had a seizure *as well*. I crawl around on my hands and knees, sucking up dust in a highly personalised manner.'

Gemma laughed. I enjoyed her laughter. No one else seemed to find me particularly amusing in those days, nor indeed now, but we are not here to talk of the present. What else do I remember? I made the soufflé, surpassing myself, and Gemma and I ate it, she emitting flattering cries of delight. I could tell from her manner, a mixture of external animation and internal gloom, that she was disturbed about something and I waited for her to be ready to tell me.

'Christopher well?' I asked, passing time.

'Yes, fine.' She stirred her salad with a fork.

'And the children?' This was more important.

'Oh, yes.' She ate some salad, put down her fork, took a long draught of Riesling. 'God, it's so funny with them both at school.'

'It must be. The great day finally came.'

'Yes, it did. I wish it hadn't.' She had a strange, lost look about her. 'Chris says I'm being silly.'

'Does he?'

'Oh well, he's being very understanding really.' She frowned at her near disloyalty.

'Of course.' It was his stock-in-trade, when not pontificating about other people's morals. Kind, well-balanced Christopher, reducing emotions to hormones and exercising his professional judgment. Always understanding where Gemma was concerned (so she said) but not above a little brisk snap-out-of-it if the case should warrant it.

'I expect I'm getting on his nerves,' Gemma said with self-pitying guilt. I picked up my cue. Occasionally she allowed me to slander him.

'What nerves?' I said.

Gemma giggled and drank some more wine. 'He's so busy,' she said, making allowances. 'It must be awful for him having me complaining about too much spare time when he hasn't got *any*.'

'He's a dedicated man,' I said spitefully. 'He doesn't want spare time, he enjoys his work.'

'Yes. I wish I did. I mean I wish I had some work to enjoy.'

'You don't really. You've been reading too many Sunday supplements. Can't you enjoy just lolling about doing nothing? Can't you sit in the garden telling yourself you're a wife and mother, backbone of the nation, and you've nothing to do till half past three, thank God?'

'No,' said Gemma. 'I can't. I wish I could. Oh, I suppose I'll get used to it. Chris keeps telling me what a lot I can do with my time.'

'Such as coffee mornings and good works?'

'Something like that. Or even studying something — God knows what.'

'How about a job?' I suggested. 'A part-time job. School hours only and fulfilling, of course. Isn't that what all the smart young mums do these days?'

'Maybe.' She looked doubtful. 'But in my case it's hardly worth it, it'd all go in tax. Besides, what could I do? I hate typing and I do enough cooking at home. I'm not trained for anything — at least not for anything I like. Mummy always said I wasn't talented and she's right, I'm not.'

'Something with children?' I said feebly. Gemma's malaise was affecting me: I could see all too clearly how ill-equipped she was to face the yawning void between nine and four. The world was out there somewhere but she was not part of it, and how could she be?

'I don't like other people's children,' she said.

'I know the feeling.'

We looked at one another and smiled. I refilled our glasses.

'Let's face it,' Gemma said, 'I'm a parasite. No, really. I'm just sponging on Chris and the kids, making them my excuse for living. I'm like one of those dreadful women you read about. I want to do something only there's nothing I want to do.'

We progressed to apple pie (home-made of course) and cream. Gemma ate like a healthy schoolgirl. 'The really awful thing is,' she said, with her mouth full, 'I feel my life is over and yet it's only just begun. I mean, here I am, nearly thirty, and I've got a nice husband and two lovely kids at school' — I noted the choice of adjectives carefully — 'and what the hell do I do with the rest of my life?'

She was a little drunk by now, of course. I must allow for that.

'It's a dreadful feeling,' she went on. 'Like going mad or losing your memory. There's something I've missed or forgotten, but I don't know what it is. Like a bit of the children's jigsaw getting lost.'

'That's a good image.'

'Oh, don't be so professional,' she snapped. And then: 'Sorry.'

I smiled at her to indicate forgiveness. 'I'll make some coffee.'

She followed me into the kitchen. 'Can I have a large brandy with it? Or a large something?'

'My dear Gemma,' I said, 'you can have a large anything you like, insofar as it's within my power to give it to you.'

Suddenly she grinned at me. 'You *are* good for me,' she said. 'You let me talk about myself but you don't take me too seriously.'

I filled the kettle and plugged it in. 'I take you very seriously indeed but I don't let it show in case you get conceited. I take all beautiful people seriously.'

'There, you see?' she said delightedly. She studied herself in the mirror I keep in the kitchen in case anyone calls unexpectedly. 'I suppose I could always grow my hair again,' she said. 'D'you think that would give me a sense of purpose?'

Book 2

'But now the calends of his hope begin'

14 September
A red letter day. Agency finally sent me out-of-work actor as promised. Wonder of wonders, he not only cleans like an angel but has mended the vacuum as well. Apparently its illness was something trivial, though too complicated for me, far beyond my great academic brain. How the intelligentsia are penalised in this mechanical world. I said as much to him as he worked but he ridiculed the idea. 'I've just got a way with machines,' he said, grinning up at me (he was on the floor reassembling it at the time). Somehow I got the impression this might mean he had a way with people too.

In fact he's a very personable young man: short and dark, with slim hips and surprisingly chunky shoulders. He looks strong, although he's very light on his feet. I shan't be afraid of overworking him as I was with Mrs Thing, who always contrived to imply imminent heart failure whenever I mentioned spring cleaning. And he's certainly more decorative to have around: the sort who deliberately wears shabby clothes to suit the job — jeans and a T-shirt — but makes sure they're incongruously clean and adds a touch of elegance with a scarf at the neck and a heavily buckled leather belt low on the hips. As if he's not really a domestic but playing the part of one — which is, of course, the case. David Meredith. He seemed upset I had not seen him on television in some police saga, or at the Royal Court doing something *avant garde*. I wished afterwards I had pretended to know his name at least. But they all look alike, these young actors with their thin, hopeful faces. Unless you have a reason to remember them, that is.

18 September
Actually, he's got quite a good face. I was studying him today

during our coffee break. In repose he can look a bit sulky — when he's listening, when the spotlight isn't on him — but as soon as he gets a few lines, starts telling a joke or a story, then he's all animation. His features are not too regular, that's the secret: his nose is very slightly crooked as if it were once broken and badly set, making him look tough. (He said yes, he'd played a lot of villains in his time and he'd got a bit pissed off with that.) But his mouth is very sensual, distracting you from his eyes, which are rather calculating. They ought to be brown as he's got such dark hair but they're not, they're a light grey-blue and very wary, as if he had good reason to distrust you. So his face isn't all of a piece, which makes it more interesting. The eyes of a schemer, the nose of a boxer, the mouth of a lover— yes, I'll certainly remember him in future.

He didn't mind being stared at, or discussing his face. Used to it, I suppose. Perhaps he even enjoyed it: they're all very conceited, aren't they? (And why not, I'd be conceited too if I looked like him.) But he can talk about his face with great detachment, as a tool of his trade, which of course it is: he showed me his good and bad sides and I saw what he meant. At some angles he's absurdly goodlooking, at others positively ordinary, even dull.

He asked me what I was working on, perhaps to reward me for taking an interest in his profession, and I told him about my translation. To my surprise, he'd actually heard of *Troilus and Criseyde*. 'That's Chaucer, isn't it? We did *The Canterbury Tales* at school.' He declaimed a bit, not making too great a hash of it. 'What's this one about?'

I considered how to make it easy for him. 'It's a love story. It's about a man who arranges an affair between his niece and his friend.'

'Why does he do that?'

'Let's say he has a heart of gold.'

He laughed. 'You mean he gets a kick out of it.'

'Perhaps.'

'And what happens in the end?'

'Oh, they get separated and she betrays him. It all ends in disaster.'

'Of course,' he said.

64

Afterwards I wondered why I had made it sound like the story of Pandarus. Is that really how I see it?

21 September
Gemma's birthday. I took her out to lunch and gave her my present, a ridiculously expensive silk scarf. She was delighted; she tried it on at once in the restaurant and people stared. I was embarrassed and thrilled. She's so spontaneous. Childlike, even. It was the only flash of high spirits, though. She ate as heartily as ever and drank a lot of wine, but her depression hasn't lifted; she still feels her life has no purpose. Reading between the lines, I diagnose a touch of frustration. Christopher, it seems, is now very active in family planning, doing extra work and giving lectures. All very admirable, of course, but it eats into their time together. 'I hardly ever see him,' she said wistfully. 'If he's not seeing patients he's out at a meeting or locked in his study. He's got mountains of paperwork — no wonder he gets so tired. I spend all my time watching television.'

My face must have betrayed me (suspicion, accusation, contempt?) for she suddenly leapt to his defence.

'Oh, I shouldn't complain; after all, he's doing it for us. I expect it's just my birthday. I hate birthdays. I don't want to be thirty. It seems so old.'

I pointed out that Christopher was forty-one. She said it was all right for men and besides, she was actually going grey. I pretended to stare disbelievingly at her hair.

'Oh, you can't see it,' she said. 'I've had a rinse.' Her eyes filled with tears and I quickly ordered her a brandy. My poor little love.

24 September
I am trying to get David to come here three times a week instead of twice. He is doubtful: he doesn't think there's enough work. I assure him there is, or there could be. I want the silver cleaned, and the windows. I want carpets shampooed and paintwork washed. The whole flat is dingy and I want it to be new and fresh. Perhaps even some interior decorating, could he manage that? A little light painting.

'You're just throwing money away,' he said. He was wearing a tight striped jersey like a fisherman, Hollywood-style. 'The flat's great as it is. You ought to see how some people live.'

I noticed the hairs on his wrists, on the backs of his hands, as he gesticulated. 'D'you want the work or don't you?' I said.

26 September
The trouble is, I have to work while he works, or he'll get suspicious. So I hardly see him to talk to, except for coffee breaks and maybe a drink before he leaves. He arrives at ten (I've told him anything earlier is impossible for me) and I greet him provocatively in my dressing-gown. It's a very nice dressing-gown but it doesn't seem to be working. He grins and says, 'Morning, professor,' this being one of our in-jokes, 'where shall I start?' and whips into the kitchen before I have time to reply. The washing-up's done in a flash and he plays the wireless while he does it; he has rubbishy tastes. I sulk in a hot bath and listen to him prowling round the flat with the vacuum cleaner; it purrs under his hand.

28 September
Gemma is not being absurd about age, or else I am. I know how she feels; I identify with her. He must be her age, or thereabouts. I am sixty-three. Is it ridiculous? Yes, of course it is. God is having one of his fiendish jokes at our expense. Why are we cursed to feel young when we are old, or old when we are young? I stood in front of the mirror today, before he came; I inspected my naked body. Pale, flabby and unappetising. We may as well face facts. Atrophied with disuse. Not that it was ever much to be proud of. I have always had to work hard for my pleasures. But this? Insanity. Crying for the moon, no less. An apt metaphor. I looked at the moon last night and I thought, no matter that they have landed on it, it's still perfect and impenetrable.

1 October
Autumn is making me melancholy. And then I think how feeble of me to be so predictable. 'Season of mists and mellow fruitfulness'. What rubbish. Season of regrets and non-events,

more like. David took the curtains to the laundrette today. What have I done with my life? I prepared a delicious salad and a pitcher of dry martini, his favourite drink. They say hope springs eternal. He came back bored and cross. 'You know, you're crazy, paying me to sit there and watch them.' He couldn't stay for lunch, he couldn't even stay for a drink. And why? Because he had an audition.

8 October
Last week was terrible. I was too disheartened to record it. The audition went badly, it seems. (Because I ill-wished him? It certainly wouldn't suit me to have him leave.) Anyway, he was in a filthy temper all week, breaking things and leaving a ring round the bath and nearly driving me mad by whistling all the time while he dusted. He actually whistles *out of tune*. I begged him not to but he said he always whistles when he's depressed and *went on* doing it, as if I hadn't spoken. But if I hadn't been so angry I might have felt sorry for him, he looked so miserable. Like a whipped puppy. The shutters came down over his face and it was sulks all the way. He even dressed for the part: black jeans and a purple jersey, as if he were in mourning for his life, like Masha. I reminded him of that, hoping to raise a smile, but no, not a flicker. He even looked more annoyed that I should presume to be so flippant.

I thought about giving him the sack, in a moment of sadism — or was it masochism? But I didn't, because if I did, then all the days would be the same. And I was rewarded: today was quite different. He arrived very late, about eleven; in fact I feared he wasn't coming at all. When he did turn up he had a crashing hangover, so I was able to minister to him. Apparently he'd been drinking to drown his sorrows: he didn't get the part. I pressed his shoulder as I handed him my patent hangover cure and said, 'My dear boy, I'm so sorry.' He looked at me strangely; he felt tense under my hand so I took it away. He said, 'That's where you're lucky, squire' —he was doing his pseudo-Cockney today, probably in memory of the part he hadn't got— 'you've got three jobs. Bit of writing, bit of teaching, bit of translating— you'll never be out of work.'

I pointed out that as I was virtually retired from all three occupations and had never been very good at any of them, I was not much better off than he was. He considered this.

'I suppose not. Well. That kind of puts us in the same boat then, doesn't it?' He downed the hangover cure and mimed an explosion going off in his head. Then he stood up. 'Right, let's get on with it.' And to my amazement he proceeded to clean the flat like an angel once more, silent and thorough, making up for lost time. I offered him lunch and he actually seemed to want to stay, but: 'I better not. Got one of my more demanding ladies this afternoon— Mrs Salmon— and she doesn't like to be kept waiting.'

There was something that alerted me (a look, an intonation?) so I said casually, 'Like that, is it?'

He grinned at me. 'Sometimes. She's not really my style but the perks are good.'

I took a chance and said, 'The perks might be good here too.'

He hesitated. 'Yeah, I rather thought they might. Pity I'm not more versatile. No offence, you understand.'

'None taken,' I said.

10 October

Strange. It could have made an awkwardness, an embarrassment between us, but it hasn't. He arrived for work today in a positively cheerful, expansive mood, obviously more relaxed with me now we've got *that* out of the way. Typically, he was more interested in my view of him than any disappointment I might have suffered. 'Did you really see me like that?' he asked over lunch. (Our first lunch.) I said no, I hadn't, and that was chiefly the attraction. 'I see,' he said, 'you like a challenge.' I thought it was rather that I liked an impossibility. I had lain awake analysing why I was not more upset. Adjusted to failure, perhaps, conditioned to expect defeat? Or do I simply prefer the conquest of the mind to the conquest of the body? It yields a more refined satisfaction, no doubt of that, and lasts longer. Now that he trusts me not to pounce he won't be so wary and I shall have more scope.

'Only it has happened before,' he said. 'I mean people getting the wrong idea. I'm only sorry I can't take advantage of it.'

I asked why he was sorry.

'Well, it would be an extra dimension, that's all. It's always flattering if someone fancies you. Like being up for a part.'

'You got the part with Mrs Salmon,' I said.

'Oh, that. Yes. Can I have some more quiche?'

'Help yourself.' (He eats as though he's starving.)

'Yes, I got that part all right and it looks as if I'm in for a long run. Only she must be fifty if she's a day.'

'And you like them younger.'

'I don't mind. Actually, I find the older ones are often more switched on. Last fling, I suppose. Anyway, this one is. Her old man left her pretty well off and she's got nothing else to do. D'you . . . like women as well?'

'Sometimes.'

'Only I was wondering . . . who's the one in the silver frame? Every time I clean it I have a good look at her. Is she one of yours?'

'My niece.'

'Oh.'

'Tell me more about Mrs Salmon. If she's so keen and she's rich, couldn't you make a living there? I mean, why bother with all this cleaning?'

He laughed. 'I couldn't stand the pace. Besides, this way, if I get fed up I can just piss off.'

He would too. He looked so pleased with himself. I had forgotten the cruelty of youth. Oh yes, I'm well out of this one. Definitely not a nice young man. But then I never thought he was. Just attractive. He would wreak havoc and disappear. Like a hit and run driver.

12 October

Telephone at dawn. Well, half past eight. Groping for the receiver, blind, in the middle of the night, it seems, till I get my mask off. 'Yes?'

'Alexander Kyle?'

A clear, light woman's voice, unknown. Not Mrs Salmon, surely, in a jealous rage. She would sound more robust and indolent. Peach-coloured and peach-scented flesh with a voice to match, I feel. 'Yes?'

'This is Catherine Meredith. I'm sorry my husband won't be able to work today, he's ill.'

'Oh.' (What?) 'Oh.'

'I'm sorry to ring so early but I've got to take the children to school.'

(Children?) 'Oh. Yes, of course. Is he——'

'It's nothing serious. He'll be back next week. But I'm sorry to inconvenience you.'

She's gone. No goodbye, just a click. And I don't trust people who apologise so often.

So now I've got all weekend to think about it. David married. David with children. Why didn't he tell me?

15 October

'Why didn't you tell me?' I said. It was all I could do not to laugh when I saw him, actually. He had a black eye, making him look more like a boxer than ever.

'Tell you what?'

'About your wife.'

'Christ, I don't know. What's the point?' He examined the eye in my kitchen mirror. 'God, I look awful. What a bitch. Suppose I'd had an audition.'

'What happened?' I asked with interest.

'She threw a bloody vase at me. I usually duck, I must be getting slow.'

'Does that happen often?'

'Now and then. When she feels like it.'

I started to make coffee since he seemed disinclined to work. 'Tell me more.'

He sat down and lit a cigarette, still gazing morosely at his damaged reflection. 'Well, she found out about Carol — Mrs Salmon. She went through my wallet when I was asleep, looking for money, I suppose, she always says I keep her short, and there was this photo. I meant to throw it away but I forgot. So we had a flaming row and she hit me with the vase and chucked all my clothes out of the window so I couldn't go to work.' He looked at me accusingly. 'I suppose you think it's funny.'

70

I hastily composed my features. 'Just a new angle on marriage.'

'Don't you believe it. Happens all the time.'

I said humbly, 'I meant new to me.'

16 October

All the same, there was something not quite right about yesterday's story. Anyone else might have believed it but to me, as a trained observer of human nature, there was a distinctly phony smell, an aura of duplicity. Why should Mrs Salmon give him a photograph when she sees him twice a week? Even if she were sentimental enough to do so, why should he keep it in his wallet and 'forget' to throw it away? *He*'s not sentimental. And his wife, that cool little voice on the phone, 'This is Catherine Meredith.' She didn't sound like a violent, jealous harridan. Not at all the sort of woman to throw vases at eyes and clothes out of windows. But the injury was real enough, so how did he get it, if not from her? And why did he get it, if not because of Mrs Salmon? Either way, why couldn't he work? There's a piece missing somewhere, I think.

17 October

I tried probing a little today. Not easy. He veers from rank exhibitionism to extreme taciturnity. Yes, he married young, at twenty, to be exact. He didn't know what he was doing. She was five years older, she cradle-snatched him, got herself pregnant on purpose. The last thing a young actor needed, to saddle himself with a wife and child, and then another child. No wonder they were always broke.

I asked if his wife could work at all, now the children were at school.

'She does a bit. She makes bags and things. Sells them to shops sometimes. Sort of cottage industry. It might be all right in the Hebrides, it's bloody ridiculous in Kentish Town.'

We were very sulky today. More sinned against than sinning, and all that. Well, at least I know where he lives.

19 October

I was in the bath when Gemma rang. He knocked on the door. 'Your niece on the 'phone.' I asked him to tell her I'd ring her back. When I came out he was waiting for me. 'She's got a lovely voice,' he said, and grinned at me. Wickedly.

20 October

Gemma claims I'm neglecting her.

'Who was that young man I spoke to?' she asked. 'Are you up to something?'

I pretended to be affronted. 'My dear Gemma, whatever do you mean?'

'I mean Oswald and Miranda, that's what I mean,' she said, quite briskly.

'I stand on the fifth amendment,' I said, 'and that was my new domestic you spoke to. My theatrical Jeeves.'

'Of course.' She sounded quite excited. 'I'd forgotten you were getting him. Who is he, what's he like?'

'His name is David Meredith and he's quite adequate, thank you.' But my last words were drowned: she positively squealed.

'David Meredith! But he's famous.'

'Come on, Gemma, don't exaggerate.'

'But he is, I've seen him, he was in *Calling All Cars*.'

'And that makes him famous?'

'Oh, you,' she sighed, 'don't you ever watch television?'

'Not if I can help it.'

'Well, he's very good. What's he doing now?'

'Cleaning my flat.'

'No, *apart* from that.'

What might I have said? Having rows with his wife. Screwing Mrs Salmon. Rejecting my elderly advances.

'Nothing much,' I said.

22 October

Now I have a choice. But I still don't know enough about him. I studied him today, very dashing in a bottle-green jersey and corduroy trousers the colour of toffee.

'You know your trouble,' he said conversationally. 'Too

many plants. They gather dust.' He flicked his duster over their leaves. 'To say nothing of all those books, but I suppose they're sacred.'

'My niece is a fan of yours,' I said.

'Really?'

'Yes, she's seen you on television.'

He had his back to me, annoyingly. Was there really a pause or did I imagine it?

'Then you should introduce us. I need all the fans I can get.'

24 October

I tried to explain about Gemma. He listened with extreme concentration, never taking his eyes from my face. He might have been learning lines: I could see him memorising everything I said.

I stopped. There was silence.

'I dunno,' he said. 'It's odd. I get the feeling you've left something out.'

I shook my head, shrugged.

'Oh, it's all right on the face of it,' he said. 'Bored married woman, two kids at school, devoted husband too wrapped up in his work — oh yes, I know all about that. Only there's something missing.'

I opened my mouth to protest my innocence. He misunderstood me.

'No, don't tell me. Let's be subtle. I like a good mystery.'

He's more intelligent than I thought. Dangerous. I don't know whether to be pleased or annoyed. Now we are both suspicious, circling round each other and sniffing, like two dogs in the park. He seemed very cheerful after this exchange, let me pour him another drink while he went on polishing the silver.

'I know,' he said. 'I'll just ask you questions and you answer them. Any way you like, of course. I'll draw my own conclusions.'

I said all right, if that was how he wanted it.

'The husband,' he said, as if Christopher had no name, which pleased me. 'Was he her first lover?'

'Yes.'

73

'Successful?'

'Presumably. She couldn't wait to marry him.'

'And since then . . . anyone?'

'For her, no. For him . . . I very much doubt it.'

'What's he like? Oh, I know you hate his guts, that's obvious, but what's he really like?'

I tried to be fair. It seemed important if we were planning a campaign. (Are we?)

'When I first met him, very diffident. Even charming. Romantic, idealistic. The last few years . . . much tougher, rather pompous. Too successful for his own good. He's got the upper hand.'

'You mean he's got out of control. No, don't answer that. I'm just making notes. Is he a kind man, do you think?'

'Yes . . . I suppose so. In his way. In a no–nonsense sort of way.'

'Gentle?'

The question struck me as odd. 'Yes . . . but what——'

'Ssh.' He smiled. 'Don't interrupt me, I'm working. Does he really love her . . . *in his way*?'

'Oh yes,' I said contemptuously. 'I'm sure of that.'

'Good. Is he a tolerant man?'

'No.' My answer came too pat; I sought to qualify it. 'He's quite religious.'

'Ah. I see. Now: if you were writing a story about him, what would you call it?'

'*A Man of Principle*.' Instantaneous reaction: I was quite surprised.

'Fine.' He started putting away the silver. 'Right; I think I've got all I need.'

'But you haven't asked about Gemma. Why all these questions about him?'

'It's the first rule. Know your enemy. She comes later. I can find her out for myself.'

'If I introduce you,' I said.

He paused at the door. I almost hated him, he looked so confident. 'Oh, but you will,' he said. 'Won't you, professor?'

'I might,' I said, 'but first I ought to know what you're going to do. *If* I introduce you.'

He smiled. Like mother with idiot child. Like benevolent dictator. Like nurse in hospital.

'I shall do what you want me to,' he said. 'Isn't that obvious?'

29 October

I spent the weekend cooking. He wanted it all to be very casual and you know how much time that takes. I excelled myself, but all the while I had the feeling that Gemma wouldn't come, or worse, that *he* wouldn't. She didn't know: she thought it was just lunch *à deux*, as usual. We'd planned it that he'd be finishing work when she arrived and I'd ask him to stay on. Not that she's ever stood me up, but knowing that it mattered . . . I just had visions of myself eating that delicious food for days on end, wallowing in anticlimax.

But he was punctual, ringing the bell at ten. I let him in and he dripped rain all over the hall, taking off his Humphrey Bogart mackintosh.

'She's coming at twelve,' I said, to reassure myself.

'Of course,' he said, enviably calm.

I locked myself in the bathroom, tensed for the telephone. The rain would put Gemma off, or her car would break down. One of the children would develop instant measles and be sent home from school. When I returned to the bedroom in my bathrobe, he was there studying her photograph, desultorily wiping the frame.

'Not long now,' he said, and grinned at me.

I couldn't work. Troilus and Criseyde seemed a million light years away. I dressed and sat at my desk staring at the rain, trying to decide if it was smoky or not. The telephone rang. I leapt in my chair and sat still. He answered it. I waited.

'Wrong number,' he called cheerfully. An omen? I went into the kitchen and put the finishing touches to everything. Then to the dining-room. He followed me there, admired the table, and mocked. 'Sure you're not overdoing it?'

'You haven't tried very hard,' I said, looking at his clothes.

'Casual,' he said. 'I told you. It's a chance meeting.'

Did he even realise how lucky he was? I went back to my bedroom, changed my tie, and sulked. I had what they call misgivings. It sounds like a badly chosen birthday present but it's very uncomfortable. I don't think I've ever waited for anything with such a clear sense of doom. Perhaps that was the chief attraction, for nothing would have made me alter the arrangements. But it's rare to be so conscious of what you are doing. We were set on collision course, as in a space fiction journey.

At ten past twelve, the door bell. 'Oh God,' Gemma said, 'this bloody rain. Just look at my hair.'

30 October
Well, they ignored me. A night's rest doesn't change that. I was just there to effect the introduction and serve the food. Otherwise I might have been invisible. *He* talked non-stop about his precious career, telling her endless funny stories and name-dropping quite shamelessly; *she* encouraged him all the way (as if he needed encouragement) by asking asinine questions and gazing at him enraptured as he answered them. Between us we got through nearly three bottles of wine, and then they proceeded to consume vast quantities of brandy. I cleared away unaided; when I came back with the coffee they were deep in discussion of the foibles of their respective children. At ten to three Gemma suddenly looked at her watch, leapt up, said she must be going, she'd have to drive like a maniac and could she give him a lift anywhere. He suggested the tube station, she kissed me goodbye with alcoholic affection, and they were gone.

No one saw fit to praise the food: they merely ate it. All of it.

31 October
'How's the puppet-master today?' he said when I let him in. 'Satisfied?' He hung up his coat, looking decidedly pleased with himself.

'I haven't heard her laugh so much in years,' I said grudgingly.

'Ah, I'm a very witty fella.'

'Not with me,' I said, advancing before him into the kitchen.

76

'Oh dear,' he said, starting on the washing-up. 'A touch of the sour grapes today, have we?'

'I didn't know you could be so amusing, that's all.'

'Well.' He glanced at me over his shoulder (a touch placatingly?). 'I always try my best at auditions, that's the whole idea. Isn't it?'

I ignored that. 'And do you think you got the part?'

He shrugged. 'A bit early to say. I think I *could* — shall we put it like that? But at the moment she's still pretending to be happily married. Any feedback?'

'What?'

'Has she said what she thought of me?'

'Not a word. She hasn't rung.' I tried to sound casual: I was secretly disappointed.

'Well.' He brooded. 'Could be a good sign. She's self-conscious maybe. Doesn't quite trust you.'

I said abruptly, 'What did you talk about in the car?'

'Nothing much.' He grinned. 'Don't worry, not about you. And I didn't make a grab at her, if that's what you mean. Much too soon for that.'

'I was surprised how confident she was,' I said. ('With ful assured lokyng and manere': the line ran in my head. But that of course was when Criseyde still thought herself unobserved.)

'Why not?' He seemed unconcerned. He jangled knives in the sink for a while, ostentatiously busy.

'Just out of practice.'

'She shouldn't be. She's very pretty — very feminine.' He said it as though it was unusual.

('Creature was nevere lasse mannysh in semynge.' I hugged the words to myself like a spell.)

He turned suddenly round from the sink. 'I hope you know what you're doing, that's all.'

1 November

The days have a purpose again; the wheels have been set in motion. I walk with a light step, like a young man. I am amiable to tradesmen. My work goes sweetly and even when it doesn't I am tolerant of myself. There is a stirring of some-

thing, more positive and less transient than happiness, an
organic growth.

5 November

My annual visit to Gemma's ritual fire-dance. She's like a child
about it, more of a child than her children. She doesn't squeal,
as they do, but she rushes about among her guests with a
suppressed excitement that is far more potent than any sound.
She is unnaturally solicitous for our welfare, our warmth and
comfort. 'Are you all right, can you see, would you like a scarf,
a drink?' The place swarms with neighbours and their children: well-bred accents float politely on the night air. Earlier in
the day it has rained, of course, but now all is damply dry.
People take pity on me as the bachelor uncle and make conversation; I know that I bore them. The air is thick with darkness,
a special night. Expectancy makes us all talk nonsense in fits
and starts: we know the true purpose of our presence. We are
not gathered together to socialise, but to watch, to be amazed.
We see each other dimly; we are not sure who the others are.
There is a constant murmur of anticipation mixed with boredom at the delay. Some people are late. A lot have come
pretending they are only here to please their children.

The bonfire has been protected from the elements by a
tarpaulin; now it is unveiled by Christopher, master of cere-
monies. The fireworks are arranged on a wall, out of reach of
young hands, gloved or otherwise. The children, deprived of
risk but assured of intact limbs, wander about feebly waving
sparklers at each other, twirling them in the air, making figures of eight out of the feathery fall-out. They offer them to
me and I refuse, generously. Bangers are banned; Christopher
considers them dangerous. Suddenly, we're off. An eruption
of gold and silver sparks rising upwards and falling in a shower
of colour. Other strange lights, red and green, and a cloud of
pungent smoke. Gemma grabs my arm; she is unfamiliar in
a sheepskin jacket and jeans, her firework kit. 'Oh,' she
breathes, 'aren't they lovely?' Around us the oohs and aahs
proliferate: from now on they will form a humming chorus
until the end of the spectacle. I wish Christopher would light
each firework singly so we could do it justice; I am confused, I

cannot concentrate. I say so to Gemma. 'I know,' she says, 'but he likes a display.' It's always the same but it still seems out of character. I am irritated by the inconsistency. (And all this time she has not telephoned me. No feedback, as David would say.) We gasp at some excessive piece of glamour; Gemma says, 'I wish I could remember their names. I tried writing them down one time but next year they'd changed them all.' She sounds so disappointed. I remember that Beatrice did not approve of fireworks so Gemma had a deprived childhood. I squeeze her hand. Will she confide in me? She squeezes back and says nothing.

The unlucky Beatrice is in charge of the chestnuts, sweating as she rakes them out of the fire. The grotesque guy has collapsed into the flames; I think it vaguely resembles her and enjoy watching its disintegration. Christopher darts to and fro, knocking corpses off his wall and lighting fresh victims. An acrid smell fills the air, characteristic of only this one night in the year, or else of war. The glow of other people's bonfires illumines the night sky, pierced intermittently by distant rockets, their stars falling like a dying bouquet. Our rockets are yet to come. Christopher's penultimate display of Catherine wheels (Catherine?) spit and spin before our dazzled eyes, a far remove from torture in the name of religion.

And then: their sticks planted firmly in earth, their blue touch-paper lit, oh so safely, in a meek line Christopher's rockets swoop into the sky and explode and flower and die, so swiftly, before our gasps of admiration fade away. Suddenly the night is very black, our eyes blinded with the imprint of colour; the fire is falling apart, pale orange and crumbling inwards, and we regroup, a little foolish, drifting towards the house and sausages, potatoes, drinks.

Gemma says in a whisper, 'Can I come to lunch again soon?'

6 November

'No, really,' she said. 'I meant just the two of us.'

'Fine,' I said casually. 'That suits me. I was only trying to be unselfish for once. You seemed to get on so well I thought you might enjoy meeting again.'

'Yes.'

There was no way to interpret that, try as I might. Her voice was quite expressionless.

'And I don't think he gets enough to eat.' Was I overdoing it?

Suddenly, she laughed. 'Oh, *you*,' she said. And hung up.

7 November

'She wants to discuss you with me,' I said. 'I think.'

'About time.' He was sulky today, up a ladder, cleaning the paintwork, his tone morose. I resented having to look up at him.

'She's worth waiting for,' I said. I wondered if he even realised the rich prize I was offering him. 'It's only been a week.'

'Ten days.'

I was gratified and surprised that he was counting. I had not thought him so sensitive. Then he added, 'I should have heard something by now,' and I realised he was still treating the whole matter as work.

'Maybe you'll have to audition again,' I said to annoy him.

He dropped the cleaning cloth and turned round dangerously on the ladder. 'I'm sick of your jokes,' he said.

'I wasn't aware I made so many.'

He looked at me with contempt and came down, jumping the last few steps. 'I don't think you've got any idea what it's like to be out of work for months on end,' he said bitterly. 'No money and the kids have got colds and Cathy keeps moaning. The water heater's gone wrong and the bloody gas board won't come — Christ, you don't know you're born, sitting here wrapped in central heating having cosy little chats on the 'phone with Madam in her detached mansion, four beds, two cars, planning to "discuss" me over one of your ritzy lunches to pass the time while I'm out there cleaning someone else's stinking house.'

We looked at each other. His anger appealed to me: he is so moody and self-pitying, even worthless perhaps. The attraction is irresistible. He is petulant and sour and destructive: he will lead us all astray, with luck.

'Can I have a drink?' he asked suddenly, smiling at me. 'It might improve my temper.'

'I was just about to offer you one.' I made martinis for both of us while he sat and watched me. The smile had made him look much younger and somehow unprotected, like a charming child when its tantrum is over.

'Christ, that's good,' he said, tasting his drink. 'You make the best martinis in the world.'

'Well, I have to be good at something,' I said.

8 November

When she had talked about everything else she finally said, 'You're quite right, I would like to see him again,' and stared at me defiantly, as if daring me to condemn her.

'Why not?' I said.

She coloured. 'And I know he'd like to see me.'

'Well, then.'

She fiddled with her glass, the cigarette substitute. I thought:

> Good aventure, o beele nece, have ye
> Ful lightly founden, and ye konne it take;
> And, for the love of God, and ek of me,
> Cache it anon, lest aventure slake.

'Why waste a good opportunity?' I said. 'You enjoy each other's company, why shouldn't you meet again?'

'You know perfectly well why,' she said gravely. 'Because we're both married.'

I affected amazement. 'Gemma, you astonish me. You've only met him once. I'm talking about a simple, harmless friendship.'

'You're not,' she said. 'Even if there is such a thing. And I didn't tell Chris about him. When I got home I didn't say I'd met him. Why didn't I?'

'Why should you?'

She shook her head. 'You're not being honest with me.' She leaned back in her chair. 'D'you remember when I was a child . . . how you used to make me stay up late, eat too much, read me horror stories, give me nightmares . . . ?'

'And you loved it,' I said.

'And I loved it,' she said, looking at me steadily.

'Well?'

'You're still doing it,' she said. 'You put temptation in front of me like a big cream bun.'

I began to laugh. 'David would love that.'

Then I noticed she was suddenly crying.

'You don't know,' she kept saying. 'You don't know.' She buried her face in her hands.

'Tell me,' I said. (My consulting-room voice.) And passed her a box of Kleenex. I could not allow myself to get carried away with emotion; I had the feeling I might be about to hear something to my advantage. 'What don't I know?'

She blew her nose loudly on a tissue and threw it neatly into the waste-paper basket. Her aim was good, even in tears. She had always been a co-ordinated person, a child who could run and jump well, if not brilliantly, whose limbs obeyed her, who had a tidy, compact body. Now that she was an adult it was reflected in her driving, her housekeeping, her handling of her children. Only her emotions were undisciplined — I hoped.

'Oh,' she said, pushing her hair back and wiping her eyes, 'I've tried so hard not to tell you.'

'Well, you succeeded.'

'Yes.' The faintest hint of a smile, gone quickly. 'Look, I do love Chris, I really do.'

'Of course.' I relaxed. I would still listen, out of curiosity, but it would no longer be strictly necessary. Once they start protesting like that, the battle's won.

'He's very good to me. And the children. He's marvellous with the children.'

And love based on merit: whoever valued that?

'Yes.' I waited for the but.

'But sometimes I feel a hundred years old.' She paused, her eyes staring vacantly into the distance as she thought what she wanted to say. 'We're like middle-aged people sitting there night after night. He comes in late, we eat, he works again, I watch TV and he joins me later and reads something while I watch. We don't talk much; we know each other so well. If we do talk, he talks about work. I talk about the children. And all the time I'm thinking, Will we make love tonight?' She was so lost in her reconstruction that she didn't even blush at this as she normally would. 'Usually we don't. We go to bed about half past eleven and he falls asleep, he's so tired. I lie awake for a bit, then I take a pill and I go to sleep too.'

Pause for a silence so intense I listened to the ticking of my own clock.

'And I keep thinking, what's it all for?' she said. 'Oh, I know marriage can't be romantic forever, but it's only ten years and I've got help in the house, we're not poor, the kids are at school, I'm not tired at half past eleven, I want to talk, I want to make love, oh, I shouldn't be saying all this, it's disloyal, that's why I didn't say it before, you always get me drunk. But we didn't get married just to have a nice home and children and sit in front of the television reading books and going up to bed like old people.'

Another burst of angry tears.

'I know,' I said soothingly. 'I know.' I felt it would be fatal to touch her, much as I wanted to: it would break the cocoon of self-exposure she had put around herself. I waited a moment, not too long. 'But when you do make love,' I said, for this was important, 'is it all right? As good as ever?'

'Yes,' she said dully; disloyalty would not stretch that far. 'But it's the *same* as ever. It's like someone who plays Chopin terribly well but they always play the same piece in exactly the same way. And they never play Bach or Beethoven.'

And David, I wondered. Would he be Brahms or Schoenberg?

'So you see,' she said, 'it's nothing to do with him.' She still wouldn't use his name. 'It might be anyone. It's between Chris and me. Only I'm vulnerable and you're taking advantage.'

I felt the time had come for some emotive words. Pandarus, I reflected, had been quick to reassure Criseyde that he was not suggesting anything dishonourable: that would shame them both.

'Gemma,' I said, my voice very serious, 'I promise you I'm not doing that. How could I? A harmless diversion, a little fun, that's all. The other day, when you met, he made you laugh. I thought it would do you good to laugh more often.'

She didn't look at me. We both felt the weight of the lie.

'After all,' I went on quickly, 'you've only seen him once. Aren't we making a lot of fuss about nothing?'

There was a long silence. She looked at me with what seemed like gratitude and terror. 'D'you know,' she said, 'when I married Chris, *dear* Chris, I thought I'd be safe from you for ever.'

10 November
Told David she was on the brink. He said it was about bloody time and he was sick of waiting.

12 November
It appears he's been telephoning her at home, on and off, just to keep her interest alive. He let it slip today. All this time, and she never mentioned it. Really, they are both behaving in a most underhand manner.

13 November
Asked what they talked about. He was evasive. Finally said, Oh, you know, stuff about what he'd like to do if he was alone with her and how he didn't want to make love to his wife any more, and did she ever pretend Christopher was him? Stuff like that. Surely I knew the routine?

I was fascinated. Gemma's extremely keyed-up state suddenly makes sense.

Later
Went to bed early but couldn't sleep. Deeply depressed that so many years since anyone made an even faintly pornographic telephone call to me. And the last time I made one, the person hung up.

16 November
Had completely forgotten my Leeds lecture next week till letter came today confirming trains, reception etc. A most unwelcome interruption. He pounced on it at once. 'Arrange lunch with her that day,' he said. 'Make her come here. She's refused to meet me in town.'

'All right,' I said, excited but uneasy. Now it will all happen behind my back. 'She hasn't told you to stop ringing her?'

'No.' He grinned. 'She won't do that. She wets her pants on the 'phone. I can say anything I like.'

Somehow I didn't like him talking about Gemma like that but I wanted him to go on.

'Such as?' I said.

'Naughty. You're peeping again.'

19 November

Will it happen? Will it actually happen? Will she take her clothes off for him in my flat? Will he have her at last — where? On the floor, on the sofa, in my bed? Will she betray Christopher *here*, cry out with pleasure *here*, beg for more *here*?

Or will she simply run away when she arrives to find I'm in Leeds?

20 November

'Don't forget to leave your keys,' he says, casual and cocky.

21 November

Fog. What if I am prevented by fog?

22 November

'I may be a little late for lunch,' she says on the telephone. 'I want to do some shopping first.'

23 November

'Course,' he says, 'it's all a load of rubbish telling her I don't fancy Cathy. Well, I don't, but Cathy wouldn't notice if I never fucked her again.'

(Distant bells rang. So why throw vases, etc.? Return to that later when my mind is clear.)

'Still,' he goes on, 'it turns them on thinking another woman isn't getting it. They all hate each other really, they're all rivals, whatever they say. Later, it turns them on thinking another woman *is* getting it. But that's later. After they think you belong to them. That's when you get them corrupted. If you betray them then, they get terribly excited, they'll do anything to get you back. But at this stage it's all fidelity and saving it up till you get them hooked. I tell you something' — and he looks at me, sure of my interest— 'I'll be relieved when we get started. All this suspense. I'm screwing Mrs Salmon into the ground, wearing myself out I am. She's delighted, of course, but I'm bloody sick of it.'

I make sympathetic noises. (Not quite the noble Troilus I might have selected but still, beggars can't be choosers.)

24 November
Go through my lecture notes on the train, sorely distracted by images of Gemma in obscene attitudes all over my neatly typed pages. Journey passes swiftly.

Deliver lecture in usual charming manner, wit and erudition nicely blended. (Well, I am all right when I have time to prepare it; it's spontaneous wit and erudition that defeat me.) Warmly received, and some not too idiotic questions. Afterwards have great difficulty restraining myself from getting drunk with my hosts. Intoxicated by thought that while I discoursed on so-called Courtly Love, Gemma was (perhaps) abandoning the sacred to embrace the profane under my roof. Have trouble hearing everything my hosts say. If the rendezvous a success, all well and good: if, however, she runs away, she has every reason to be very angry with me for arranging trap. Have not considered this before: why not?

Go to sleep after heavy meal and dream of Christopher. (Never before, as I recall.) We are walking about a minefield, he and I, looking for Gemma, who has suddenly become very small. I know she is somewhere else but I can't tell him where because I am secretly hoping he will step on a mine. At the same time very much afraid I will instead. Sense of fear extremely vivid in dream. Also maddened by conflicting goals: destruction of Christopher, preservation of self. Why can't he go on looking for Gemma in minefield and let me go safely home? For some iron reason not clear in dream, this cannot be.

Wake in small hours. Never sleep well in a single bed. And I have indigestion. Take pill. Picture Gemma lying (how interestingly ambiguous the word lying is) beside Christopher in the dark, reliving adultery — or thanking God it never happened. Which? How long before I'll know? Will he tell me tomorrow? Will he tell me the truth? And she?

Take another, final pill, and sleep.

25 November

On way back reflect on unfairness of life. Pandarus not sent off on train just when his best efforts were coming to fruition. He was there, stage-managing everything. Instead, they have banished me. Man opposite me on train has extraordinarily obnoxious habit of interlocking fingers and cracking joints. Amazing how loud a noise this can be. I jump as if I'd been shot, each time, in an effort to deter him, but to no avail. He is innocent and insensitive. He does not appear to notice what he is doing and yet every time he does it an expression of pleasure and relaxation passes over his face, like a dog masturbating.

Later

It seems strange to be home. I've been all over the flat carefully, like a detective looking for fingerprints. There is nothing to indicate what, if anything, has occurred in my absence. I don't feel I can relax till I know: the furniture holds a secret. For the first time I am uncomfortable in my own home. I stare at the telephone, but the obstinate beast will not oblige me by ringing. I examine the carpet for stains, I sniff the sheets. My home is not my own. They haven't left a trace. Not a scent, not a mark, not a single erotic clue. I am excluded.

Book 3

'Pandarus had accomplished his intent'

'Dear David,

When I woke up this morning there was a moment before I remembered, when I thought it was just another morning, and then I did remember and I got such a shock, I could feel myself blushing. Wasn't that silly? I'm sure you'd have laughed at me if you'd seen.

I wanted to reach out and touch you but of course there was only Chris. I felt embarrassed when I saw him so I turned over and pretended I was still asleep and thought about you waking up in bed with Cathy. I hope she didn't notice anything different about you last night. When I got home I felt ever so shaky and very very odd — not like myself at all. I was afraid Chris would ask me what was the matter but luckily he was reading and he didn't notice.

You were absolutely right when you said we mustn't let this affect our marriages. If we start feeling guilty it will spoil everything. But as long as we don't hurt anyone there's nothing to feel guilty about, is there? I always used to be afraid that having an affair would mean not loving Chris any more and falling in love with someone else, and what a ghastly mess that would be, with the children and everything. I didn't see how it could possibly work. That's partly why I didn't do it — that and never meeting anyone really special. But of course it doesn't have to mean all that, it can just be what you said yesterday, a sexual friendship. I'm glad you called it that, it sounded so nice and solid — made me feel I could write to you as well as go to bed with you.

Take care.

Gemma'

Now I don't want you to suppose that Gemma habitually posted her letters unsealed and neatly numbered for future reference, nor that this particular letter just happened to fall out of David's pocket while he was cleaning the loo and I innocently chanced upon it. No, there's a little more to it than that, I fear: not entirely to my credit but ultimately justifiable. David did not turn up for work; Gemma did not telephone. I placed the letter on the mantelpiece and went about my business. It was not an immediate decision. I began the day with every intention of passing the letter on to David undefiled. At least, I think I did. But each time I passed it Gemma's writing reproached me, those careless squiggles of violet ink, which in anyone more sophisticated would be an affectation. Don't you care? it seemed to say. Don't you even want to know what I've written? A eulogy? A rebuke? A farewell?

I boiled a kettle for fresh coffee and the kitchen filled with steam. David might lie to me about the contents of the letter. Gemma might be too proud to confide in me if she needed help.

I have always been good with my hands. The secret is not to hurry or it will tear. To wait and to be gentle, judging the moment. If I did not read the letter, the symmetry of my design would be incomplete, my creation unfinished. And I was consumed by prurient curiosity. I squirmed with delicious guilt in the steamy kitchen, but my hands were steady. And afterwards, a mere moment with the photo-copying machine, a lucky purchase years before, because I always disliked carbon, it somehow contrives to soil my fingertips and lurk under my nails. I numbered the copy at once because I knew there would be more now she had begun and I like to be orderly, especially in emotional matters.

Making the letter whole again was trickier but I persevered, having no alternative, taking my time. I likened myself to a Japanese surgeon repairing a ravished maidenhead. I was probably even more careful than necessary, in my usual perfectionist way. People do not generally examine the backs of letters very closely, as far as I can tell. They do not expect them to be tampered with, any more than they expect to find their nearest and dearest has committed murder. It is too radical a crime to be perpetrated by somebody one knows intimately. And yet the majority of murders take place in the home, so we are told.

The letter itself was such a bonus. Unoriginal in content and undistinguished in style, it nevertheless represented a degree of intimacy I could not achieve any other way. Because it was not intended for me, it showed me a side of Gemma I had never seen, that no amount of conversation could have revealed because she would have known she was talking to me. It was as if I had watched through the keyhole while she undressed. An unlooked-for gift. I had not thought of her writing letters. I had imagined inhibition, prudence, idleness — all would prevent her. Did I perhaps not know her after all? I had imagined a greater degree of guilt, too; guilt there certainly was, if only in her denial of guilt, but I had expected more. I had not anticipated this lightness, this positive enjoyment. But I was responsible for it. She lay in my hand, exposed.

'I ought to be very cross with you,' she said when she finally rang.

'I can't imagine why,' I said primly. 'It was an accident of fate. Didn't he tell you? I was called away unexpectedly and it was too late to let you know. You'd already left.'

She actually laughed. 'I wonder why you're so bad at telling lies,' she said, 'when you get so much practice.'

Sex with David seemed to have sharpened her wits.

'We're going to be very sensible,' she said, 'and not let it affect anything. He still loves his wife and of course I love Chris.'

'Of course.'

'So it's not a love affair, it's a——' She hesitated and I wondered if she would actually use his words. But evidently they were too private, for she went on, 'just an adventure.'

I wondered if she knew yet that was not what she wanted.

'It will do you good,' I suggested.

'And my marriage,' she said quickly. 'I won't be so tiresome and Chris will be happier with me.'

'And you with him.'

'Yes.'

There was a long pause: I almost wondered if she had gone away to fetch something. Sometimes she did disappear without warning if one of the children suddenly needed her.

She said, 'Was David pleased with my letter?'

I smiled. 'He hasn't got it yet. He took the day off.'

'Oh.' A world of disappointment in her voice.

'You must have worn him out,' I said.

'I wish you wouldn't make jokes like that, you're going to spoil everything.' She sounded quite cross.

'I'm sorry,' I said. 'I didn't know it was sacred.'

'It's not . . . it's just . . . oh, I hate not having any privacy.'

I said, 'I shall make myself as unobtrusive as possible.'

'I know you will.' As always, she softened instantly, one of her most endearing qualities. 'So my letter's still there.'

'Sitting on my mantelpiece. It's quite safe.'

When he had finished reading the letter he looked smug and put it in his pocket with the casual air of a man who was accustomed to such tributes.

'The fish is hooked,' he said.

I thought this remark in poor taste but ignored it and asked instead why she had written. I was interested to see how far he would lie if I gave him the opportunity.

'It's another way of touching me,' he said.

I was impressed: I had not credited him with so much perception.

'She's so lovely,' he said, leaning back in his chair. (I could see very little work would be done today.) 'She really is. She deserves someone nicer.'

'She already *has* someone nicer,' I said. 'That's the whole point.'

He smiled. 'It's like seducing a child,' he said. 'She's soft and gentle, ignorant and curious.'

'You seem to know a lot about it.'

'I was in a play about it once.' He shrugged, looked away, evasive. I wondered how much of his life was rooted in unreality. 'That was a line from the play, if you really want to know.'

94

'It doesn't sound like a very good play,' I said critically.

'It was all right. At least I was working.'

I said, 'She rang up.'

'Yes. She would.'

'To talk to me,' I said. 'Not to you.'

'Same thing. You're a link. I bet she talked *about* me.'

'You're very confident,' I said, 'aren't you?'

'You set it up,' he said. 'You've only yourself to blame.'

I did not like the associations of the word 'blame'.

'For what?'

'Anything that happens. It's out of your control now.'

'Don't be too sure,' I said.

'Oh, believe me. There's nothing you can do but watch. But that's all right. You enjoy that, don't you?'

He had my measure. I watched him uncomfortably, annoyed that he was looking more than ever attractive, as if Gemma had rubbed off on him.

'You'd like me to tell you all about her,' he said. 'Wouldn't you?'

'In the Middle Ages,' I said, 'lovers had to be discreet.'

'So the next time we want to meet here, you'll discreetly go out?'

(2)

'Dear David,

I feel such a beginner. I don't care what you say, I simply don't believe you haven't done this lots of times before. You know all about it and what to do and say. I don't just mean making love — although I'm sure you've had much more experience than me — I mean the whole thing of how to behave— how to conduct this sort of affair. I don't think you can possibly remember what it's like to be new to it all. Like changing schools and you don't know the rules or the slang— or going on holiday and suddenly everyone's talking a foreign language and driving on the wrong side of the road.

I don't even know if you like my letters. When I was engaged to Chris I used to write to him and he wrote back. It was only after we were married he told me he thought it had been silly writing letters when we lived in the same village.

But I don't think that's the point of letters — you don't have to be miles apart — it's the thing of being able to talk to someone whenever you feel like it, and you can't always pick up the phone. Half the time I don't even know where you are and I have to wait for you to ring me. I think I wait much better if I can write letters.

Chris still hasn't noticed anything. I'm very glad but isn't it odd? Because I think I'm so different. I don't want him to notice but I feel he ought to. When someone you've lived with for years doesn't notice such a big change it makes you wonder what else they can't see.

Lucky for us, anyway.

Gemma'

She was begging him not to be like Chris, ever, in any detail. And disappointed at the same time that Chris was not instantly transformed by her adultery. (Wasn't it magic after all?) I invited myself to tea for the novel pleasure of observing the complacent cuckold at close quarters. He greeted me absently; he was deeply engrossed in some volume detailing the latest refinements in rubber, plastic and chemical devices for circumventing the tedious consequences of human fertility. I wondered which method he and Gemma favoured. The tedious consequences of their own fertility, the socially acceptable pair, played at our feet. They were not nearly as attractive as Gemma had been at their age: they had inherited too much of their father — a tribute more to Gemma's fidelity than her good taste. But it could have been worse: they might have resembled Beatrice.

I had not seen Gemma since the affair began, David having banished me before she arrived for their second tryst. Seeing me might make her self-conscious, he said, and the second time was always tricky, neither novel nor established. I went out reluctantly, yet with relief: I was not sure I felt ready to face them both together. The happy couple I had created. I walked a little, but it was a dispiriting winter's day so I went to the cinema and watched an indifferent film. When I got home they had gone but they had been more careless and relaxed: towels ruffled and the bedspread creased, a couple of windows conspicuously open to destroy the scent of love. I was rewarded for my co-operation. They had given me a little more of themselves.

Now I searched Gemma's face for signs of change — sensuality, anxiety, fatigue — but she looked exactly the same. She was excessively nice to her husband, though; I thought he must be a fool not to notice something was wrong. I studied him with satisfaction: it was my doing that his wife was unfaithful and he did not know. He was an ancient figure of fun. So much for his boasting that he and she had a perfect understanding. So much for his attempts to exclude and humiliate me. I was sweetly revenged.

Gemma cornered me in the kitchen. 'Oh, it *is* good to see you,' she said, kissing me with sudden fervour on the cheek, adding swiftly, 'I do hate weekends now.'

I saw what she meant: no hope of a telephone call, no chance to write letters.

She said, 'When can we come to the flat again?'

'Whenever you like.'

'We weren't sure.' The pronoun gave her obvious pleasure. 'It seems awful asking you to go out. And of course I mustn't come up to town too often or it will look funny.'

The intoxication of deceit made her tremble slightly. She looked very beautiful and I wanted to kiss her.

Later on Beatrice arrived, admired the children and pretended to be pleased to see me. We all ate an uneasy tea together.

'Gemma looks well,' said Beatrice, puzzled. Like a dog, she picked up the scent; I had not bargained for that. But she lacked the skill to interpret.

Gemma avoided my eyes.

'It does me good getting up to town more often,' she said.

'I hope you'll do the Christmas shopping while you're there,' Christopher remarked. 'Less than three weeks to go now.'

We all received this startling information with the silence it deserved.

'Of course I will,' Gemma said eventually. 'That's the whole point.'

'If I knew when Gemma's going to town,' Beatrice said, aggrieved, 'I could ask for a lift.'

I noted that for the second time she had not addressed her daughter directly but commented upon her to the rest of us, as if she were a household pet.

'But you like to plan ahead,' said Gemma. 'And I usually go at short notice. On impulse.'

'Or when I invite her,' I added helpfully. 'I'm very impulsive.'

Beatrice said, 'I haven't seen you, Alex, for a long time.'

'No, I've been busy.'

'Still on *Troilus and Criseyde*?' Christopher asked. He always remembered. I was pleased and yet I resented his courtesy. He was only polite because he thought he had won. He discounted me.

'Yes.' I amused myself picturing the horns on his forehead.

Beatrice said irritably, 'Aren't you ever going to get to the end of it?'

'It's a very long poem.'

The children whined to get down from the table.

'Perhaps Gemma could help me with it later,' I said, glimpsing a plan. 'Do some typing. Take dictation now and then.'

Christopher said, 'Gemma? You might enjoy that. You're always saying you don't have enough to do.'

Beatrice said, 'Can't you use a dictaphone?'

I said, 'I hate machines.'

Gemma said, 'I might come. If you ask me nicely.'

(3)

'Dear David,

Such an awful weekend. Friends of Chris to dinner on Friday and they stayed late and drank a lot and I had such a headache. My own fault, I suppose, for drinking brandy, but I had to do something to stay awake. Then Chris felt sexy after they'd gone — the first time since you and I began — I was amazed, usually it's me running after him, especially late at night. So I had to be nice to him. I felt very odd. I tried to analyse it so I could tell you. I was sort of excited but reluctant as well. And I felt a bit of a scarlet woman. He also seemed

98

much more of a stranger. Does any of that make sense? Anyway it was all right eventually. It took longer than usual because he'd had so much wine, and I kept thinking of you and then wondering if I ought to. I don't mean pretending he was you or anything like that, I couldn't do that, but just remembering and wondering if anything I've learned might show up — would he think I was different? I know you said it ought to help and make it more exciting and in a way it did, I suppose. Anyway it's over and that's a relief because I've been dreading it as a sort of test. Silly, I know.

Then on Saturday we had a children's party because Jonathan and Stephanie have been to so many. I used to hope just two a year, for birthdays, would be enough but it wasn't so now we have one midway between, *plus* Christmas. It really is a lot. I'm not sure who it's for really — them or Chris's patients so they'll all think how lovely he is. Anyway what seemed like *hundreds* of children turned up (I think it was fifteen really) and made the most incredible noise all afternoon playing games, and ate and drank like pigs, and then some of them were sick before we could get them to the loo and others kept crying and one in particular — a real little Hitler — bashed another one quite badly and I had to explain to his mother why he was going home covered in sticking plaster when he'd arrived perfectly fit. She didn't take it too well and I can't say I blame her, poor woman. Chris thinks the Hitler child is disturbed and maybe he is, I don't really care, I'd just like to stop him bashing other kids — and thank God it wasn't one of mine he bashed or I'd have had to explain to his mother why I'd murdered him. By the time they all left I was so exhausted I had to have three gins before I could even think of putting my two to bed and getting supper. (Chris was out on a call.)

I'm so glad you have children too. I don't think I'd dare write all this — or even say it — to someone who hadn't. And it means we really understand each other's point of view in other ways too. About marriage and everything.

Sunday was better, thank God, because Uncle Alex came and actually dropped hints in front of Chris about me going to work for him in London. Just think — we could meet more often — it would be a perfect alibi. Wasn't it sweet of him? Chris seemed to think it was a good idea too! (I was very casual about it.) But it spoilt it a bit that Mummy was there — I couldn't really relax and enjoy myself. She was in an awfully strange mood and kept giving me funny looks. She can't possibly suspect anything, that would be ridiculous, but she was sort of watchful and grumpy. Of course she and Uncle Alex have never really got on, it could be just that. I wonder if you'll ever meet her. I bet you could charm her. She loves Chris of course because she thinks he's so suitable for me, and she's a bit of a snob so she adores him being a doctor. It's funny. You would represent everything she dislikes — but I'm sure you'd get round her somehow.

It amazes me to think of Cathy not wanting you any more when I want you so much.

See you soon.

Gemma'

He said furiously, 'Another time just you keep your nose out of my affairs.'

I was surprised. From my own point of view I had found the letter wanting in sensuality and heavy with domesticity, but I could not see why it should enrage him. And he certainly could not know that I had read it: I had resealed it with particular care. A work of art, no less.

'I don't understand you,' I said mildly, impressed by my own forbearance. The soft answer that is alleged to turn away wrath. I had learnt from my mistakes with Christopher that it does not pay to lose control of a situation by losing one's temper, although the appearance of doing so can of course be useful at times. This thought immediately led me to wonder if David, as an actor, was in fact acting now. The rage seemed disproportionate.

'She says you've offered her a job here. So we can meet more often. You must be out of your fucking mind.'

I said, 'I thought you'd be pleased. She's very keen.'

'I know that, for Christ's sake. But she won't be if you set it up so she sees me every bloody day.'

I said, 'You're very modest.'

100

'Jesus, don't you know anything? What's all that reading done for you, what about the course of true love and all that not running smooth? God almighty, you're trying to make it so fucking smooth we'll skid right off the end.'

I was amused and impressed. I have always been generously inclined to encourage the talented few.

'That's a very vivid turn of phrase,' I said approvingly. (It was more: it was accurate.)

'Don't give me any of that academic shit. It's my life I'm talking about. It's me who's having Gemma, not you— much as you'd like to— and it's my decision how often I have her.'

'In my flat,' I said.

Suddenly he sagged, like a puppet, Petrouchka, the sawdust draining out of him.

'There are other places we could meet,' he said, with child-ish bravado. 'I've got plenty of friends.'

'Of course.' In fact I could not imagine him having any, given his neurotic and moody disposition. 'But isn't it safer and easier and more comfortable for you to meet here?'

There was a cold silence, while we surveyed each other. We were, of course, discussing supremacy rather than conveni-ence or erotic tactics. Who, in vulgar parlance, was to call the shots. We were carving up Gemma between us as if she were Poland at the Congress of Vienna in 1815. Presently he agreed that it *was* safer and easier and more comfortable for them to meet here, but I felt there was something suspect about the way he said it. He seemed so relieved to be able to agree with me, I began to believe then (as I still do) that there was something in him that corresponded to something in me, that we were equally corrupt, a matched pair, and that it satisfied this something in him to use my flat as much as it satisfied this something in me to have it used. He did not want to meet Gemma anywhere else and he was grateful to me for making it possible for him to go on meeting her here, for practical reasons, without loss of face, without admitting the truth. Meeting elsewhere, in the home of one of his hypothetical friends, would have evaporated some essential spice, the scent of evil, the aroma of corruption— whatever you like to call it.

The affair would have become antiseptic, bland. It needed to be acted out in the same environment where it had been generated, under my aegis.

None of that could be said: we picked it out of the silence. Looking at him as we waited, dark and sulky, chewing his fingernails, fidgeting, glancing out of the window, lighting one cigarette from another, I thought that despite his distressingly offensive personal habits, which I tried in vain to overlook, he and I were in fact very much alike. Devious planners, both of us. Scheming and plotting in the heavy silence. Otherwise he would never have acquiesced to my dream so readily. He was on my wavelength. We were related.

'The point is,' he said, breaking the long silence and papering the cracks very obviously, 'she's got to *want* to see me more often than she *can* see me, otherwise it won't work.'

'Right,' I said.

'These early stages are very delicate,' he went on, like an artist or a market gardener. 'You've got to get the balance exactly right. Later on it doesn't matter so much.'

'You mentioned true love,' I said avidly.

'A figure of speech.'

'But surely that's what she really needs.' It was certainly what I myself needed her to have. I was bored with the limitations and inadequacies of sexual friendship and adventure. Was that all I had exerted myself for? Where, to put it crudely, were all the blood and guts? Troilus and Criseyde had not messed about like this, enjoying a pale safe imitation of the real thing. 'Isn't that why she keeps writing to you?' I demanded crossly.

'She writes because she's lonely.' He made the statement as though it were obvious and any fool should know it. 'She thinks she wants sex but really she needs someone to talk to. Mrs Salmon was the same. Most women are. They just want someone to hug and someone to listen. It's ludicrously simple. If the average man only realised that, he could have the time of his life.'

I considered this piece of wisdom, so carelessly dispensed. It seemed desperately sad, but I could not afford to let myself become sentimental at this stage in the game.

'Anyway,' he said, without real interest in the subject, 'why are you so obsessed with true love?'

I answered snappily, 'Perhaps because I've never experienced it.'

'What about when you were young?' An unnecessarily cruel thrust, I felt.

'It's not a matter of age,' I replied with dignity. 'It's a matter of temperament.'

'Come off it. We've all been through the mill at least once.'

Really he was so crude. All this coarse and outdated slang. It was just as well for him that he was good-looking or he would never have had any success in life at all.

'Perhaps some of us learn from experience sooner than others.'

That would have to satisfy him. I was concerned with other people's exposure, not my own. He actually laughed.

'What's that supposed to mean?'

'Let's just say I grew up at a very early age.'

He lit yet another cigarette from the stub of the old one, a detestable habit. It was extremely irritating that I still found him attractive. I hoped something bad would happen to him, and soon. A domestic disaster, since his career was already gratifyingly in ruins: perhaps the geyser could explode, his wife and children fall ill, the landlord suggest eviction. It was, after all, too early for Criseyde to betray Troilus. The affair had not yet run its appointed course.

'It sounds to me,' he said judiciously, 'as if someone hurt you pretty badly.'

I poured myself another martini, ignoring his empty glass. 'You've been reading too much paperback psychology,' I said.

(4)

'Dear David,

Sorry I had to hang up so quickly only Chris walked in just at that moment. Of *course* I was thrilled about your part — it's *marvellous* news — but does it really mean we can't meet for two whole weeks? Seems an awfully long time and with Xmas so near — I don't know, I find this time of year so depressing nowadays and I used to enjoy it, I suppose because when I was young it was all done for me whereas now it's up to me to do it all. It just seems like a lot of shopping for food and drinks and presents, all for people I don't really like— well, most of them anyway. We *will* be able to meet before Xmas, won't we? I was so looking forward to having a really leisurely lunch with heaps of time to make love, and I've got such plans for your present.

I suppose it really is impossible to meet if you're rehearsing every day and I know work has to come first, but if you do get any time off do ring up, won't you, I can get up to town at very short notice to do shopping or have lunch with Uncle A.— at least till the children break up, then of course it takes more organising. Anyway, I hope the rehearsals go well.

Keep in touch.

Gemma'

In terms of content, hardly worth the effort of opening and resealing, I thought crossly as I made it good. However, the plaintive tone was appealing and I was quite fascinated by the child-like confidence with which she revealed her feelings. No attempt at dissimulation. No suspicion that anything she said might be used against her. She was so simple and trusting. It was probably that very quality that endeared her to both of us — and would doubtless be her downfall.

I invited her to lunch: she was pale, restless, lacking her usual appetite. I thought I even detected reluctance to come to the flat knowing *he* would not be there, which annoyed me: I did not want to be dependent on him for her visits, when it should be the other way round. She fidgeted, didn't appreciate the food, drank too much and seemed to wander about touching the furniture to soothe herself— as if where David's duster had rested, she too could be at peace. It was true that he had a job: he had told me about it with disgusting smugness. But it certainly didn't mean he had no time to meet Gemma: that was policy. He was in fact still cleaning my flat (though at peculiar hours such as seven o'clock at night) and the part he was so nauseatingly triumphant about only amounted to a few lines, as I later discovered when I forced myself to watch it on the television. He was playing another of his petty crooks (which seemed appropriate enough) and playing it rather badly. I suppose when you work so seldom you get out of practice.

Gemma, however, was clearly bored by his absence and anxious about the Christmas festivities. As if to reassure herself that these would actually take place, she asked, after a lot of fumbling around the subject, if they could use my spare room. She meant with their own sheets and towels and bathrobe, as a sort of holy place undefiled by me (unlike my bed, my sofa and my carpet) but it took her a long time to say so. 'Just to have somewhere private that really belongs to us,' she said finally, then added with a flash of her old spirit, 'like renting a room without actually paying for it. You wouldn't mind, would you? Our own special place, in your flat, only separate. Where we could leave things and come back to them.'

I couldn't resist saying, 'You mean like Oswald and Miranda?'

She looked at me calmly, her eyes unclouded: the vision of the room, like a shrine, had uplifted her. 'Oh. I'd forgotten about them.'

After she had gone I inspected the spare room. It had an impoverished air, like all rooms that are seldom used: it seemed to have collected the worst furniture, and not just the worst but the most ill-assorted. Nothing matched; periods were jumbled together; the curtains and bedspread were thin and cold. It would require a lot of doing up, and it needed a large mirror. Gemma deserved the best. On the other hand I resented the very idea of spending money to benefit David, to whom I had already handed a pearl beyond price. It was an interesting problem, a genuine dilemma, and I lit a rare cigar and poured a not so rare brandy so that I might perch on its horns in greater comfort. I liked the idea of creating a love-nest; I liked even more the idea of disporting myself in it after the lovers had gone. It would remove once and for all the bother of working out where the action had taken place — all that undignified sniffing and peering. It would concentrate the essence of the affair in one room, rather like having a chapel in one's own home. I could light candles and burn incense, if the spirit moved me. I was impressed that it was Gemma who had thought of it, out of a desire for privacy, no doubt, which she had mentioned before; but it was nevertheless a creative idea and I had not thought Gemma capable of such artistry. I only hoped she did not plan to add a key: I doubted if I could be as adept at picking locks as opening letters, and it would be boring to be forced to behave like a burglar under one's own roof.

When David arrived to do his post-rehearsal stint and collect his mail, I was tempted to tell him what Gemma had suggested, but I restrained myself. It was amusing to know something he didn't, so instead, as a kind of compromise, I got him to clean the spare room; I pretended uninvited guests. He was tired and bad-tempered, requiring several drinks, but it was worth it to me, knowing that he was himself preparing the temple for his own use. I had been annoyed and jealous that his policy with Gemma was working so well, that his scheme could induce pallor and tension and anxiety so simply, and I had not thought of it, because of my impatience for action. But this, listening to the growl of the vacuum cleaner, watching him dusting and polishing, this made it all worthwhile. The balance was restored.

(5)

'Darling David,

God, it was fantastic this afternoon. I didn't know I could come so many times so quickly — I really had no idea it could be like that. What are you doing to me? You're going to make me so dissatisfied at home — no, I don't mean that, it *will* be all right, the way we said it would be right at the start, but it *is* going to be harder than I thought, like being two people. I feel so split — the good wife at home going through the motions once a fortnight and then today with you when I went right over the top so many times. I wish to God I could describe it properly so you'd really know how fantastic you make me feel but I can't — oh, why can't I? That long slow climb — only no effort — and then at the very top knowing I'm going to go right over the edge and nothing can stop me and down I go like that dream of falling only marvellous not frightening like blacking out for a second because the feeling's so strong it's as if I'll explode if I stay conscious. No wonder people used to

106

think it took years off your life — or was it days? Worth it anyway. Who wants to live long without that feeling? I keep thinking of skiing — the chair lift and the downhill racer — but that just makes it sound silly. Oh *hell*. I do so want you to know the pleasure you give me — I can't believe I do anything like as much for you but I wish I could. God how I wish I could.

It was amazing when you rang — I really was resigned to waiting two weeks — as soon as I heard your voice I got such a pain because I wanted you so much. I'd been trying not to think about it because I didn't want to masturbate, it always depresses me afterwards. And I thought I'd hate us only having half an hour but instead it was wonderful.

Oh I must stop, I'm just rambling on and not saying half what I want to say. I'll keep my fingers crossed about Xmas but at least we've had today. I must be very careful or Chris really will get suspicious if I keep going around with a goofy smile on my face!

Don't get run over, will you?

Gemma'

Well, that was better. Worth all my manual dexterity and the steam and the glue and the photo-copying machine. Worth it to know that Gemma had finally discovered the delights of multiple orgasm. (I envied her.) Worth it that I had been summarily turfed out into the cold street so that they could have what David inelegantly described as a quickie. Myself, I would have thought that a quickie involving multiple orgasm was a contradiction in terms, but his definition was half an hour hard at it with no time for chat. Even more to the point, Gemma had been summoned at only two hours' notice after ten days' starvation: it was a kind of test case, apparently, to see how highly motivated she was to rearrange her domestic life on the instant in the interest of sexual fulfilment, and she had passed with colours flying. Her reward was to be a leisurely erotic and gastronomic treat on the eve of Christmas Eve, but she didn't know that yet. 'I suppose you want me to cook,' I said to him, and he said well, he couldn't and wouldn't, having neither the talent nor the wish. And he certainly couldn't afford to take her out, he added, in case I was thinking of suggesting that. As with Beatrice, I felt uneasy at the mention of money: was he perhaps angling for a rise? It seemed more appropriate that he should pay me, or at least work for nothing to show his appreciation of the privileges I was bestowing on him; and in any case were the television people not foolishly paying him some vast amount for his dubious services — enough at least to buy Gemma a meal? Tactfully, I attempted to imply all that, only to be greeted with a diatribe: Cathy was (allegedly) shrieking like a fishwife about unpaid bills and the impossibility of providing Christmas festivities for the children on the pittance he gave her; the gas, electricity and telephone seemed in imminent danger of disconnection. All in all, my ill-wishing had worked well: the picture painted was of such financial blackness that his only hope of a square and romantic meal this side of next year would be one provided by me.

And of course I wanted to do it. Only not to be taken for granted. I like to be cajoled. As often as possible.

After he had gone (the so-called quickie representing a rehearsal unexpectedly cut short), I brooded. It sounds like something connected with old women or hens, but there is no other word for it. Obsession is a strange device for concentrating the mind: it takes over your life: it replaces everything else. I looked it up in the dictionary once and it means (in practice) exactly what it says (in theory) — not something that can be claimed for every word in the language, alas. 'The action of besieging,' I read, 'investment, siege.' I had certainly invested a great deal in Gemma, and my flat was frequently assailed. 'Actuation by the devil or an evil spirit from without; the fact of being thus actuated.' My only quarrel here, perhaps a little petty, was concerned with the direction from which the evil spirit came. I preferred to consider it very much a spirit from within; I flattered myself that I could produce, with total concentration, as much mischief as the devil in an idle moment. One yields to the experts, of course: in my case, more effort was required. The amateur cannot hope to surpass the professional in any sphere, but I believe equality can be achieved by perseverance and dedication and a bit of overtime.

Perhaps my dictionary had been compiled before it was acceptable to assume responsibility for such matters oneself: they had to be superstitiously attributed to a supernatural agency or else the sky would fall in. (Not that such an event would be entirely unwelcome: it would at least make a change and, incidentally, fulfil one of my favourite fantasies.) Finally, 'the action of any influence, notion or "fixed idea", which persistently assails or vexes'. Well, that seemed to me exactly what Gemma's and David's affair was doing to me — persistently assailing and (occasionally) vexing. And it certainly was a fixed idea: no other notion or influence ever entered my head. You may ask, But surely there were other people, friends, work, leisure activities? and I answer, Yes, there were, a few, or at least the choice of them, but they did not count, they were motions to be gone through, trivia, refuse; they might as well not have existed (and in a sense they did not). My whole life was given over to the creation of a doomed love affair; and why not indeed? Sufficient artistic preoccupation, you might think, for anyone.

So I brooded: hen, old woman, obsessive — what you will. Which is why Gemma's letter afforded me particular relief. I did not much admire her style, the ineffectual efforts to describe orgasm (a rock on which far greater talents have perished) but I did admire her courage in attempting such an unlikely feat. A noble failure, I thought. And it was rewarding to know that the whole scene (as Oswald and Miranda would have called it) was hotting up nicely.

At my age you do not expect surprises, nor are they welcome; so I was most disagreeably taken aback when the telephone rang next day and a cool, unmistakable voice I had heard only once before said, 'Mr Kyle?' in tones of resignation.

I said yes, as one is bound to do.

'This is Catherine Meredith,' the voice announced unnecessarily, for who else could it have been? That light, clear voice was unforgettably recorded in my head. Neither pleasant nor unpleasant, in fact conspicuously neutral, but instantly recognisable for the rest of my life, if I live (which God forbid) for a hundred years.

'I'm afraid we really will have to have a talk,' said the voice, not angry, not sad, but suggesting duty and commonsense like a dentist. 'Would tomorrow suit you?'

'A talk?' I said, playing for time and feeling it run out simultaneously. 'What about?'

'You're an intelligent man,' said the voice wearily. 'About your niece and my husband, of course, what else? And tomorrow really is the best day because David's in the studio, as you must know, so we're bound to be undisturbed. Unless your niece turns up, of course.'

She made us sound like conspirators already. (But how had she found out?)

'Mrs Meredith,' I said, 'why do we have to have a talk at all?' I was cooking at the time for David's and Gemma's love-feast only two days ahead; she could hardly have rung at a more unsuitable moment. 'I'm sure I'll be delighted to meet you at any time, but what is this urgency?'

She sighed. 'Surely you realise there may be a tragedy if one of us doesn't take steps to prevent it.'

There ensued a long silence which it occurred to me Mrs Meredith had no intention of breaking. Short of hanging up on her, which etiquette forbade, I was obliged to answer.

'All right, Mrs Meredith,' I said. 'I'll see you tomorrow. What time would be convenient?'

She answered crisply, 'Any time between nine and three.'

I shuddered at such possibilities. 'Shall we say half past eleven?' That way there seemed a good chance of getting rid of her before lunch, although I very much wished I had the courage to suggest half past two.

'That'll be fine. I'll see you then.'

She seemed about to go; I was forced to add, 'Don't you want my address?'

'It's on the envelope,' she said, and hung up.

So that was how she had found out. I warmed to Mrs Meredith, a reader of other people's letters, like myself. My curiosity was aroused; I should be happy to meet her. Mrs Meredith was clearly a woman to be reckoned with. But tomorrow? It was rather soon. I returned to my pâté, my chestnut stuffing, my chocolate mousse (for obviously as much as possible must be prepared in advance to be eaten cold in order to allow the heat of passion to rage freely.) I was less relaxed; there was no doubt about that. Only the roast would be actually cooking on the day, and they could lift that from the oven and carve it without too much effort, and content themselves with cold vegetables. What was I to say to Mrs Meredith and, worse, what was she to say to me? The chocolate mousse, normally the easiest thing in the world, promptly gave me trouble, as if sensing my agitation.

I slept badly that night. The hours raced and crawled with a peculiar jerky motion all their own. I took pills, slept, woke, drank water and looked at the clock. The night seemed endless. Catherine Meredith, unknown and inescapable, loomed before me. I longed to dream of her, as if to prepare myself, but she eluded me, very much a waking phantom, a hideous (or delectable) reality. David's wife. What was I expecting? I tried to get foreign stations on the radio to ease my suspense and fell instead into a jumble of sound. Towards dawn I slept soundly, exhausted by my imagination; at eight the telephone rang. It could be no one else: she must be ringing to cancel our bizarre appointment. I seized the instrument and croaked a greeting. Pips. Then a dialling tone.

After that there was no hope for me. A wrong number or a cruel joke, it made no difference; I lay awake, my head throbbing, while I pictured David and Catherine, Gemma and Christopher, all cosily tucked up in their respective beds. Or were they already rising to deal with their revolting children? No matter. As far as I knew, they had spent the night in peaceful marital slumber. They had not been racked as I was by doubt and uncertainty, or if they were, they were not alone to endure it. Moreover, Gemma was looking forward to the trysting day, David and Christopher were absorbed in their work, and Catherine Meredith, who would no doubt turn out to be a prize bitch, was preparing to make my life a misery. Why had I ever imagined it would be a pleasure to meet her?

Somebody once said that not sleeping doesn't matter so long as you are resting. I lay in bed stubbornly until ten o'clock, trying to rest, but the fact that I had not slept preyed on my mind. At ten I rose and went lugubriously through my

111

morning routine: breakfast, bath, clothes. There was no post. No letters to steam open. (It was surprising I did not open them all that way by now.) And just as well; my hands would have been unsteady. I was totally preoccupied with the irrational fear that Catherine Meredith would somehow get the better of me.

I was ready early, sitting miserably waiting for her. For a man of my age to feel at such a disadvantage was ludicrous and undignified. I should have been excited. I should have laid plans. I should have had the upper hand — or at the very least felt assured that we would meet on equal terms. Instead I sat huddled, a miserable sight in the mirror, like a chicken fluffing out its feathers. I awaited my fate.

She was precisely on time, as I had known she would be. I would have staked what was left of my life on that. The owner of that voice could not be late. The bell struck a solid chill into my soul, like an ice cube descending whole into the stomach. On my way to the door I felt myself putting on a brave face: I knew the feel of the stiff mask over my skin.

'Mr Kyle.'

'Mrs Meredith.'

I was so nervous I hardly saw her as I let her in. Once in the sitting-room she glanced all round it searchingly as though looking for dust. I half expected her to run a finger over the furniture. While she inspected the room, I began to look at her.

'Well,' she said at last, drawing out the word, 'he certainly does you proud. I'm glad about that. I'm glad he's good at something.'

She sat down and lit a cigarette.

I said, 'Mrs Meredith, what can I do for you?'

'You might as well call me Catherine.' She sat unmoving, unblinking: as cold and still as a corpse. Whatever I had expected, I had not been prepared for this extremity of thinness and pallor. Her hair was pale brown, her eyes grey, her skin beige. And not an atom of make-up. I was used to women who painted their faces. There seemed no colour in any part of her, just luminous bones. Even her clothes were neutral: a straw-coloured shirt and a long woollen skirt the shade of putty.

'After all,' she said, 'we're probably going to see a lot of each other.'

I thought that extremely unlikely and said so, hoping I had not also revealed the intense panic I felt at such a prospect.

'Oh yes,' she said, her voice quite expressionless. 'These things always take time, Mr Kyle. Believe me.'

'In that case,' I said politely, 'would you like to call me Alexander?'

She studied me and shook her head. 'No, I don't think so,' she said. 'After all, you're a lot older than I am and I don't think it's very polite calling older people by their first names, do you?'

Had there been any wind in my sails, that would certainly have taken it out. Both she and David seemed hell-bent on reminding me how old I was — as if I could ever forget it. In my mind the sand slipped through the hourglass continuously, causing me both terror and relief.

'At my great age I hardly know any older people.' It was not that I was offended exactly: her manner was matter of fact enough to take the sting out of her words. But I judged it best to lighten the proceedings if I possibly could.

She smiled. 'I'm not planning to use your name very often anyway,' she said. 'I don't like names much, I don't find them very useful. There's no doubt we're talking to each other, so what do we need names for?'

'Quite.' It occurred to me that she was perhaps slightly mad, but in a very logical way that appealed to me. I began to like her and my apprehension eased. 'Nevertheless, I intend to use your name a lot,' I said, with more of my old glib style, 'because it's so pretty.'

'Yes, it is, isn't it?' she said, as one might remark on the weather. 'It's the prettiest thing about me. Not as pretty as *her* name, though. Gemma.'

The name fell between us like a challenger's gauntlet.

'Now that really is a pretty name,' she went on smoothly. 'Does it suit her?'

'Yes.'

'Good. I thought it probably would. David usually chooses pretty girls. I think it's because he's so pretty himself, it's a

113

kind of mirror thing. I was an aberration on his part, but that was so long ago, he hadn't really got his eye in.'

Then she shut up and stared at me. Was I supposed to contradict her? She was certainly not pretty but there was something obliquely attractive about her. However, in my (albeit limited) experience, that is not the kind of remark that passes for a compliment among women.

'Well, Catherine,' I said uneasily, glancing at my watch, 'can I give you some coffee? Or a drink?'

It was twenty-five to twelve. I could hardly believe it. Only five minutes had passed.

She said, 'Thank you. I'd like a large scotch. I drink rather a lot, I should warn you, but I never get drunk. It seems rather a waste.'

I poured the scotch, and gin for myself. She declined soda or water.

'Ice?'

'Neat.'

I splashed tonic into my gin; I needed all the courage I could get, no matter from what source. I added one ice cube and then I added some more gin.

'Thank you.' She took a large mouthful of scotch: no one could have called it a sip, and a gulp suggests panic, which she was obviously far from feeling. 'Well,' she said, lighting a fresh cigarette from the stump of the old one, just like David, 'I suppose I should come to the point. All I really want is to save your poor niece from my husband.'

I swallowed gin and tonic and gin rather rapidly.

'Unless she wants to suffer, of course. If she does, she's really chosen the right person.'

I leaned back in my chair. 'Tell me more.'

'Well, if you care for her at all, you'll want to save her too.' She downed some more scotch. 'Oh, it's not entirely his fault. Being out of work so much doesn't help. If someone would actually pay him to create drama, he wouldn't need so much of it in his spare time. But since all his time is spare, as it were, what else can he do to justify his existence? I almost feel sorry for him at times.'

'And for Gemma?' I was beginning to enjoy myself.

'Oh yes.' She looked surprised. 'Of course. *She*'s not to blame. David can be quite irresistible when he chooses. He even was to me, once, though it's hard to remember now.' She drained her glass. 'Funny thing really. He's a very good actor in private life. It's only when he's working that he's so bad. I suppose that's why people don't employ him very often. It does seem ironic, doesn't it? He spends his life acting, he really ought to earn his living at something else. That's why I'm so glad he's got this cleaning job.' She looked round again appreciatively. 'I mean, this room is beautifully clean. What a pity he thinks it's beneath his dignity as a career.'

Her monologue had been delivered in a calm, reflective voice as if I were in her consulting room, not she in my home, and we were discussing a patient.

I asked, 'Then why does he do it so well?'

'Because he's acting the part of a cleaner. You're just lucky he's chosen to act a good one.'

I reached out a hand for her empty glass. 'Catherine,' I said, 'let me get you another drink.'

'That would be lovely. You see, I talk a lot as well.'

I poured her another large scotch and topped up my gin.

'Thank you. Actually, you seem to drink as fast as I do.'

I was startled by this observation, coming from someone who thought it impolite to use my Christian name.

'Sometimes,' I said cautiously.

'I'm always cheered when I meet another drinker. It's one of the few things David and I have in common — apart from the children, that is. Of course he always says I drove him to drink. That's one of the best things about marriage — having someone to blame.'

Again she stopped and stared at me. 'You're not married yourself.'

'No.'

'No, well, it doesn't suit everyone. Oh dear, I'm getting off the point again.' She paused and swallowed half the scotch in her glass. 'Look. About your niece. She really is going to get hurt, you know. We've got to do something.'

I said, 'You mentioned a letter.'

'Yes, I thought the last one was a lot more steamed up than

115

the others. I probably should have rung you sooner but the kids have had sore throats and it slipped my mind.'

It was my turn to stare at her. 'Do you always read your husband's letters?'

'Not the boring ones on the mantelpiece, no. Only the ones he tucks away in his pockets. He knows I go through his pockets, that's why he leaves his love letters there.'

'You mean he wants you to read them?'

'I imagine he must do. That way we both know what's going on without the effort of talking about it. Much easier.'

'I thought you said you liked talking.'

'Oh, only to strangers, not to David. Not after ten years. I mean— we've said it all. What is there left to say? I think most of the pleasure in conversation comes from the novelty, don't you? Now *you*'re a novelty. It's usually husbands and fathers I have to go and see. I haven't had an uncle before.'

I refilled both our glasses without asking, since it was obviously going to be necessary.

'You make a habit of this?'

'Well, David does, so why shouldn't I? Look, I don't think you realise how serious it is. Your niece is all set to fall in love with my husband.'

We were agreed on that at least. Joy sang in my heart.

'She told me it was just a casual affair,' I said innocently.

'Oh, he *always* starts them off like that. If they're married they feel safe and if they're not married, it's a challenge. Then after a few weeks he turns on the heat and suddenly it's a great love.'

I considered this with interest. 'D'you mean he falls in love too?'

She shrugged and poured more of my scotch down her throat. I wondered if I should put the decanter near her so she could help herself and save me all the bother of getting up and down so often. But it seemed a discourteous idea.

'God knows,' she said. 'I can't tell what goes on in his head. Sometimes he pretends he doesn't love them when he does and sometimes he tells them he does love them when he doesn't— I don't know, I can't keep track of it. He's always acting and turning all his feelings inside out. It's that mirror thing again.

116

That's how I think of him really. Permanently in front of a mirror. Admiring himself and reversing everything. It's all opposites. Left for right. And it feeds his ego. Maybe if he was working all the time he wouldn't do it so much.'

There was a pause. Predictably, she finished her drink.

'You must love him very much,' I ventured, 'to go to all this trouble.'

'Love?' she said reflectively. 'What's that? I like a quiet life. Every time he has one of these affairs some wretched woman goes berserk and I don't get a moment's peace for months. They ring up at all hours, they take overdoses, they come and weep all over me begging me to divorce him and their men get cross and beat him up and then he can't work.'

A memory stirred. 'Really? Who did that?'

'Oh, didn't he tell you? That woman in Golders Green, her husband caught him in bed with her and gave him the hiding of his life.' She frowned. 'I rang you. It was you he couldn't work for that day. Don't you remember?'

'Mrs Salmon,' I said.

'That's the one. Nice woman but she went off her head. Must have been the menopause, poor thing. And her husband was such a *big* man.'

'I thought she was a widow.'

Catherine Meredith smiled. 'Oh, is *that* what he told you?'

'But why? Such a pointless lie . . .'

'Well, he has to keep in practice. Like saying he's twenty-eight when he's thirty-two. Besides, it probably sounded more flattering — rich widow desperate for sex. Better than married woman having a bit on the side.'

'Like Gemma.'

'Exactly. You see how I get off the point. Now he'll have to turn that into something dramatic, he's bound to, he really needs it, and she sounds like a pushover — can't you do something to stop it before she gets hurt?'

I poured us both drinks. My head was beginning to swim, but Catherine Meredith, as promised, seemed perfectly sober.

'But what if she wants to go on with it?' I said. 'Who am I to interfere?'

She sighed. 'The one before Mrs Salmon jumped out of a window and broke her leg,' she said. 'Do you really want your niece to do that?'

I said gravely, 'I think I can promise you she won't do that.'

'Well, she'll do something. They all do. David only picks women like that. I don't know how he can tell but he can. One of them crashed her car into our garden and set it on fire. A woman who just shrugged her shoulders and said better luck next time, now she wouldn't be any use to him. Where's the satisfaction in that?'

'You talk as if all the affairs have to end badly.'

She looked at me as though I were stupid. 'Well, of course they have to end badly. Otherwise all these silly women wouldn't feel desperate, would they?'

I said craftily, 'But what if one of them rejected him?'

She shook her head. 'Oh no. That never happens. He can see it coming a mile off — he's got a sort of radar. No, he always gets in first.'

I rose unsteadily to my feet. My watch had stopped, but an enormous amount of time seemed to have passed and I was ravenously hungry, my stomach awash with nearly neat gin.

I said, 'Catherine, can I offer you some lunch?'

She looked startled. 'Oh no, I never eat during the day. But you go ahead.'

Considering the amount of whisky she had consumed, I marvelled that she even got through the day.

'I thought I might make myself an omelette,' I said feebly.

To my surprise she suddenly stood up. 'I expect you'd like me to go now,' she said. She seemed to specialise in the unanswerable.

'You must do exactly as you wish.' I thought longingly of eggs and butter.

'But you won't do anything to save her.' She began moving about the room in small circles that were obscurely threatening, as if she might spring on me at a moment's notice.

'What do you suggest?'

'Well, you could try giving David the sack. Then they wouldn't have anywhere to meet. That would be a great help.'

'That would make my niece unhappy. Besides, you said

yourself how efficient your husband is. I don't want to lose him. And you can't want him to be out of work.'

'That agency would find you another cleaner. And they'd find him another job. It would really make everything much simpler.'

I said, 'They'd only meet somewhere else.'

She eyed me strangely. 'I'm not so sure. David's very lazy— he hates making arrangements and asking favours of people— and he's much too mean to take her to a hotel. He usually sees them in their own homes when their husbands are out but he can't in this case, can he? So it all comes back to you.'

A chill of fear, temporarily held at bay by the gin, began to creep back.

'There's something odd about you,' she went on, quite casually. 'There's something odd about this flat. I get the feeling we've been at cross purposes the whole time. We're not talking about the same thing at all.'

Through the haze of protective alcohol, some paradoxical maxim about the interchangeable nature of attack and defence floated luckily into my mind.

'You mean in reality you're a jealous wife wanting revenge and you're only pretending you want to save my niece.'

She laughed quite heartily. She really was the most annoying woman. I could see I would have to make an ally out of her somehow, so as not to lose out utterly. The laughter was incongruous, seeming too strongly coloured with emotion to belong to such a neutral person.

'Oh really,' she said, 'you can do better than that. You're up to something, aren't you? I thought so all along, the funny way David talked about you. Is it something to do with writing, is that it? Are you collecting material or something?'

'Far from it.'

'If I hadn't read her letters I'd think you were all having a jolly little threesome. But that's not it. She's not that kind of girl, is she? I mean, those letters — they're so innocent. Positively childish.'

I said, 'I really will have to see about that omelette now.'

She smiled. 'All right, I'm going.' I began to follow her to the door. Suddenly she turned round to face me, so suddenly

119

that I nearly fell over her. 'You don't fancy him, do you?'

To my horror I heard myself saying, 'I beg your pardon?'

'You *know*. He's had several offers. You might be gay for all I know — I can't always tell. In fact I've often wondered if David is and doesn't want to admit it. Might account for him chasing so many women. At least, that's what it says in books.'

I managed to say, 'My dear lady, what an extraordinary idea.'

She shrugged and turned away. 'Oh well, I'll find out eventually. I always do.'

I accompanied her to the door, furious to find myself the victim of such a banal response as my heart knocking against my rib-cage loudly enough, it seemed, for her to hear it. She paused on the doorstep and held out her hand. I was obliged to take it; it was icy cold. I tried not to tremble at her touch.

'Thanks for the scotch,' she said cheerfully. 'It was very good scotch.'

'Yes,' I said. 'It was.'

She smiled. 'By the way,' she said, 'has he told you his life story yet?'

I shook my head.

'Try not to let him. It takes hours and he comes out a cross between Winston Churchill and Oliver Twist.'

The feast day came and Gemma arrived early. I was reminded of the far-off days of Christopher the eager puppy, when she had felt confident enough to be late. I put the finishing touches to the table. Gemma hovered. We were both nervously excited.

'It looks beautiful,' she said.

'I hope so.'

We both stared at it as if to make sure it did not change before our eyes.

'It's fantastic,' she said. She kept darting off to brush her hair in front of the mirror and apply more scent. She smelled so delicious it was all I could do not to pounce on her.

'I've got him a silk dressing-gown,' she said. 'I do hope he'll like it.'

120

'He'll love it,' I said, indignant at any other possibility. 'How could he fail to love it?'

She looked at me with the same big frightened eyes as in the old days when I had read her X-certificate fairy tales. 'It's Christmas. Our first Christmas. I couldn't bear it to be a failure.'

'In my spare room,' I said, 'how could it be?'

She froze; then exploded with joy. 'You darling. Have you really?' She hugged me and I felt for a moment the wildness of her that he knew and I did not; her scent made me dizzy. 'May I look?'

'I'll be most offended if you don't. I've gone to a great deal of trouble.'

She ran off like a child to find a toy. I followed her slowly, followed the cries of delight that were coming from my spare room, no longer spare but filled with a sense of purpose she had once hoped to get from growing her hair.

'Oh, it's marvellous. You've done wonders. It's all new.'

I stood in the doorway looking suitably modest. 'I've added a few things here and there.'

'You're an angel.'

She looked about to burst into tears. I reflected how beautiful she was. I had not been wrong when I looked at that child of four: she had been worth waiting for. No wonder we all wanted to possess her.

I said, 'I think I'll go now. Before he comes.'

She seized me by the arm. 'Oh no. Stay and have a drink with us.'

'I'd really rather not. I've been told I drink too much — and anyway, all this emotion, at my age it's bad for the heart.'

She studied me while I got into my coat, my winter favourite, mutton got up as Persian lamb.

'You put on such a cynical act,' she said tenderly, 'to hide how kind you are.'

'Just remember to take the roast out at one o'clock.'

I went to see *Gone With the Wind* for the fourth time and sat there, an exile from home, analysing my reactions to Catherine Meredith, while Scarlett pursued Ashley, Rhett pursued Scarlett, and Melanie smiled at everyone. It was comforting to have a familiar background against which to do my thinking. When you have seen a film four times in thirty years, it becomes like reading a diary: yourself when young springs out of every frame.

I wanted to find out more about David and Catherine, but if I did it would be superfluous information: I could not incorporate it into my design. Criseyde had been a widow; well, that was all right. It was both easy and pleasant to imagine Christopher dead. But it was not fitting that Troilus should have a wife. She gave him a less romantic, more homespun image; she might upset all my plans; she represented events beyond my control. And she had brought a most unwelcome blast of cold air into my carefully nurtured hot-house atmosphere, with her careless talk of broken legs and burning cars. A note of ridicule indeed. My tender plants might not survive the icy breath of laughter. How dare she mock all I had struggled so long and so hard to create with true high seriousness: my own private living work of art.

As usual I wept when Scarlett vowed never to be hungry again, and the lights for the intermission came up and caught me wiping my eyes and my glasses. The last time I had seen the film I had been in America, surrounded by teenagers who had come to mock and remained to cry. This generation seemed more robust, queuing dry-eyed for ice-cream and soft drinks. Well, it was their loss. Myself, I could have done with a hard drink, but it was not that kind of cinema.

I was not even bothering to imagine the erotic antics in my spare room; yet today was the peak of my achievement so far. I wanted to see Catherine Meredith again, and not just to keep her under surveillance. She fascinated me: the drinking, the talking, the new angle on David. His lies — or were they hers? The truth about Mrs Salmon? They could not both be telling the truth, so one (or both) of them must be lying. How far could I pursue my double mirror image, I wondered, for here might be a unique opportunity to observe not only one but two couples in action. I felt slightly disloyal because although I loved David and Gemma in my own fashion, I found

122

Catherine more interesting. She was intelligent; I was afraid of her. I thought David was probably afraid of her too. And yet I felt that if we could join forces, she and I, we would be invincible.

And if not? I borrowed Scarlett's philosophy: I would not think of that now. I would think of it tomorrow.

When I got home I was amazed and rewarded for my fortitude: David was still there. Still in fact wearing the new silk dressing-gown, which turned out to be a rather strange colour that looked expensive rather than attractive and was probably called aubergine. He was sitting on the dishevelled bed of the spare room with a dazed expression on his face. I asked if he should not be at home by now, but he said he had told Cathy he was having drinks with a casting director.

'Happy Christmas,' I said. To tell the truth, though pleased to see him, I was almost embarrassed at my nearness to their love-making. Gemma's scent was everywhere in the room. Alone, I could have enjoyed it properly; with David there I was wrong-footed.

'The food was terrific,' he said. 'You did us proud.'

His last words echoed because Catherine had used them. It must be a family expression; I had noticed before how married people often talked alike. To get away from the tantalising smell of sex, I wandered into the dining-room.

He called after me, 'It's all right, I've cleared up in there,' and so he had, as if the feast had never been. I went back to the spare room and found him getting dressed: his body was covered with dark curly hair and he was circumcised. Suddenly I felt ill with envy; but which of them I envied most I could not have told you. An extraordinary feeling, so intense as to leave me physically weak: I had to hold on to the door for a moment. But it passed, as all feelings pass.

'Look what she gave me,' he said, hanging the dressing-gown on the back of the door. 'It must have cost the earth.'

'She's very generous,' I said. He was like a child, enchanted by a present. Or did he think mere expense made him more worthy?

'She stayed till four,' he said. There was something odd

123

about his voice: a stunned quality. As if he was telling me that she was generous with time as well as money and he was surprised.

I said, 'D'you want a drink?' It was after six and I needed one badly.

He shook his head. 'No, I don't think so. We had rather a lot — she brought champagne and so did I.'

He was dressed by now. He surveyed the room. 'I just didn't want to clear this up too soon.'

'Shall I help you?' I moved forward slightly. My sick feeling had passed; already I was able to enjoy seeing the lipstick marks on the pillow, the semen stains on the sheets.

'No, don't help me, I'd rather do it.' He began to do it in a reluctant desultory style, not at all the way he dealt with the rest of the flat. He said, 'You're going there at Christmas, aren't you? To her home?'

'Yes, I always do.'

'Then give her this and pretend it's from you. I mean she'll know it's from me but let the others think it's from you. Then she can wear it all the time.' He put a small, badly-wrapped package into my hand.

'I shall have to wrap it better than that,' I said, 'or no one will believe it's from me.'

'Do what the hell you like with it, only give it to her. She won't be expecting it, she thinks we've both had our presents today, but I want her to have something extra on the day.' He reached for his jacket, then as if changing his mind sat down suddenly on the bed. 'I think I love her. My God, what have you done?'

Book 4

'Those who serve love have painful things to do
From time to time, if they would have the joy.'

Christmas Eve

As usual I stayed with Beatrice. A strange convention but one accepted by us both, that since we were related by marriage and lived alone, we ought to be together at Christmas. No amount of tacit dislike could get around that, it seemed. I drove down there on Christmas Eve and I returned home on the day after Boxing Day. Nothing less would have sufficed: it was traditional. We had both long since given up considering how much we resented it, or perhaps we had simply gone past resentment. There is, after all, something restful about knowing exactly what you will be doing for three days every year, particularly when all your eating and drinking is at the expense of others.

My chosen contribution was champagne (also traditional): six bottles in a box on the back seat of the car, produced with a flourish like the conjurer's rabbit and greeted by Beatrice with cries of amazement and wonder, as if I had never done it before. After that, I could relax: no further effort was required. I had only to be even-tempered and appreciative.

Between six and eight Beatrice kept open house for neighbours, some of whom brought small presents and all of whom consumed large drinks. (Not our precious champagne, though; that was for family delectation only.) I was usually introduced as a visiting celebrity ('This is my brother-in-law, Alexander Kyle; I expect you've heard of him.') to new neighbours; old ones were supposed to remember me from last Christmas. It was all fairly embarrassing, as I grew more obscure every year and few of the neighbours had the slightest idea who I was, though some of them were polite enough to pretend, however unconvincingly, that they had.

Promptly at eight, like well-trained dogs responding to a

127

high-frequency whistle, they all departed and Beatrice and I sat down to our solitary dinner together. Beatrice cooked turkey on Christmas Eve in order that Gemma might cook goose on Christmas Day. Each year I found myself wondering how a woman with so little imagination could be such a good cook. Eventually I decided that all Beatrice's latent energy, all her creative talents that might otherwise have been channelled into eroticism or wit, had discharged themselves in *haute cuisine*, an art she had certainly concealed from her daughter.

Christmas Eve was also reminiscence night, and over the first bottle of champagne Beatrice dug out her memories: my dead brother, their idyllic courtship and marriage, her tragic loss, Gemma's birth, the trials of her upbringing, the triumph of her marriage and the joys of grandchildren. (Beatrice, like most women, had lived her life vicariously.) All that was routine and usually took us up to the plum pudding; I had only to listen and grunt. But tonight she seemed to gallop through it all, cutting short her customary eulogy of the children and doubling back to Christopher before we had finished the turkey. I listened uneasily: any departure from tradition at this time of year had to be suspect.

'Poor Christopher,' she said, sighing a little. 'It's such a pity he has to work so hard.'

'Does he have to?' I asked. 'I thought it was his choice.'

'Well, he's very dedicated, of course.' She approved of the dedication; I could see her casting around for a way to criticise it without compromising her principles. 'Too much for his own good, I sometimes think.'

I refilled her glass. She went on as if I had asked her to explain.

'Well, it doesn't leave him much time with Gemma and the children. I often think it's a pity Gemma's always had help in the house — all those silly foreign girls and that cleaning woman — it leaves her with a lot of time on her hands.'

Was I imagining a look of suspicion, interrogation, on that large bland bovine face?

'She hasn't always had help in the house,' I said. 'Only since the second child.'

'Well, nearly always. I never had anyone to help me with

128

Gemma, there simply wasn't enough money. I had to struggle on alone as best I could.'

Christmas, I thought, was an unlucky time to be reminded of Beatrice's everlasting poverty.

'You had a cleaning woman for years,' I said. 'I distinctly remember her. She had varicose veins.'

'Oh, Mrs Hodges. Yes, but you could hardly describe her as a help.'

I refilled my own glass. If Beatrice was determined to play the martyr, I might as well get quietly drunk. She went on with a nasty edge to her voice:

'I wonder sometimes if Gemma appreciates how lucky she is.'

I said smoothly, 'Oh, I'm sure she does.'

'When I compare her life to mine— well, I just wonder if she realises, that's all.'

'But you wouldn't have wished her to suffer like you, surely?'

'No.' She sounded uncertain, as if, with hindsight, she felt a little suffering might have done Gemma good but, in her maternal role, dared not own up to such an idea. Or was that amount of sadistic commonsense beyond her?

'After all, it was always your ambition she should marry well,' I reminded her. 'And she has.'

'Yes.' Again she sounded doubtful. 'Too well, perhaps.'

'You mean you envy her?'

'Of course not, don't be ridiculous. I just mean she's had a very easy life.'

'Well, it's not over yet,' I suggested. 'Perhaps the worst is yet to be.'

'Now, Alex, that's not funny at all.'

'Who's trying to be funny? Isn't that exactly what you were advocating — a little healthy disaster to make her count her blessings?'

We had clearly finished with the turkey. Beatrice compressed her lips and gathered up the plates. I watched her broad shape disappear into the kitchen; I should have to be very careful. Her instincts were still making her pursue the scent she could not identify. But that only made it more exciting. She

129

was not a worthy adversary but she would add a little spice to the game. After all, without the Nazis, there would have been no need for the Maquis.

Christmas Day

Christmas morning meant church with all the family. Agnosticism was no excuse and I had long ago decided to give in gracefully. Besides, I enjoyed the ritual, enjoyed hearing the music and inhaling the incense and wondering how high Beatrice's favourite vicar really was. Religion, like money, was a subject I preferred not to discuss with her, but it amused me to sit in the pew beside my relations (making six of us in all) and play the conformist. Now and then I would steal a glance at Gemma's profile, so pure and serene (what a pity the children had not inherited it), and wonder if her conscience troubled her at all, particularly in this holy setting. But for most of the time I simply shut my eyes and gave myself up to the delight of erotic thoughts. My first night in the spare room had proved most satisfactory.

After church we all assembled at Gemma's house, armed with two of my precious bottles of champagne, and started drinking to deaden the sound of Gemma's children playing with their toys. Santa Claus had arrived at half past five, Gemma told me, miming exhaustion with a charming bend of the knees.

'This is very good of you, Alex,' Christopher said, opening a bottle.

'It's the least I can do,' I said modestly. I was enjoying myself; I always enjoyed myself in Christopher's presence since the affair began. It was as if I had been granted perpetual double vision: every time I looked at Gemma and Christopher, I saw Gemma with David. And it was all my doing. The sense of power made my head swim long before I tasted the champagne. I could hardly wait to get back to London to continue my machinations, yet the enforced hiatus was almost attractive, giving me time to savour my own anticipation.

Gemma's goose was not a success, but we all pretended it was. I hoped her typing would prove more reliable, should I ever have occasion to test it. Proof of her more than adequate talent for flower arrangement was all around us throughout the year. I used to think that Beatrice had maliciously withheld her culinary arts from Gemma, until I recalled that she had parted with her most precious commodity — money — in order to entrust Gemma's education in these matters to others. It was ironic and appropriate that of the three skills Gemma had acquired only the least useful and the most decorative. Meanwhile, I entertained myself during lunch with variations on the theme of her goose being cooked, since the conversation was generally reduced to the lowest common denominator of the children, and therefore left a great deal of time for private thought.

Grown-up presents were exchanged after lunch, again according to a tradition whose origins no one could remember but which struck me as foolish, since by that time the children had forgotten the avalanche of parcels they had received in the morning and demanded more, becoming fractious and greedy. A few small extra gifts (apart from ours) were put by to pacify them: not for the first time I marvelled that a man who was otherwise so coldly rational could as a father be so indulgent. I even wondered what character changes I might have undergone had I ever become a parent. Fortunately, there had never been the least danger of my finding out.

We all assembled in the sitting-room and the ritual began.

Beatrice gave Gemma a book, Christopher a record, and me some driving gloves. I was a most difficult person to buy presents for, she reminded me, and we all laughed, for no apparent reason. Everyone then marvelled at what had been unwrapped. Gemma and Christopher kissed Beatrice. I smiled at her.

Christopher gave Gemma a blue cashmere jersey, Beatrice some scent and me some cigars. He apologised for his lack of originality. Gemma kissed him. Beatrice kissed him. He and I shook hands.

Gemma gave Christopher a shirt, Beatrice a nightdress, and me an onyx cigarette box. We all kissed her and sat down again, exclaiming that she had given us just what we wanted. There was a lull. I had been waiting for it with fearful delight.

I gave Christopher a bottle of brandy, Beatrice some slippers, and handed Gemma the newly wrapped gift from her lover. She looked puzzled; she had been expecting her usual bottle of scent (now reposing on the mantelpiece of the spare room.) She could tell from the shape of the parcel it was not scent.

Beatrice and Christopher unwrapped their presents and told me what an excellent choice I had made. They did not feel compelled to touch me to prove the point. Gemma was slow with her parcel and suddenly just as she opened it I realised she was going to blush. I quickly diverted Beatrice's and Christopher's attention to some nonsense with the children and their toys so that I could watch, enraptured and in perfect safety, the deep flush of colour in Gemma's face. She looked up and caught my gaze; she knew. I nodded.

She took out a silver pendant on a silver chain and slowly hung it round her neck. On the medallion was her Zodiacal sign of Virgo. Until that moment I had been quite angry with David for not researching the matter: the present was totally out of keeping with my character. But the look of enchantment on Gemma's face made me forgive everything.

'Whatever's that?' said Christopher, turning round from ruffling his son's hair.

Gemma said carefully, 'It's a pendant with my birth sign on it. Isn't it lovely?'

Christopher actually laughed. 'So you finally got one.' He turned to me. 'I didn't think you believed in all that nonsense.'

'I don't,' I said, 'but Gemma does.'

'Oh, Gemma certainly does. She's been nagging me for years to get her something like that.' Alcohol had made him almost jovial.

Beatrice said sharply, 'I thought you always gave Gemma scent for Christmas.'

'Time for a change.' I beamed at her in my best jolly-uncle style. 'I suppose I really should have thought of it in time for your birthday,' I said to Gemma.

'Oh, this is much nicer. More of a surprise.' She was holding the medallion loosely in her hand, moving it to and fro on its chain.

'I even wondered if I should have got them to put Libra on

132

the other side as you're nearly on the cusp, but the man in the shop advised against it.' Was I overdoing it?

'My word,' said Beatrice, 'you *have* been reading it up.'

'Maybe Gemma's been dropping hints,' I said, passing the ball.

She fielded it neatly, as I expected. 'Fancy that, you actually remembered me saying I used to read both horoscopes to get the best of both worlds. Well, I don't do that any more.'

'Then I made the right decision,' I said, trying to sound bored with the subject.

'And Gemma got her own way again,' said Beatrice.

'Well, why not?' said Christopher genially, pouring us all brandy. 'It *is* Christmas, after all. If a silly present like that makes her happy — no offence, Alex, you know what I mean — well, why shouldn't she have it?'

And then to my amazement I heard Gemma say, 'Well, I couldn't get it from you so I had to get it from someone else.'

Luckily at that moment one of the children stepped on a toy, overbalanced, fell and hit its head on the corner of a chair. All hell broke loose, distracting us perfectly. Beatrice and Christopher sprang to the rescue at once but Gemma was swifter and had the child in her arms before they could reach it. At intervals it paused to draw breath and there was a brief but welcome silence before the next bellow. The other child watched with what appeared to be mild interest and total unconcern, confirming my belief that the basic callousness of human nature is determined at an early age, and Christopher's views on family planning were absolutely justified.

Nothing else of interest occurred, and at six o'clock tradition decreed that we should leave, so that Gemma and Christopher could be alone with their children and Beatrice and I could be alone with each other. We were all destined to consume cold meat in solitude that evening when we might — who knows? — have preferred to go out and get drunk at the local inn (was it open?) or retire early to bed to sleep — or weep for our transgressions. But variations on the theme were not permitted. Christmas must be played according to the rules, or not at all. I hoped David and Catherine were having a fairly dismal time in Kentish Town.

133

On the way back in the car Beatrice said to me coldly, 'You're spoiling her.'

I considered the implications of this, spoken after a long silence; in particular the interesting ambiguity of the word spoiling. Did Beatrice have in mind indulgence or ruin; and did one, in fact, automatically lead to the other? I thought for some time about what my answer should be: a polemic or a dignified silence. In the end I settled for enigmatic neutrality, which spared me a lot of effort.

'Of course,' I said.

Boxing Day

I still had not been alone with her.

Boxing Day was a gamble: it could go either way. Dregs or bonus. Gemma and Christopher were obliged to lunch with us, but beyond that nobody quite knew what to do with the time. It was a left-over day: we had all eaten and drunk too much, drowned in presents, seen each other too often. We had run out of steam. I was not allowed to depart, although I am sure Beatrice hoped I would. Everyone was beginning to wish that life could be normal again, and then feeling guilty for wishing it.

Still, if I were lucky or clever, there might be a chance. I could tell Gemma wanted to talk: she had a furtive, shifty expression on her face and she kept trying to manoeuvre the lunchtime preparations and aftermath so that we could be alone together. ('Uncle Alex and I can get lunch for you, Mummy; it's only cold, isn't it?' Or: 'Mummy, why don't you sit down, you're doing too much. Uncle Alex and I can do the washing up.')

But Beatrice foiled her, martyr to the end. Not for nothing was it the feast of St Stephen, and Beatrice intended to make us feel every arrow.

'Nonsense, Gemma, you know I enjoy it. And anyway, you look worn out.'

It was unfortunately true. Gemma did look pale and tired — drawn, I believe the word is, only that reminds me of seasonal poultry, or felons on the Elizabethan scaffold. I wondered if

134

Christopher had been claiming his rare conjugal rights as a Christmas treat.

As if accused, he now looked up from the *Radio Times*; he was strangely addicted to old films on bank holidays, though too disciplined to succumb to them on other occasions.

'Does she? I thought she was looking rather pretty today.' He caught hold of her hand as she passed him, squeezing it briefly. I thought I saw Gemma flinch, but that may have been wishful thinking.

'I've eaten too much,' said Gemma inconsequentially. 'I'm going to be fat as a pig. D'you fancy a walk, Chris?'

She must have known he'd refuse.

'Well, I rather fancied watching *The African Queen*.'

'Oh, is *that* on again?' said Beatrice and stopped short, having fallen neatly into Gemma's trap.

'I'll come for a walk with you, Gemma,' I said casually. 'I could do with some fresh air.'

That left Beatrice with a dilemma. According to her own etiquette, it would be impolite to leave Christopher alone in front of the television, however much he might desire such a fate. Obediently she switched on the set, and shot me a glance that was almost pure hatred. I was surprised; I had not thought her capable of such extreme emotion.

'Take the kids with you, Gemma,' said Christopher over his shoulder. 'Then we'll get a bit of peace.'

It was a nasty day, typical of the English winter at its worst, not the Christmas card variety, picturesque with snow, but dank, raw, clammy weather like November. There was nothing crisp and clean about it, as winter should have been, only a misty chill that seeped into your bones as you walked. The children didn't notice, mercifully; they ran ahead shouting and throwing sticks for the dog. In the distance, a few other families were bent on the same errand; otherwise the common was deserted.

'Alone at last,' I said to Gemma.

She giggled; not a habit I like in others but in her it was charming, full of childish mischief without the other disadvan-

135

tages of childhood. She was tactfully wearing Christopher's present over her jeans and under her sheepskin (firework) jacket. The blue matched her eyes almost exactly. It was like Christopher to select the obvious colour: I was pleased to find him so predictable. And round her neck, proudly, defiantly, hung the medallion for all to see.

'I think your mother guesses,' I said.

'Yes, so do I. At least, she thinks there's something but she doesn't know what.'

Silence. We walked on. Alone again with her after what seemed an eternity, I felt I was reclaiming her, like land from the sea. Too many tides had washed over her: David, Christopher, the children, Beatrice, but at some fundamental level she was still mine. I wondered why I wanted to risk losing her: all my schemes, first with Christopher, now with David, took her temporarily out of my orbit. Some kind of potency test, perhaps, or else the ultimate gamble for a jaded palate. For if I lost Gemma I would lose everything.

Suddenly she said vehemently, 'Well, she can rot. She can't prove a thing.'

The violence amazed me; what passions had David awakened? I was pleased. 'She, she — the cat's mother, they used to say when we were children. It was very rude.'

'Yes. I hope so.'

'It's odd that she's noticed and Christopher hasn't.'

A long sigh. 'Oh, he's too close. He can't see what's under his nose. Or he doesn't want to.'

'That's more important. You need him to be blind, don't you?'

She didn't answer. Just as suddenly, after another silence, as if starting a new conversation, she said, 'God, I hate her. She's never stopped watching me — she used to know when my period was due before I did. She just sits in a corner watching and waiting like a bloody great spider.'

The analogy pleased me: Beatrice was terrified of spiders.

'I've always hated her,' I said smugly.

'You used to hide it.'

'I used to do lots of things I don't do now.'

'Besides, it's all right for you. You can afford to hate her, she's only your sister-in-law. But it's awful to hate your mother.'

'Awful it may be,' I said, 'but it seems to be very common. And it isn't all right for me — I absolutely dispute that. Nothing is all right for me. Far from it.'

But she wasn't interested in me; she was too young. She was only interested in herself.

'It's terrible to hate your mother when you never knew your father,' she said. 'It's worse than being an orphan.'

Another silence. I felt we were leading up to something.

'He's an orphan,' she said.

'Yes, I know.' Christopher's parents had conveniently died in the classic car crash the year after he qualified, as if they had wanted to make sure of his education and then relieve his future wife of the encumbrance of in-laws.

'I meant David.'

It was then that I knew, really knew for certain, for the first time, that she was in love. The way she said his name was unmistakable: the proud casualness mixed with the tender lingering verbal caress, as if no one else in the world had ever had a name. I wondered if I had misunderstood her deliberately in order to make her say it so that I could hear it.

'He's had a terrible life,' she went on. 'His parents divorced when he was five and he was shunted between them. Then his father died and his mother remarried and didn't want him — imagine that, not wanting your own child — so he went to foster parents. But they said he was too difficult to keep — because he was so unhappy, of course — so he went to another lot, and another, but none of them worked out, and then his mother said she'd have him back after all, only then *she* died so he ended up in a children's home.'

She said the word with such horror that she made it sound like Auschwitz. I was reminded of Othello and Desdemona: something about 'She loved him for the dangers he had passed And he loved her that she did pity them.' I had never found that particularly convincing, but obviously Shakespeare as usual was right and I must revise my ideas. However, I also remembered Catherine Meredith's warning, and I wished I had paid more attention to Oliver Twist and Winston Churchill, at least in their youth.

'So of course he got married young just to have a home of his own and someone to love. But after the children were born his wife said she didn'want him any more.'

I cast about vainly for something to say that Gemma would consider adequate. It was, after all, the first time in her life that she had had any one to feel sorry for. A luxury.

'Extraordinary,' I said.

'So now they stay together because of the children. He can't bear his children to go through what *he* went through, you see, and he's afraid they might, if there was a divorce. So he stays. He'd rather he was unhappy than risk upsetting his children.'

She sounded as if she were nominating him for the Nobel Prize for sanctity.

'It sounds grim,' I said.

'It's terrible.'

She seemed really upset when she ought to be grateful: if he were happily married he might not be having an affair at all. (I say 'might' advisedly, as I am far from expert on the matter.)

'You knew at once about the present,' I said to change the subject.

'We talked about it once. He said if he ever——' She stopped and seemed to change her mind. 'He said it was something he might give me one day. He knew I wanted one. He believes in it all. He's Gemini. We're not supposed to be compatible.'

Perhaps answers were not really necessary. Perhaps she was talking to herself. In a moment she might tell me his collar size and his inside leg measurement, the colour of his socks and the design of his underpants, what kind of shampoo and toothpaste he used and whether he believed in deodorant or sweat. Any amount of random trivia might pour out of her because, if it pertained to him, the vital him, it was of supreme importance. I dimly, enviously recalled the feeling. Every scrap was valuable. (I had once stored someone's nail clippings in an envelope.) When the beloved crossed the room you stared in wonderment at the miraculous way he or she moved. Look, they can walk, aren't they wonderful, you thought quite seriously.

Sensing her recklessness, I said, 'You took a chance yesterday, saying what you said to Christopher.'

'I know. I couldn't stop myself. I was suddenly so angry with him.'

'Why?' This was progress.

'Oh— for having everything. And for being so pleased with himself. And for being so bloody sensible.'

And for not noticing, I thought.

'I wouldn't mind if he had faults, like Mummy,' she went on. 'She's a bitch. But he's a good person — really good. He's kind and generous and he never thinks of himself.'

'And he never thinks of you either.'

'Well, he's always thinking of other people. Their welfare and all that. It makes me want to scream sometimes but how can you scream at someone like Chris? I mean, he'd be so surprised and hurt. And then he'd make allowances for me. He really hasn't any faults— oh, I know you don't like him much, but really, he hasn't. He makes me feel terribly inferior. I used to think I was all right— not good, not bad, just all right— but living with Chris . . . ' She fell silent, as though living with Chris left her speechless; she tried again. 'Well, he's so *adult*. Whereas David and I are like children playing together. I feel we're equal. We don't want to hurt anyone but we do want to be happy. Now I don't suppose Chris has ever thought about whether he's happy or not — that's simply not the way he thinks.'

She stopped. I thought it all sounded most promising and was about to press for more when a piercing shriek distracted me. In the distance the younger child had fallen over. The elder one yanked it to its feet, then stood and watched it bawling. Gemma stared in the direction of the accident but did not move. The moment was frozen, one of those trivial incidents that would be timeless, forever fixed in memory for no apparent reason.

'Mummy,' Jonathan yelled without emotion, sounding rather bored. 'Stephanie's hurt herself.'

'Coming,' Gemma called back, but she still didn't move; she fiddled with the fastenings of her coat and said to me in a low voice as if we might be overheard, 'D'you think it's possible to love two people?'

I felt it was a rhetorical question and did not answer: in a moment she ran ahead to join her children.

Next day I escaped and went home with a letter in my pocket. She kissed me goodbye with tears in her eyes.

(6)

'Darling David,

I don't know what to say to you about my lovely lovely present. It's perfect, exactly what I meant, and as soon as I saw it I heard your voice saying, If I ever give you something like that you'll know I'm in love with you. Darling, did you mean it? I can't bear it if you don't. I think I fell in love with you ages ago only I wouldn't admit it, I was too scared. After all you said about us having a sexual friendship I was afraid my being in love would put you off, and I was afraid for myself too — afraid I couldn't look Chris in the face if I actually loved you. So I pretended I didn't — it was safer. I fooled myself so I could fool him. Now I can't any more. I ought to feel guilty but I'm too happy. It's as if you've said it's all right for me to love you — I couldn't quite let myself till you gave me permission. Now I feep terribly free. I can be myself. When I'm with you I feel completely different from when I'm at home — I'm another person and I think that person is really me, or at least a side of me I can't express at home. It's so awful feeling only certain bits of you are acceptable and you've got to sit on the rest and squash it down because it's nasty or silly.

Darling, I'm wearing your present day and night. It was so clever of you to think of giving it to me that way so no one could object, and Uncle A. played his part beautifully. (I think he enjoyed the intrigue.) Chris made fun of it, of course, and I wanted to hit him. He can't stand anything like astrology and he always makes fun of things that upset him.

It's awful being Virgo, can you imagine the jokes at school I had to put up with? I do wonder though what it would have been like if I'd been a virgin for you, if we'd met in our teens and I hadn't married Chris and you hadn't married Cathy. It's tempting to imagine us living happily ever after but that may

140

be just a silly fantasy — perhaps we only get on so well now because of all we've been through already. The thing that worries me now in spite of being so happy is about whether there's enough love to go round. It works all right with children — I mean you don't love the first one less after you have the second — but that's different. Can it work in a case like this? (You ought to know — come on, tell me what happened before in all those affairs you pretend you didn't have!) Already I don't want Chris to make love to me, I only want you. And I used to be so angry with him when he didn't feel sexy — now I'm angry with him when he does. And then of course I feel guilty because I ought to be pleased and he's probably only trying to please me because I used to complain — or maybe I'm more attractive now I've got you? — but anyway it's no good, all that stuff about rights and duties doesn't mean a thing when you're in love, in fact it's pretty revolting. Chris has rejected me so often, why should I accept him now when I don't want to? I wish we could live like brother and sister, then we might get on perfectly well — if I could see you as often as I like, a bit much to ask, even of a brother!

I find I keep thinking about you and Cathy and wondering, if you really love me, whether you still want her. I know you said she doesn't ever want you but I find that so hard to believe. Not that I think you're lying, just that I can't imagine anyone not wanting you. In one way I feel very jealous when I imagine you both together, quite sick with jealousy, but in another way I almost hope you do make love because if I can't be with you I'd rather you had someone, even her. I know how much sex means to you and I can't bear to think of you feeling deprived. And because she's your wife it doesn't seem quite so bad — as if it doesn't really count. If it was another woman I'd die of jealousy but you wouldn't do that to me, would you?

I'm sure there must be something wrong with marriage if we all end up like this.

Christmas was simply awful — packed with relatives and friends all eating and drinking too much and talking about nothing and watching rubbish on TV. Thank God it's over. If I was God I wouldn't have a birthday. Do you think that's blasphemy? I know you said you don't believe but I bet you do really even if it's only on the 'old man with a beard in the sky watching us all' level.

If it hadn't been for your present I think I'd have gone mad over Christmas. In fact if we hadn't met I really don't know what I'd be doing now, I can't believe we're meant to spend our lives like this. It's incredible that we only met in October and we've only been lovers for a month. Oh, darling, I do love you so much.

What I want most now is to be with you on New Year's Eve somehow. Obviously we can't manage the evening but maybe we could manage lunch. I do loathe all these stupid family festivals that keep getting in our way. If only we could have a night together sometime — d'you think we ever could? If we told enough complicated lies perhaps — I could be staying with Uncle A. if he was ill or it was foggy and you could be on tour in Aberdeen or somewhere. Oh, could we? I can't bear to think it will never happen.

Darling, please forgive this scrawl but I've had to write all over the place, mainly in the loo as there's nowhere else I can lock the door and be alone, especially at Xmas. That's another awful comment on marriage. Do you think we should introduce Chris and Cathy? They might get on fine and all our troubles would be over. I ache to be with you and I don't know how to wait till the next time. I did a silly thing the other night after I'd had my bath, I got a brown towel and put it between my legs and stroked it and pretended it was your head. I wasn't going to tell you but now I have. It didn't feel right, velvet would have been better but I haven't got any brown velvet. Anyway it gives you an idea how much I want you.

Darling my love, please be extra careful crossing roads and do let's meet soon. Now we've got our own special room it all seems so lovely and private.

All my love,
Gemma'

January
It should have been the happiest time of my life but something went wrong. What went wrong (for me) was that nothing

142

went wrong (for them). They were too cosy; they got highly organised very quickly; they dug themselves in. David bounced back from the Christmas recess demanding twice or thrice weekly meetings under the banner of my employing Gemma to type. (They had not managed New Year's Eve, which made them both rather twitchy.) When I reminded him of the howls of rage that had greeted that idea when it came from me, he actually laughed. I was most offended by the laugh. He said it was different now, surely I realised that. Monday, Wednesday and Friday would be just about right. I said I hoped he wasn't expecting me to cook and he said no, she could do that or they could go without or get takeaway Chinese, there was no problem, they could even have a cold picnic on the floor. The fact of there being no problem enraged me. There ought to be a problem, so that I could solve it. I had made everything too easy for them and now they had rendered me impotent. When would the work get done? I asked. Oh, before or after her visit; I wasn't to worry. Everything would be all right. And where was I meant to be, every Monday, Wednesday and Friday, walking the streets? Well, I might be lucky, even at my age. Then he saw my face and rearranged his own: of course they were grateful and of course they realised they were inconveniencing me, but I could always go to my club or the British Museum, couldn't I? In fact, *he* wouldn't mind if I stayed in the flat but he thought Gemma might be embarrassed.

I watched them together, the next time they met, steeling myself to have a drink with them. They were both extremely high, as if they had arrived drunk, only I knew they had not. A feverish excitement burned between them. They fed on each other; they laughed overmuch at one another's jokes. The glances they exchanged were hot with longing but they were also sure enough of themselves to enjoy the delay before they could touch. My presence was a tantalising aphrodisiac. I toyed briefly with the idea of announcing I would not go out, I was ill, it was too cold, but decided to keep that possibility for another time: it was useful to hold something in reserve. But I accepted another drink, for the fun of seeing anticipation turn to anxiety. They instantly became very solicitous, assuring me that Gemma would really type while David cleaned; it was so kind of me and they were so grateful (and now would I please go, I could see them longing to say, so they could fall into each other's arms and my spare room bed). I mentioned maliciously that I could not afford to pay Gemma for typing as well as David for cleaning. Instantly they both offered to work for nothing. And that, I suppose, is love. Defeated and triumphant, I went out and found it really was cold. (One of the few disadvantages of living with central heating is that you do not form any impression of the temperature outside). At my age it is positively dangerous to wander about in the cold, but the B.M. and my club were not attractive alternatives. On an impulse I went into a phone booth and looked up Meredith, D. There were not as many as I had expected and I found it easily, Meredith, David, printed in full through vanity, no doubt, vainly hoping to be plagued by fans. I jotted down the number and dialled. It rang for a long time. Finally, when I was about to give up, the unforgettable voice answered.

'Hullo?'

I hung up. I did not have the correct small coins and I was not certain what I wanted to say. Instead I went to the cinema, my favourite place for thought, as I have mentioned before. Besides, once you have decided what to do, you do not have to do it immediately.

I sat in the dark and considered the matter, while the screen antics moved in front of me like comforting shadows. I was disappointed in Gemma's letters: they were so ordinary. The stolen-fruit quality was still pleasing, but unfortunately the quality of the stolen fruit was not very high. If the letters had been handed to me open, I doubt if I would have bothered to read them. Beatrice had been right all along: Gemma was not clever. She had no special talent. Her ideas were commonplace; she dealt mainly in feelings and even there she had no originality. David had also been right all along: she was lonely and she wanted someone to talk to, someone to hug. She had fallen into my trap only because it was so exactly the trap she would have set for herself, had she had the intelligence. She was beautiful, spontaneous, affectionate — and rather stupid. Well, that was probably enough. They were all qualities I

144

lacked conspicuously, and so far her life had been far more rewarding than mine.

My other complaint was more serious: I had done myself out of a job. Like an impresario, I had succeeded too well. My protégée was launched, and all that remained for me to do was make the bookings and collect the percentage. Only the percentage was not high enough, and I had noticed before in biography and autobiography how boring the story becomes once the early struggles are over and before the doom and destruction begin. The halcyon plateau of success is delightful for the protagonist but infinitely dull for the observer. In *Troilus and Criseyde* it comes as a shock when we are told that the affair has lasted for three blissful years. Time has passed imperceptibly: there was nothing for Pandarus (or Chaucer) to do while the lovers disported themselves in ecstasy. But as soon as the liaison is threatened, he is as busy again as when he first acted as their go-between.

Happiness, then, is not very interesting — unless, of course, it happens to be your own. You could, I suppose, put my dissatisfaction down to simple envy, but I happen to think it was a little more subtle and complex than that.

When I got home at half past four they were both still there, drinking tea and gazing foolishly at each other across the table.

'Oh, you're back,' they said. I had the impression they spoke as one, though that is probably not factually true.

'Yes, I live here.' I smiled to soften the words. I was surprised (in view of how well I thought I knew myself) at how angry I felt: rage spilled out of me like the semen that was doubtless trickling down Gemma's legs.

'Would you like some tea?'

'Yes, I would.'

They were so happy, they had more than enough kindness to spare for the ugly, bitter old man they had exiled from his own home. Gemma poured me the tea, with lemon and no sugar, just as I like it. She smiled at me. She looked like pictures of the Virgin Mary, young and innocent.

'Thank you.'

I sat at the head of the table as was proper, forming the apex of a triangle with them.

'I'll have to be going,' she said to David.

'I know,' he said.

She didn't move. Their hands met and clasped across the table. They were quite oblivious of me. I drank my tea, watching them avidly, against my will. Gemma's make-up was smudged, nearly gone, and she looked exhausted; but not, I felt, merely through sexual excess. It seemed like the exhaustion of spent tenderness, of giving out emotion, like a mother when her child's bedtime finally comes. David looked exhausted, too, but in a different way, as if he had had a long and exciting day and been kept up too late: he looked young and vulnerable, as I had never seen him before. They had made the difference in each other's faces, something I could never do.

'Darling,' she said, 'can I give you a lift?'

'Thanks, just to the tube station.'

'Oh, good.' She smiled at him: a few more golden moments together. Again no one moved.

'How was the typing?' I asked unkindly.

'Oh.' She flushed. 'I did it all. I'm a bit rusty, I had to do some of it twice. But I think it's all right.' She was talking to me but her eyes were on him. He looked at her tenderly as she described her exertions, as if she had spent the afternoon down a mine.

'Come on, love,' he said. 'We'll have to go.'

She got up obediently; she kissed me on the forehead while he fetched her coat and helped her into it, an amazing courtesy, I thought, for him.

'Day after tomorrow,' he said to me curtly, shepherding her out with an arm round her shoulders as though she might break.

When they had gone, I poured myself a large drink, got into their stained and rumpled sheets and made love to myself, since there was no one else to do the job. A lonely enterprise. Was it perhaps that one did not value what was so easily gained? Or did the very certainty of success detract from the anticipation? Anything, anything, rather than dwell on the fact

146

that one had been rejected by the entire world. Here, in their sheets, where they had been two, I was one. There were no miracles.

'I didn't expect to see you again,' Catherine Meredith said. 'Not so soon.'

We were eating some rather disgusting moussaka in a Greek restaurant in the back streets of Camden Town. She had selected the restaurant because it was cheap, thinking of her own poverty rather than my relative affluence, although I was paying. She had also selected it because it was convenient — for her, not for me. When I rang up she had sounded immensely surprised; I treasured the sound of surprise in her voice: Catherine Meredith, whom I had thought never to take unawares.

'I got bored,' I said. 'They're using my flat three days a week.' I paused. 'They're there now.'

She crammed her mouth, chewed, swallowed and drank. 'I imagined they must be,' she said, 'when you asked me to lunch.'

'They're in love,' I said.

She smiled and poured herself some more retsina. 'Yes,' she said, 'they would be. It's about time. Her letters are very sweet, don't you think?'

I was nonplussed. 'How d'you mean?'

'Oh, come on,' she said vulgarly. 'Don't tell me you haven't read them.'

There was a long, long silence. I avoided her eyes. Finally, deciding to laugh, I forced myself to look at her.

'How did you know?'

'I used to steam open letters. They look different, that's all. If you've ever done it, you can tell. Other people can't, don't worry. David doesn't know. He doesn't look at details like that.'

'Why aren't you jealous?' I said, much too abruptly, riveted by her unconcern.

'Oh.' She swallowed a lot of wine. 'I'm past all that. That was a long time ago.'

'You mean you were jealous once.'

'Yes, of course. In the beginning, like God. But it passes.'

'He told me,' I said, overcome by our proximity in the scruffy, steamy restaurant, her pale face and pale hanging hair, the black jersey I vaguely recognised as belonging to David, our sleazy intimacy in this unlikely spot, 'he told me you threw a vase at him and his clothes out of the window when you found Mrs Salmon's photograph.'

A frown creased the smooth forehead.

'Photograph?'

There was a pause, during which I felt a fool. 'There never was one? Nor a vase? Nor a scene?'

She smiled gently. 'He has fantasies. Like everyone else.'

'He says you're frigid.' I was getting more reckless.

'If I don't fancy him I must be frigid.'

She spoke with such calm, amused contempt that I stared at her, fascinated.

'Why don't you divorce him?'

'Why should I?'

She made it sound like a genuine question.

'Well, it doesn't sound as if you're very happy together.'

'No, it doesn't, does it?' She swallowed another huge mouthful of moussaka. For someone who never ate during the day, she seemed to have an enormous appetite. 'But then I'm not sure marriage is meant to be happy. I think it's a twentieth-century fallacy.'

I thought of Gemma and her pathetic idealistic hopes, and I could see Catherine's point.

'But might you not be happier with someone else?'

'I don't see why. After the first few years I'd probably be just as bitchy, whoever I was with.'

'You could live alone. Like me.'

'Ah, but living with David I can feel superior all the time. I like that.'

'You're very honest,' I said.

'Am I?' she said. 'How do you know?'

'Well, at least you don't say you stay together because of the children.'

'No,' she said. 'At least I don't say that.'

There was a silence. She did not help me to break it, merely

148

drank more retsina and looked at me. Challenging me to continue? I wondered how old she was. It was an unlined face.

'That's what David told Gemma,' I said. 'About the children.'

'What else could he say?'

'You mean it's not true?'

'If I said he couldn't live without me, would you believe me?'

Black made her look younger than the pallid colours she had worn to my flat. And she had plaited her hair so that it hung like two ropes framing her face. Thick fat plaits held with rubber bands, like a little girl in the school playground.

She said, 'Well, anyway, he's got to support his children, he wanted them, I didn't, so he might as well support me too. He certainly can't afford two homes. I think it serves him right, don't you?'

I said, 'I didn't think you'd come to lunch. After all you said about not eating in the daytime.'

She laughed. 'So now you're wondering if I'm just as big a liar as David. Poor Mr Kyle. Don't worry, you'll get used to us. I told you it would take time.'

Afterwards we walked by the canal. The temperature was unpleasant for sightseeing but I was reluctant to let her go, and she did not invite me home. Indeed I was proud to be seen with her in her black flowing cloak, as I had been proud of being seen with Gemma when she was a conventionally pretty child, and later Miranda when she went around with pre-Raphaelite hair smelling of incense. It seemed a privilege to have some of their incongruity rub off on me: there is little enough beauty or mystery left in the world. Catherine was better equipped for the weather than I was, with David's sweater and some bisexual jeans tucked into seven-league boots that seemed made for striding along river banks in winter.

'I don't know this part of London,' I said to break the silence that had iced over our conversation.

'No, I didn't imagine you would.'

She tried pointing out landmarks to me while I tried steering her back to David and the children. She seemed bored with the subject now: all she would say was that David simply loved her being pregnant but he wasn't so keen on the actual children. (This was awkward, since one stage lasted so much longer than the other.) Whereas she quite liked them once they were here, but found the nine months very tedious. I pressed her for reasons.

'Oh,' she said, sounding cross, 'I think it's feeling my body doesn't belong to me, it's been invaded. Which is probably why David loves it.'

She seemed more vulnerable in the open air: altogether gentler and softer once exposed to the elements. I wanted to put my arm round her.

'So I just hope your niece is on the pill,' she said lightly. 'There's nothing he likes better than impregnating women all over the place. He won't admit it but I think he gets a kick out of seeing them swell up and knowing it's all due to him.'

'That's all right,' I said. 'Nothing to worry about. Her husband's a doctor and he's very keen on family planning.'

She smiled. 'I wish I could say the same for my husband.'

That night I could hardly sleep. The idea of Gemma pregnant by David excited me beyond measure. Her other pregnancies had taken her away from me because they were Christopher's, but this one would surely bring us closer together. If David and Gemma were to have a child, the three of us would form an unholy trinity, united beyond the grave, and I would be revenged forever on Christopher. He would be condemned to support another man's child till he died. Longer: he would surely make bequests.

Moreover, it would be a supreme test of my ingenuity.

The letters stopped: the two of them were too much together even for Gemma to have need of letters. But I panicked, plunging into a paranoid fantasy. They had discovered me and were being clever, playing it carefully, covering their tracks. I knew this was not true, but the idea roamed, like an animal escaped from the zoo.

Their room became full of objects: scent, hairbrushes, make-up, dressing-gowns, things for the bath. Another life went on in there, just through the wall from my room, where no life went on. They were more than visitors: it was like being dispossessed by squatters, disguised as charming children. I had the feeling that everything was gaining momentum, rushing out of control. Had I not said at the start, no, before the start, that we were set on collision course?

He sang her praises as if he had invented her. Week after week, on Mondays, Wednesdays and Fridays, he talked about her non-stop from ten till twelve while he dusted and polished — that is, if I stayed in the room with him. But he did not tell me anything about her because he talked in generalised superlatives. She was magic. She was so giving. She was so warm and gentle. She transformed him.

('When I think of that bloody cold bitch at home——' he said once and stopped short, abruptly, as if someone had turned him off by flicking a switch.)

She laughed at his jokes, she took an interest in his work, she made *him* laugh, she could cook. (Cook!) She was sexy. She was innocent yet uninhibited. (But that did not tell me what she was *like* in bed.) And she was so affectionate he felt no one had ever really loved him before, even his mother. Correction: least of all his mother. In a word, she was perfect.

It did not seem to occur to him that he was indebted to me for finding this paragon and delivering her up to him; or if it did, he did not see fit to say so.

I thought about mirrors. It would mean going back to my old haunts and no doubt prices had gone up, but it was a mirror that the spare room lacked and needed. A mirror would make it come alive for me. I now regretted, of course, getting rid of Oswald's and Miranda's mirror, but in those days I had favoured the clean sweep theory of getting over distress and had jettisoned everything that reminded me of them. An expensive method of avoiding heartbreak.

Then at twelve (and always punctual now) Gemma would arrive and we would all three have an uneasy drink together while they gazed at each other and pretended to be talking to me. At quarter past twelve I would leave, returning at three sometimes to find they had gone, occasionally to join them for tea and more foolish glances. Then they would leave together.

In short, I was never alone with her. On Tuesdays and

151

Thursdays, when they did not meet, she would ring me up to complain about this deprivation and to explain how wonderful he was, how lucky she was, and how benevolent I was. At least she was appreciative; I must give her that. Almost monotonously so. She went on and on about how grateful they were to me for bringing them together and allowing them the use of my spare room, and whatever would they do without me, but it did not occur to her to do anything *for* me in return, such as visiting me alone or talking about something other than David. I had forgotten how selfish lovers are: like children they are interested only in themselves, and they prattle away unselfconsciously, insanely convinced that what is of devouring interest to them must necessarily fascinate everyone else. If it were not insulting it would be comic.

One week Stephanie was ill and Gemma could not come on Wednesday. She spent half the morning on the telephone to him when he would have been better occupied with the vacuum cleaner. Thursday produced this:

(7)

'Darling love,

Thank you a million times for being so sweet about Steffie. Much sweeter than I could be, I'm afraid. We've had a miserable afternoon playing games very half-heartedly and the more I looked at my watch thinking of where I should be, the more she went on about her sore throat and her tummy ache and the pain in her head and how she was hot/cold/hungry/sick and wanted a drink of water. I know she felt rotten and I *was* sorry for her (I think) but at one remove somehow. I mean I know it isn't serious and she could have managed without me, even Chris said so when he took a look at her this morning and I'm sure Inge could have coped. What's more, she'd have played games a lot less reluctantly than me! Now of course — now I've finally got S. to sleep and I'm racing to catch the post — I feel full of guilt for being such a rotten mother. Poor child, she *did* feel awful, she *was* all hot and cold and funny and just wanted me to be there, but I wanted to be somewhere else and there were moments this afternoon when if I'm honest I've got to admit I resented her like hell for

152

stopping me — even hated her — I felt she was doing it on purpose— every time I went near the telephone she yelled as if she knew — I swear she's got wind of something she can't understand on her radar, just like my bloody mother.

Darling, please don't stop loving me because it looks as if I love you more than my own child. Even writing that scares me. It can't be true, can it?

Love, love, love and more love,

Your Gemma'

February

She started sounding me out about my holiday. 'Are you going away as usual?'— 'Yes'— 'To the same place?'— 'Yes' — 'How lovely. Lucky you.'

Each year I spend my birthday in the sun. The Caribbean sun, to be exact. It seems to me, born at such a desolate time of year, the least I can do to console myself, and, with advancing years, almost a medical necessity.

'You'll come back all brown,' she said enviously.

'That's right.'

'And I shall hate you.'

I smiled. 'But you're young and beautiful and happy. You shouldn't expect to be brown as well. Think how much compensation I need compared to you with all your advantages.'

There was a silence while she thought about it. I had an idea what she was coming to, but it was amusing to let her get on with it.

'Of course,' she said, as if it had just occurred to her, 'what I should really do is ask Chris if I can go with you this time. Then he'd give me the money, David and I could stay at your flat, he could pretend he was on location, I'd give *him* the money and we could both go under the sunray lamp every day.'

'What a brilliant idea,' I said. I was impressed by the amount of detail she had gone into, as well as her carefree disposal of Christopher's money. 'What a pity it's not possible.'

'Oh, I was joking,' she said quickly.

My instincts told me she had in fact been deadly serious, needing only my encouragement.

'No, I meant the flat won't be available. Otherwise you could probably get away with it.'

The silence on the other end of the phone was eloquent with pain and surprise.

'Won't be available,' she echoed faintly.

'I'm afraid not. I promised it to a friend— oh, ages ago. Last year. Before you and David ever met.'

'You mean we can't use it at all?' Stricken.

'Well, no. Not really. I'm sorry.'

'Who is he, this friend?'

I had expected David to ask questions, so had my answers ready.

'He's an American academic. This way he can have a cheap vacation, staying in my flat.'

'Funny time of year for an academic vacation.'

'He's on sabbatical to write his book.'

David was sharper than I had given him credit for.

'What's his name?'

'Morris Abrahams.' The answers flowed so readily, I was proud of myself. I began to see the man, neatly bearded but going bald, I thought, an alert Jewish face with dark intelligent eyes and a dry sense of humour. About fifty. His students liked him. He deserved to have the use of my flat. He would be more grateful than David and probably leave me a duty-free bottle of bourbon.

'Won't he be going to the British Museum like you?'

'Oh yes, I expect so.'

'Couldn't we come to an arrangement— sneak in while he's out?'

'That would upset Mrs Abrahams.' She would be in the kitchen a lot. Morris had married out, to the distress of his family, so Mrs Abrahams was trying to make amends by practising kosher recipes. She was a second wife.

'So you don't want me to come here at all while you're away — to clean or anything?'

'No. Of course I'll pay you just the same.'

With Gemma it had been all disappointment. With him it was rage. But there was nothing he could do.

'He's in a filthy temper,' Catherine said. 'What's gone wrong? It ought to be too soon for trouble.'

We were eating lasagne in a nice Hampstead restaurant (my choice). I explained about my holiday and the visiting American professor. She listened attentively and then began to laugh.

'I don't believe a word of it.'

I tried to assume an innocent, injured face, but it didn't work too well. She knew me already.

'You're just doing it to be spiteful,' she said.

'Well . . . it *is* my flat. Why should they have it when I'm away?'

'I wonder if he'll find somewhere else to meet her. I'll soon know if he doesn't.'

'How?'

'He'll start making love to me again.'

I asked if she minded and she looked almost gleeful.

'I shall lie still as a stone and make him feel it's rape.' She smiled. 'All that lovely guilt.'

'His or yours?'

'His, of course. I never feel guilty about anything.'

As you can see, we were rapidly becoming more intimate. My attentiveness was paying off. I felt privileged every time she told me something new. Often if I made no reply but merely studied her bony, mobile face, leaving a space for her to speak, she would go on.

Now she said, 'D'you like Wagner?'

'Yes. Very much.'

'I don't. I often think Wagner must have made love like David. A long, exhausting performance full of noise and false climaxes. By the time you get to the end, you're too worn out to enjoy it. I'll settle for a quick bash on the surgery floor any time.'

I must have looked surprised for she pretended alarm and added, 'Oh dear, now I've given the game away.'

'What game?' I asked obediently.

'I'm having an affair with my doctor. It's terribly convenient. David thinks I'm a frightful hypochondriac. I've been dying to tell someone about it and you're the obvious person.

You really treasure secrets, don't you? No wonder you like having David and Gemma in your flat.'

But my mind had stopped five sentences back. I was stunned. (Was it true?)

'Are you really having an affair?' It would explain everything: the alleged frigidity, the unconcern, the air of wellbeing.

'Oh dear, now you're doubting everything I say. It's David who tells lies, you know, not me— well, not often. It rubs off a bit, I suppose.'

'You're not answering my question.'

'Yes, of course I'm having an affair. It's lovely. Perfectly safe for me and terribly dangerous for him. God knows what he'll do if he ever wants to end it — I could wreck his career.'

'But you wouldn't — would you?'

'I might . . . who knows what I might do if I felt spiteful enough? But he won't, he loves me.'

'And do you love him?'

'I don't know about love any more. Perhaps.'

'Doesn't David suspect?'

'No, of course not, he's far too conceited. That's why he thinks I'm frigid — he thinks I can do without.' She smiled. 'I'm talking too much and it's all your fault. You're a true voyeur, aren't you — a professional.'

On the strength of that, I ordered the mirror. My friends in Paris warned me prices had gone up.

'You'll miss seeing Chris on TV,' said Gemma listlessly. 'He'll be on while you're away.'

'Whatever for?'

'He's in a debate about contraception and abortion. They're terribly pleased to get a doctor who's in favour of both and religious as well.'

She reeled off the information as if she were reading a publicity handout, but she seemed very doleful about it.

'You must be proud of him,' I said.

'I suppose so. It's very nice for him to be asked. All his hard work's paid off at last. All those long evenings.' She sounded oddly bitter.

I said thoughtfully, 'Funny they should both be on TV.'

I had to pick my moment carefully. I waited till he was up a ladder cleaning paintwork so he could not see my face (I am not as skilful a dissembler as I pretend) and I busied myself with dusting and rearranging books on their shelves. So we were both fully occupied and far apart within the confines of the room.

I said, 'Her husband's going to be on TV.'

He echoed my words most gratifyingly. 'Whatever for?'

'He's talking about sex.'

He laughed. 'What the hell does he know about that?'

I laughed too: it was a comfortable feeling, making us into allies, men of the world. 'No, not making love, prevention and cure, that's all. He's in a debate about abortion and contraception. He's the Christian doctor on the panel.'

I expected a ribald joke; instead he said seriously, 'I don't approve of abortion. Cathy had one once. I didn't like it at all.'

I said, 'Well, I expect Christopher sees it as a last resort. The lesser of two evils and all that.'

He said, 'It's not right. There's no excuse for it.'

It seemed unlike him to be so sternly moralistic. I said soothingly, 'Well, Gemma's never had one. She wanted more children but he wouldn't let her have them.'

A silence fell: I was alarmed. Visions of a sniper flinging his grenade, a saboteur planting his gelignite flashed across my brain. I could see why brains are described as fevered. A strange hot sensation ran over my forehead. I had planned this moment so carefully: was there to be no reaction at all?

He said, 'More fool him.'

I said, 'She was very disappointed. She really wanted more. I think that's why she got restless. Ironic, isn't it?'

Another silence. I was desperate but counselled myself to be patient, to wait, as if it did not matter.

He said casually, thoughtfully, 'I suppose that might explain it.'

I did not want to seem too eager. 'Explain what?'

'Why she's so careless. I've often wondered. She keeps on and on about how we must be careful, but half the time she

157

leaves it all to me.' There was a shamefaced edge to his voice, as if he did not feel it quite proper to be disclosing these intimacies to me, yet found it impossible to resist. 'You'd never think she'd been married ten years. God, I've had teen-agers who knew more about it than she does.'

'I suppose he takes care of all that.' I didn't like the words I had chosen but they seemed suitable, redolent of women's magazines: precautions, methods, that side of marriage. 'Have you asked her?'

'No, not really. I tried but she wouldn't talk about it.' His voice was full of tenderness again: she was the perfect one, inviolate, her faults a delight. 'There are things she won't say — you can't really discuss him with her properly.'

I thought of the letters: was that all she would expose? End-stopped conversation: she revealed what she chose and no questions answered. I thought too of our chats when we were alone. Not enough.

He said gently, admiringly, 'It's like a kind of protection. I suppose she doesn't like to betray him twice.'

I longed to say more but dared not. Instinct told me it was better to let the matter rest. I might well have done enough — we would see — and if not, I could always re-open the subject later. Much too dangerous to press it now, however terrifying the renewed silence. I had planted the seed (how gratifyingly sexual these metaphors are) and that must suffice.

On the last night, all the same, while packing my holiday clothes, such as they were, I made a thorough search of the spare room. They were a messy couple and I discovered all sorts of debris: hairpins, champagne corks, stained towels, used tissues and old lipstick, but I persevered, and at the back of a drawer I finally found Gemma's diaphragm. Very carefully, slowly and delicately, I punctured it several times with a needle. I am remarkably ignorant of these methods and their sabotage, but it seemed worth a try, just in case my revelations had fallen on stony ground. It did occur to me to wonder if she had a similar device at home (would it be indelicate to use the same one with lover and husband, and why were her methods so primitive?) or was Christopher in sole charge and did he spring forth like Minerva fully armed? But I did not wonder for very long; I was tired and I had a plane to catch in the morning. As I fell asleep my last conscious thought was of Troilus and Criseyde and a problem I had never considered before: how had they avoided pregnancy? Three years of coitus interruptus (for what else could it have been?) seemed to take a lot of the glamour out of their romance. Perhaps it merited a footnote.

March

For the first few days they did not exist. Annihilated by the heat, the flowers, the hovering humming-birds, the darkness of the nights, the blaze of day. They were people I had dreamed of in another life. I was glad of the peace: I found myself exhausted by contrivance — six months since David came to me — and the recent inexorable flow of Mondays, Wednesdays and Fridays relentlessly following each other like soldiers on the march. I needed a rest.

As always, I had not quite remembered the exaggeration of the tropics. In theory, of course, I knew from experience exactly what to expect, but the reality always took me a little by surprise. The sun in the sky was hotter and brighter than the sun in my memory; the nights more densely black, a thick, soft colour that descended more abruptly than I could ever expect. It was another world: absurd to concern myself with people in England who were not real.

Every day after breakfast, a stroll through the hotel gardens then down to the beach, a fearsome drive, my bones and teeth rattling, but worth it to find a stretch of sand where even I did not mind exposing myself. It is not easy for a voyeur to become an exhibitionist, though that perhaps could be as good a definition of holiday as any. After lunch a languid siesta by the pool until the sudden sunset. A rest and a shower before dinner. And afterwards no more than two drinks, to avoid socialising, and early to bed for two hours' work before sleep overcame me.

Slowing down the pace of life makes details stand out: the highspot of my day became watching the lizards on my veranda and trying to persuade them to pose for photographs.

Their wrinkled, primeval, *jolie-laide* faces reminded me of my own: I felt the tug of kinship. But they evidently did not. Too often at the last vital moment they darted away.

The first gin and tonic of the morning (around half past eleven) was another peak. I could walk fifteen minutes along the beach to the nearest hotel for it, or take the magic ingredients, with ice in a flask, and mix it myself. I usually preferred the latter, the personalised ritual. The barman at the hotel was not attractive, and there were too many American matrons revealing themselves with rather more courage than tact. Alone on my private beach I could swim and drink, balancing the liquid within and without; read and sunbathe, laze and drowse. I even began to imagine that if my whole life could be spent like this, I might acquire a nicer nature.

Catherine wrote:

'Dear Mr Kyle,

I thought when you gave me your address it probably meant you wanted a letter. Are you enjoying yourself? I don't see you as a holiday person, you seem to need your own environment. David and I don't have holidays because we can't afford them but I've always liked the idea of going somewhere new and strange for two or three weeks and telling some outrageous lies. A great opportunity to be someone else, holidays. David has borrowed a flat from a friend of his but it's very grotty (I know the friend) so I don't think she'll like it. Anyway it means I won't get raped by Wagner after all which will please my doctor who gets terribly jealous. I can't understand jealousy myself any more. I know I did once but now I can't remember how it felt. One body is very much like another, after all, it's what goes on in the mind that counts. She's written to him at the flat already, it's a nice letter, do you want me to make a copy of it? They have a photostat machine at the post office that only costs 5p.

Love (whatever that is),

Catherine

P.S. I saw her husband on TV the other night, he seemed to have all the right attitudes. I also thought he was rather good-

160

looking—I like that hollow sunken-cheeked style. Or maybe I just have a thing about doctors. C.'

And then I began to miss them. All three of them. They were my children. What was I doing in this strange foreign place?

A honeymoon couple arrived to torment me. They were young and dark and thin and they kept touching each other. Apart from that, they did not do anything overtly embarrassing (in fact they were rather off-hand with one another verbally) but I resented them nevertheless. They were both very pretty and full of energy; they shone like well-groomed horses. The excesses of the night left a gloss of satisfaction on their faces as they chewed their breakfast paw-paw; afterwards they would play tennis and I would hear them shouting to each other, making fun of their bad shots, before I went down to the beach. They were younger than Gemma, and there they were, pledged for life, and seemingly delighted with the arrangement. About twenty-four, I thought. And rich enough to come to the island for their honeymoon. They always went to bed in the afternoon (I used to stroll past their chalet to soak up the sounds) and reappeared early in the bar, every night in new clothes, browner by the hour and smiling kindly at the rest of us. Like Gemma and David, they had a lot of goodwill left over.

It all turned sour after that. I began to notice VD posters scattered around the island for some kind of health campaign; it struck me as I drove about that the older inhabitants were obsequious and the younger ones arrogant; even the weather did not seem as perfect, a few showers and a high wind at night. I started to dream, not the sort you remember in order to recount but those that leave you vaguely uneasy, knowing you have slept badly but relieved to wake up. Suddenly paradise was a hostile place.

Gemma wrote:

'Dearest Uncle Alex,
  I hope you're having a lovely time but I can't wait for you to

161

come back. We are borrowing a flat belonging to a friend of David's but it's not a bit like your lovely spare room. The sheets are filthy and there's a horrid atmosphere. Still, we're grateful to have anywhere — though we daren't risk going there more than once a week. I can't justify any more trips to town with you away. Hurry back!

Chris's TV thing was a great success but he wasn't a bit excited about it, in fact he's been very funny lately. He can't suspect anything, can he? He's very quiet and sometimes he looks so sad I just want to fling my arms round him and say I love him although of course I don't— except that in a way I do. And then I feel disloyal to David. Anyway I can't hug Chris, however much I sort of want to, and I think by now he'd be surprised if I did. I'm worried about him though— suddenly he looks so much older or else not well— I've tried to get him to have a check up but you know what it's like trying to make a doctor do that.

I wish you were here to talk to. I know I haven't talked to you much lately but now you're away I really want to. Because of Chris being the way he is and me feeling so guilty, I can't argue with him about anything, and now he's saying we must go to Majorca in June instead of Cyprus because of the troubles. I'm sure it's all quiet there again now and would be quite safe to go but he won't listen. I have this awful feeling he's just making excuses and really he only wants to go to Majorca to have a second honeymoon with me. I keep telling him it will be horrid and touristy and spoilt— not at all like it was ten years ago — but he won't listen. He insists there are still some nice quiet places left — I think he expects Robert Graves to ask us to dinner or the ghost of Chopin to materialise with a brand new nocturne— it's going to be *awful*, I don't know how I'll bear it. After all this time away from our room, to be marooned on holiday with Chris being terribly affectionate is more than I can stand. It's like a jail sentence.

David and I have such fantasies about running away together one day. At least I suppose they're fantasies. The trouble is he can't bear to leave his children and of course I couldn't possibly leave mine so it would mean taking four children with us and he'd never earn enough to keep us all and I

162

could hardly work with four children to look after. That's quite apart from all the upset for them, and hurting Chris and Cathy. And of course they might both fight for custody. Now I've written it down it looks quite ridiculous and yet we talk about it all the time. We ought to be satisfied with what we've got, I don't know why we want more, we're really very lucky. But it seems to be a terrible craving like for drink, to plan a future we know really we can't ever have. We even talk about the sort of flat we'd get and how we'd furnish it.

You must think I'm mad. Hurry back. Maybe I'll be sane again once we're back in our lovely room.

Lots of love,

Gemma

P.S. I almost forgot to tell you the other awful thing — Inge is leaving. I've been so busy with myself lately I didn't even notice there was anything wrong with her but she's just announced she's pregnant — it must have happened at Xmas when she went home — and she wants to go back to Germany and marry her boyfriend as soon as possible. She keeps apologising for all the inconvenience she's causing us (I'm sure we'll never get anyone so ideal again) but she looks terribly cheerful all the time and I'm so envious I could hit her. Being in love doesn't seem to improve one's character, does it?'

On my last morning the honeymoon girl appeared pale and tense at breakfast. I imagined a quarrel but it turned out she had hardly slept because a large red spider had got into their room and her husband had failed to catch it. Wafts of reminiscent terror emanated from her, palpable even at several tables' distance. The maids were sent in; at lunch they announced, triumphant, that they had captured the beast. Were they really sure? she demanded. Oh yes, they had kept it for her as proof. She shrank away under her husband's shoulder. 'No, no, don't let them show it to me, please.' He comforted her and reassured her they wouldn't; everyone laughed good-humouredly, the maids' large white teeth flashing, their eyes puzzled by the exhibition, but her terror and panic were real and I felt them. For one night at least her honeymoon had been ruined and she would remember.

I flew back home vindicated, reading Gemma's letter over and over again. Treasure trove.

April
The pleasures of homecoming: an even tan masking nearly all irregularities, making me almost enviable; the contrasting pallor of an English spring and the surly unconcern of the natives; and my flat, familiar yet strange after absence, full of contradictions. It looked larger and smaller, lighter and darker than I remembered it. Empty and hollow, yet containing so much of me that I half expected to meet myself coming down the corridor.

Gemma was ecstatic. 'You look marvellous — oh, it's so good to have you back.' It was my spare room she was really talking about as she hugged me.

David merely said, 'Yes, you're very brown, it's all right for some.' Then he looked round the flat suspiciously with his expert's eye. 'They were very clean and tidy, your friends. Not a thing out of place.'

I said smugly, 'Americans are great respecters of property,' and went out. I had a lot to do and so, presumably, had they.

The mirror was a huge success. I had been right to be apprehensive: the price brought tears to my eyes. But it was worth it, once they got it installed. Just like old times in its accustomed place: boldly on the wall in their room, safely behind the tapestry in mine. I could not afford to take any risk of David finding it in the course of his cleaning.

I trembled a little as I looked at it: the culmination of a dream and the nearest I would ever get to paradise. I had been a fool to quibble at the cost. You cannot measure such privilege in terms of mere cash.

There were of course certain practical problems to be overcome or perhaps simply risked. David would have to become accustomed to my locking my bedroom door occasionally when I went out — better still when I went away. They would think themselves doubly alone then and be more relaxed. If I made sure he cleaned my room on Wednesdays, I could say I was going away for weekends and watch safely on Mondays

164

and Fridays. The excitement was almost too much for me; I feared for my heart. If the very thought of watching them had this effect, what would the reality do to me?

In case you are wondering, I had no guilt. I was not stealing, merely taking what was my due, which they had withheld. They had stopped talking to me and they no longer wrote letters. They would not be the poorer by my action, for they would never know.

Catherine said, 'You seem very restless. As if you were expecting something to happen.'

We were walking by the Serpentine, a new meeting-place, in the pale spring sunshine. I was surprised to have succeeded in luring her so much nearer to my territory, so far from her own.

I said, 'Not expecting, my dear Catherine. Merely hoping. I get bored easily, you see. Any event would be welcome.'

She walked slowly in her flowing caftan, her hair loose. The garment was sea-green; it was the first time I had seen her in a primary colour. She seemed a different creature with the change of season: there was colour in her cheeks (though still no make-up) and she walked with a lighter step. She seemed younger, nebulous, floating. For a mad moment, making nonsense of my mirror and all the expensive delights to come, I thought David must be crazy to prefer Gemma to her. Gemma had proved so attainable.

'Well, it's too soon for disaster,' she said equably. 'I told you that before.'

'I remember.'

Back home they would be making love in front of my mirror, unobserved. A kind of undress rehearsal (I permit myself the occasional pun). It was a Wednesday, of course. David would clean my room either before or after the performance. I was getting them accustomed to the new regime, and I did not grudge the delay. True artistry cannot be hurried: it grows slowly, like a plant. In truth I was a little afraid to face the moment when I was to watch for the first time. There would be no way to recapture that novelty, however many times I watched and however much variation I saw.

165

Catherine asked, 'So what are you hoping for?'

'Satisfaction,' I said, feeling that to say happiness would be over-reaching myself.

She laughed. 'Are you in love with them? Are they doing it for you?'

So casually asked, it threw me. I could not answer. The Serpentine spun in the thin April sunlight.

She went on, 'Satisfaction through others, it's only saints and voyeurs who can live like that. The man in your poem, David told me about that.'

I said faintly, 'It's Chaucer's poem, not mine.'

'Well, you know what I mean. You're making it yours. That man was in love, wasn't he, supposed to be anyway, with someone who never rewarded him?'

I was taken aback. 'You've actually read it.'

'Oh yes,' she said, 'a long time ago. I'm not as ignorant as David. I was going to do English before I switched to Art. Only I never really believed in Pandarus having a lady, however cold and distant. I think that was just an excuse he used to put people off the scent. I think he was in love with Troilus and Criseyde.'

She was going too far, too fast. I was scared of her again. 'I think he was in love with power,' I said.

'Oh, that's just a smokescreen.'

There was a long silence.

'Poor you,' she said gently, to my amazement taking my hand. 'Has no one ever loved you?'

'Not your pity,' I said. 'Please. Spare me that.'

'You mustn't mind,' she said. 'It's the kindest emotion I can feel. And I told you I'd find out eventually. But it doesn't matter, really it doesn't. Love is such a myth.'

I had the intercom installed. I told the man that the child of a friend of mine was coming to stay and I must be sure to hear her if she cried in the night. He tested it for me with one of us in each room, but after he had gone I put the radio on their bed and went back into my room. I folded back the tapestry and hooked it out of the way; then I lay on my bed. There through the glass I could see the radio lying innocently on the winter

166

quilt. And I could hear it: every word, every note of music. There would be two bodies coupling and I would see every movement, hear every sound. I would share their love at last; I would be part of it.

David got a job. Only a small one, of course, a guest appearance in some long-running TV series in Birmingham, but it meant being away for a week. I was disappointed and angry at first, then I thought that perhaps it was just as well: a break in routine at this point might make him less likely to notice or question my new habits and the locked bedroom door. He was jubilant, of course; I assumed it was merely actor's ego, but when I saw a strangely intent conspiratorial look on Gemma's face I knew there was more to it than that.

'If you'll help,' he said, oddly diffident for him, 'we can have a night together. It's our only chance.'

'Please,' Gemma said. 'You will help, won't you?'

I liked their soft words and pleading faces. The plan was simple: David would go up there for a week, all *bona fide*, and Gemma would join him for a night, pretending to be with me.

'A Saturday night would be best,' she said. 'It's very awkward now Inge's gone and the new girl hasn't arrived.'

I was amused at the intrusion of these domestic details into their night of bliss.

'I won't be there on a Saturday, it's Monday to Friday.'

'Then make it Friday and we can travel back together on Saturday.' Her face lit up at the added bonus: on top of a whole night together, their first, the joy of a train journey as well.

'Yes, I'll tell Cathy there's a party or something, she won't care.'

'And you'll have finished work, so I won't be distracting you.'

They were both trembling with excitement, as if they were planning a bank raid.

'I never thought I'd be so pleased about going to Birmingham.'

They both laughed as if this were terribly witty. Then they looked at me.

'You will, won't you?'

'You don't have to do a thing. Only say I was here. Just pretend, in your head. You don't have to stay in or anything. You can go to the pictures if you like.'

'My children,' I said, 'how can I refuse you?'

'*Oh.*' She hugged me so hard that for a moment I could scarcely breathe. On David's face I saw no gratitude but intense relief.

'Now,' I said. 'To be practical.'

'Just remember to say I was here for the night on Friday if anyone asks. That's all. I'll explain to Chris.'

'No,' I said. 'There's a little more to it than that. *Why* are you here?'

'Oh.' She pondered. 'I'll think of that later.'

'You're ill,' David said promptly to me.

I said with a smile, 'You needn't sound so pleased. And I don't like pleading illness to a doctor.'

'What d'you mean?'

Happiness had made them stupid.

'Your husband,' I said, 'might ring up.'

'Why should he?'

'Why shouldn't he? To speak to you. To ask how I am. *To check up.*'

There was a short pause. I could almost hear them thinking, like the ticking of a clock in another room.

'I know,' Gemma said. 'We'll do it in easy stages. Then he *can't* ring up. I'll come here at lunchtime as usual to type. Then in the afternoon I'll ring Chris and say you're ill and can I stay. He's bound to say yes. Then it's all spur of the moment and I've spoken to him and he won't ring up. You'll have nothing to worry about.'

'And if he does ring up?'

'He won't.'

'But if he does.'

She looked exasperated at my obstinacy; I was spoiling the dream by conjuring up reality. I represented all her worst forebodings and she would not admit them so she must condemn me instead.

David said, 'Oh God, it's easy. I'll leave my Birmingham telephone number with you and if he rings up, you ring us and

168

Gemma can ring him back. Tell him she's in the bath or something.'

It was easy; he was right. 'And how serious is my illness?'

He went on smoothly. 'Food poisoning, I think. You went out to a heavy lunch. Oysters, probably, followed by pheasant. You're allergic but you won't admit it. There's nothing Gemma can do but you don't want to be alone. He'll tell you to suck ice cubes. It happened to me once.'

'Perfect,' I said. 'Provided he doesn't come rushing up here to minister to me.'

'He can't leave the children,' Gemma said quickly.

'He could ask your mother to babysit.'

'He won't.'

No. He certainly wouldn't. My health was not a matter of much concern to him.

'There's nothing anyone can do,' David said with authority, 'not even a doctor. You feel so ill you just want to die.'

'But not alone.'

'That's right. Now you've got it.'

I remembered to say, 'And I was planning to go away for the weekend.'

'Oh well,' he said, 'you can go another time, can't you?'

On the appointed day she did no typing, needless to say. She arrived late, overnight essentials hidden in her handbag, her face such a mixture of happiness, fear and excitement that I did not know what to say to her. But I doubt if she'd have heard me if I had spoken. She was hardly in the world at all.

'When I was a child,' she said, 'and I read love stories, I always thought there was something magical about the night, about actual sleep. Two people together in darkness, unconscious . . .' She balanced on the edge of her chair, rocking it gently. 'That seemed to be what made the bond between them. Anything could happen. Giving your unconscious to someone — I thought that was why there was all that fuss about the wedding night. It seemed the essence of marriage somehow, being together asleep in the dark.'

And of course Christopher telephoned. About nine, when I

was beginning to feel secure. Gemma had done her bit in the afternoon, ringing neighbours to collect the children, ringing Christopher to describe my symptoms and ask permission. I was surprised how genuine she sounded, what a competent actress she had become. Perhaps David had been coaching her.

But was she good enough? The telephone bell sent chills through my stomach, momentarily making me feel almost as ill as I was alleged to be. It could, of course, have been anyone, even Gemma herself. But I knew it was Christopher. I had foreseen it from the time I cross-examined the guilty lovers and David concocted the plan.

'Yes?' I hoped my voice sounded suitably weakened by vomiting.

'Oh.' He seemed slightly taken aback. 'Alex. I thought you'd be in bed.'

'I am.'

'Oh. Yes, of course. It was only that I expected Gemma to answer as you're not well.'

A pause. He had not asked, but I suddenly felt obliged to answer his silence.

'She's in the bath,' I said.

'Oh.' He sounded—what? Relieved. Disappointed. Disbelieving. All three. And something more: the unutterable sadness that Gemma had described in her letter to me, that invaded his voice and, dislike him as I might, totally overwhelmed me. But it was not a time for sentiment; rather was it a time for a calculated gamble.

'Shall I call her?' What was I to do if he said yes? Why had I chosen to take such an appalling risk?

'No.' I had of course known he would, he must say no. 'It's very trivial, I only wanted to ask her where she put some notes . . .' His voice trailed off.

'I'll get her to ring you back.'

'No. Don't bother her. No need.'

For a moment I was insanely convinced he knew.

'No bother.' Was my charade effective?

He pulled himself together, put on his doctor's voice. 'How are you feeling, Alex? Any better?'

'Pretty weak. You know what these things are like.'

'Yes, indeed. I told Gemma to tell you, just suck ice cubes. There's nothing else for it. Don't even swallow water till tomorrow, you'll only be sick again.'

'I know, she told me. And before that — I found out to my cost.'

'It's a wretched business. Give it twenty-four hours though and you'll be amazed at the difference. Well, I must get on. Goodnight, Alex.'

He was gone. I hung up slowly, half expecting to see Gemma emerge from the bathroom wrapped in a towel, her face full of guilt and apprehension. I had convinced myself at least. But then I have always had a talent for make-believe. What surprised me was the lack of gleeful conspiratorial response. I felt instead — well, no, not guilty, no, but embarrassed. His pain was in the room with me. Did he really love her that much?

I was wasting time. I looked up the number and dialled. It rang several times. A cross sleepy voice answered; they must be in bed already.

'David,' I said sharply, 'get Gemma to ring home, would you?'

There was a startled pause. Then:

'Christ. He actually rang.'

'Yes. He actually rang.'

'I never thought he would. What did you tell him?'

'She's in the bath. I didn't change a word of your dialogue.'

Silence. Then Gemma came on the line. 'What did he say?'

'Nothing much. He asked for you, of course. Something about some notes — he said it was trivial.'

A long sigh. 'Oh God, yes. I was typing something for him — he's going to a conference next week — oh God, I suppose he couldn't find it. I should have thought.'

Her remorse irritated me profoundly. 'Look, instead of explaining to me, why don't you ring him?'

She didn't even notice my irritation. 'Did he say anything else?'

'Not much. He asked how I was.'

'But did he sound all right?'

'You'll know if you ring him,' I said, 'won't you?'

'You don't think he's guessed?'

'How can I tell?'

'It might have been an excuse about the notes. He might have been trying to catch me out.'

'Then he'd have made me call you, wouldn't he?'

'Oh yes. Yes. That's right.' What was that extra note in her voice beyond the relief? Disappointment?

'Look,' I said, 'I don't know how long you usually take in the bath, but hadn't you better ring him back?'

'What's the matter?' she said abruptly. 'You don't sound yourself.'

'I'm not feeling well,' I said. 'Have you forgotten? Something I ate disagreed with me.'

May

Oh, but I forgave her everything when I saw her. It is not granted to many to witness such perfection. I was reminded of the Bible: 'They were swifter than eagles, they were stronger than lions,' although strictly speaking, speed and strength were not what I saw. But as a measure of sublimity the ancient words echoed in my head. What I saw was love. When Gemma kissed David all over his body it was because she loved every inch of him, as the saying goes, literally, and this was her way of showing it. I followed her tongue with my eyes, my own lips sensing the feel of the curly black hairs. Her body arched over his, charming in its imperfections, breasts sagging a little since the last child, stomach a little stretch-marked and curving with maturity. I loved her imperfect body and so did he. Lying there like a Sultan in his private ecstasy, he was of all men most enviable. All I lacked was the smell of his sweat and the warmth of his skin under my face. And he looked so young. As Gemma moved, I glimpsed his face behind her tangled hair and his youth hurt me even more than his pleasure. No one had ever kissed me like that, and now it was too late: no one ever would. I was ugly, and I was old. I was undesirable in every sense of the word: sexual, aesthetic and social.

When he made love to her I was enchanted again and in a different way. I had expected a marathon, to judge from

172

Catherine's jokes and Gemma's letters, and that to me suggested coldness and endurance, a long-distance battle of wills. Instead there was a young man struggling to hold himself back, to give pleasure, to prolong the magic or to repeat it. And when I heard that strange lost cry from Gemma's throat, I did not marvel that he should strive so hard to conjure it. Kingdoms had been well lost for less. She clutched at him as if she were dying, as if he were a raft in the sea or her last hope of spiritual salvation. Her fingers dug into his flesh, her mouth closed on him, her arms dragged him closer till it seemed he would go right through her and they would both suffocate or drown.

There was so much I had forgotten: wilfully, I suppose. In a spirit of self-preservation. So as not to go quite mad. The contorted faces of those in the last extremities of sexual pleasure: a weird sight indeed. Like victims struggling under torture. Was that how the whole sado-masochistic sexual mythology had arisen, by chance, from an observed phenomenon? It was so long since I had had a partner and I was not in the habit of watching myself — in my case there was no pleasure to be had in that. But the typical interplanetary visitors, beloved of newspapers and science fiction, reproducing like the amoeba or the fish, how astonished they would be if told that these were lovers enjoying the highest form of physical delight vouchsafed to mankind. They would never believe it. These twisted features, these cries of rage and pain and loneliness — no, never. Everyone knew that these people were torturing each other. Any fool could see that.

I had forgotten how they spoke, too. All that loving chat, and the jokes. Unfinished sentences. A word, a look, a laugh. How easy it was for them. It flowed. There is no way I can describe it as it was: even now your memories will have to do their work. For they moved from caress to speech, from activity to inertia, and back again. To recount it is to make distinctions, and it was all one.

When he came he sounded angry. As if his seed were being wrenched from him.

Afterwards they were very still and silent, like the dead. They had the same repose and exuded the same air of invul-

173

nerability. They were beyond everything, out of harm's way. 'Fear no more the heat of the sun' was in my mind as I watched them. They lay in a huddle of limbs, flopped down where they had fallen and wrapped around each other, sweating and breathless and silent, still as stones. Until they opened their eyes and smiled at one another; smiled and began to talk. And to kiss.

If I had forgotten the foolish words and the caresses, the endearments and the silly jokes, still more had I forgotten the kisses. The afterwards kisses, for love only, not to excite, when there was nothing more to gain, different by a world from those lavished on the body to arouse. Kisses on the mouth and eyes to say Thank you, to say Goodnight and go to sleep, my love, and rest, you're safe with me. No, I had not forgotten. They were something I had never known.

I watched through a mask of tears and I was not ashamed.

Gemma noticed the innovation at once. 'I like the new mirror,' she said to me on Wednesday.

'Yes, I thought you deserved something better.'

God, it was a happy time. It did not seem much hardship now to have endured sixty-four wretched years to reach this state of joy. Twice weekly, Mondays and Fridays, in my own private cinema, a programme fixed but infinitely flexible, and on Wednesdays lunch with Catherine. Three matinées a week, starring all my favourite people.

Of course I was terrified at the start. On the first Friday, terror almost overcame excitement. It took a real effort of will to install myself behind the locked door, unhook the tapestry and wait. I wanted to run away. Quite frankly, I could have (almost) abandoned the entire scheme there and then. The waiting was so long. Once David had arrived (about eleven, late because he thought I was away, I noted) I was of course a prisoner. Too late to retreat now: the die was cast with a vengeance. I had to lie quiet in my room, trying to give out emanations of emptiness, and listen to him bustling about with dusters and polish; the chink of washing up, the roar of the vacuum cleaner. These familiar sounds seemed very foreign because I was not supposed to be there. I was reminded of the first day he had come to me, when I was very aware of everything he did around the flat because he was a stranger. It is an eerie sensation to be in your own home, on your own bed, pretending to be away, while another person makes free with your other rooms and your cleaning equipment. I could hear my heart beating. I was terrified. That was absurd, of course. The worst that could happen was that he would try the door and find it locked. That in itself was no crime, merely odd, perhaps not even that. But of course he did not try the door: why should he? He had cleaned the room last Wednesday and had no reason to go in it till next Wednesday. All I had to do was keep silent. Unless I made a sound, I could not be found out. Immediately the greatest temptation in the world was to sneeze, cough, scream. Even that he made easy for me. He turned on the wireless. It was bizarre to lie there, a helpless victim of popular music, waiting for the greatest experience of my life.

Gemma arrived about twelve. I thought they'd be sure to go straight to bed but they were ages in the kitchen and living-room, eating and talking. I could hear the sound of their voices but not what they said — an infuriating predicament. When they finally came into the spare room the angle of vision prescribed by the mirror prevented my seeing everything they did: by focussing on the bed I had lost the rest of the room. Somewhere in a private recess they were undressing and I could see nothing, only hear tender banalities: 'God, you're so beautiful,' and 'Darling, I do love you.' So it was a shock when they finally came naked into my sight and began to caress each other. There is something touchingly vulnerable about the naked human body. But I do not want you to imagine I was obsessed with anything so crude as mechanical performance. As always in these situations, the most titillating sensation arises first from anticipation, next from the feeling of power and privilege that watching unobserved can give you: the secret intrusion into privacy, the furtive participation in inti-mate rites. Of all stolen fruits, these are surely the most delicious.

'You're looking very cheerful,' Catherine said. (Tea at the Savoy.) 'Has something happened?'

'My work's going well,' I said.

They were not sexual athletes like Oswald and Miranda, but I got some wonderful photographs all the same, despite the difficulty of working at an oblique angle. Nothing new, not more than half a dozen basic positions in all, but some lovely movements with all the grace of dancers. I concentrated on their faces: there is, after all, nothing more erotic than the expression on the faces of two people in love who are giving each other pleasure. I did not find out anything new about sex but I learnt a great deal about love.

Oswald and Miranda had in some ways been a disappointment. Young and beautiful though they were, they seemed to me to experiment too much. They were not truly in love. When I look back over their photographs, I am struck by an air of strain, of improvisation for the sake of novelty. Sometimes, anyway, it was as if they were trying something new simply because they had heard about it, like a drug or a T-shirt, or because someone was paying them to pose for a calendar. They lacked tenderness.

In the streets as I went about my business, shopping or strolling, I half expected to be arrested. I felt my air of satisfaction and well-being (which Catherine had noticed) was conspicuous to passers-by, and anything so blatantly happy must surely be an offence.

Perfect love casteth out fear of germs. I was impressed and envious at the mutual worship of genitalia that was going on in my spare room, all that licking and sucking, like animals devotedly grooming one another. They had pet names for each other's sexual organs and lay staring at them for long periods of time, saying at intervals, Isn't he (or she) lovely, in the same tender rapturous tone that they used when talking about their children.

One day they didn't make love at all but lay on the bed with their arms round each other, naked, silent. They kissed for a while. I waited for the action to start but nothing evolved. I took a few photographs and began to get bored. Then:

'Leave him.'

'Oh darling, don't.' A long sigh from Gemma. 'Not again. I can't bear it.'

I switched on the tape recorder.

'If I get that job we'd have enough money.'

'Not for four children.'

'Just bring yours. I've given up. I don't think Cathy'd let me have mine anyway — not really. She's a cow, she'd fight me all the way and the bloody courts would back her up.'

Silence.

'I can't do that to Chris.'

'What about what you're doing to me?' Very sulky little boy voice full of injury.

'Oh, *darling*.'

A lot more kissing and hugging; an air of desperation. Nothing I could record. Then she sat up, arms round her knees, legs apart, breasts hanging loose, hair tousled. I took a photograph; she looked very appealing.

He said, 'You couldn't just leave them, could you?'

'I've thought about it.'

'God, are you serious? I thought you'd be shocked.'

She said very sadly, 'I was shocked at myself when I first thought of it. But I'm not shocked at you. I'm glad you've said it.'

'But you won't do it, will you?'

'Oh God.' Another long silence. 'I wish I could.'

He said with sudden furious energy, 'I just can't bear to think of you on holiday with him next month. He'll get randy in all that heat, won't he? He'll be at you all the time.'

She turned to look at him; she shook her head. He pulled her down to kiss him and she ran her hand up and down his body, lingering on his cock with sad proprietary tenderness.

'I love you,' she said presently, very slowly and seriously like a pledge.

'Then leave him.'

Silence. The tape recorder ran on, wasting itself.

He said abruptly, 'I'm so lonely. You've no idea. There's nothing like living with Cathy to make you feel alone in the world.' He paused. 'And there's something about this place I don't like.'

'Our lovely room?' She sounded shocked and puzzled.

'Yes, it's worse in here, but the whole flat, there's something——' He stopped. I held my breath.

'What?'

'Your uncle gives me the creeps, if you really want to know. I bet he comes in here and wanks after we've gone, poor old sod.'

'Don't say that, it spoils everything.'

'Why? Surely you know he fancies you. And me, come to that.'

'Of course he doesn't, he's just lonely.'

'He's a weirdo.'

'No he isn't.'

'Kinky then. You know he is, why not admit it?'

'He's a bit eccentric — all right — but he can't help it — he's alone so much.'

'I'm not surprised. Who could fancy him the way he looks?'

'Darling, don't. I've known him all my life — and look how good he's been to us. Where would we be without him?'

'Better off.'

'We'd have nowhere to go.'

'If you'd leave Chris we could have our own place. I'm sick of meeting you in a dirty old man's spare room.'

Well, that was what you got for trying to help people, for providing all the comfort and convenience of a brothel without the expense. They say listeners never hear any good of themselves but there is no excuse for rank ingratitude.

Catherine said, 'I can't think how you're going to manage the ending. He's bound to leave her first, he always does. I warned you about that.'

I shook my head. 'Criseyde left Troilus in the end.'

'I know that. But it was wartime, she was a hostage. You can't reproduce all that. What can you possibly do — persuade her husband to emigrate and take her with him?'

'That's a bit too drastic, I'd never see her. Besides, he wouldn't go; he's a pillar of the local community.'

'I was joking,' she said gently.

'She has to meet a new lover, that's all.'

'Diomedes.'

'Of course.'

'I always fancied Diomedes. I remember thinking Troilus was a bit wet, really, always bursting into tears and not eating, but Diomedes was sexy. I always liked Greeks after that.'

We were walking in Hyde Park. It was turning from a warm spring into a hot summer and office workers, wage slaves, lay sprawled on the grass in various stages of undress. Catherine picked her way delicately through them, looking absurdly young in jeans and a diaphanous shirt. I was proud of her.

On the last day before the holiday they made love with particular beauty and skill. I could not hear their voices clearly, they were muffled against each other's skin, but David was saying something urgent to Gemma about not letting Chris make love to her. They both wept a little in their embrace, I remember, and I found that more moving and erotic than anything else they had done. For a moment I almost felt an intruder.

While he was dressing she got up, still naked, and wandered across to the mirror to brush her hair. I held my breath; we were inches apart; she looked as if into my eyes and saw, of course, nothing but her own reflection, while I felt I gazed into her soul. It was what I had always coveted.

They were so preoccupied with themselves that never once did they try the locked door or question my new habit of going away at weekends. They never even asked if I enjoyed myself. Love makes people very selfish. I have noticed that before.

June

I thought I would miss them and all my new-found delights, but in fact I was glad of the rest. Like a too rich diet, my observations had weighed me down. I was heavy, exhausted, satiated.

179

David cleaned sullenly. He arrived late and left early. He took frequent breaks for coffee and martinis. He talked round the subject, nothing of interest about himself and Gemma, but a lot of veiled malice about Christopher and a constant peevish refrain about why Gemma was afraid to leave home. He tried to present this as a temporary fear, as if he were certain that she (or he) would overcome it. I was not sure if he was trying to convince himself or me.

'She doesn't love him, you know,' he said insistently. 'She's just sorry for him. She doesn't know how to tell him it's all over.'

He looked peculiarly attractive: it was pleasant to have him all to myself again. Of late I had been wondering sourly what Gemma saw in him (a foolish question to ask of lovers) because he was so removed from me. She had stolen him away and so, for the loss to be bearable, the prize must be worthless. But now he was given back, albeit on loan. Redeemed, like a pawnbroker's pledge. I looked at him closely. He had one of those faces that was always changing: it could be very attractive and then just as suddenly plain, so that you were puzzled by your own allegiance. At some angles it was even lop-sided. The sulky shutdown look that moods evoked suggested more was going on in his head than (I suspect) actually was. Watching him as he stood there in his jeans and jersey, the belt on the hips, the scarf at the neck, his face a brooding mask as he cleaned my silver and reflected on his life, I was enslaved all over again and angry with myself for being so. If he could reject Catherine for Gemma, I had never stood a chance. I knew he was shallow and worthless, that was why I had chosen him, to give us all the maximum trouble. I could not go back on my bargain now and wish him more amiable. I should not complain that there was not enough inside his lovely shell. So why did I still hanker after him? I had seen the extent (and limitations) of his sexual performance; I knew (at one remove) every detail of his body; I was satisfied that there was little of interest in his head. But — and perhaps this is true of all people who sell themselves for a living — the elusive essence of self was exceptionally fascinating, for that was all he had to offer. The play of light upon his face, the way it changed from

180

little-boy-lost actorish puppy charm to dangerous crooked devious malice. He in himself was not really powerful except in this one aspect of quick-change artist. It left us all not knowing quite where we were, a delicious uncertainty. Kicking and stroking were interchangeable. The waif we had rescued might turn on us yet, all gratitude gone, steal our silver and kick us in the teeth. Or (if we were very lucky) kiss our feet and weep to be forgiven. It could go either way; that was part of the fascination. But — and this worried me — uncertainty too could become boring, a habit like any other. Suppose I should tire of him before Gemma did? What if my spare room became a permanent refuge for two people who no longer excited me? How would I bear it? How (more important) would I ever get rid of them?

He talked a lot about Catherine too: how she suspected; how she was jealous; how she kept pretending she was ill in order to capture his attention; how surprised she would be when he left her and how it would serve her right for being such a cold-hearted bitch. He said all that in a sour, aggrieved, obsessional tone, often repeating himself. I said nothing but listened attentively. One day he suddenly rounded on me. 'You must be very pleased with yourself,' he said savagely. 'You've really messed things up good and proper.'

Gemma wrote from Majorca:

'Dear Uncle Alex,
   I'm enclosing a letter for David, please don't tell him what's in your letter. I've made a big effort to be cheerful in his letter.
   I am afraid I may be pregnant. I can't tell David yet in case it isn't true, please God it isn't, telling him would make it more likely somehow. I don't know why I'm telling you really except I must tell someone. I was late before we left but put it down to the worry about leaving David and going on holiday with Chris etc. But I am still late, in fact now I am twelve days late and I have never been twelve days late in my life without being pregnant.
   I can't be pregnant, it's absolutely impossible. I can't worry David with it, it's too silly. But if I am pregnant I've got to

181

have an abortion and I'm terrified of abortion, I always have been, the more Chris tells me about how simple and easy and painless it is these days the more I curl up and die. I mean when he tells me about abortion in the course of his work, *not* that he's got any idea about me. But can you imagine if I am — the effort of keeping something like that secret from your husband who also happens to be a doctor?

Please please make me not be pregnant. I've never prayed so much in my life as I have this week but nothing happens. Do you think God doesn't hear me? Why can't he be merciful and let something happen? The awful irony as you know is I've always wanted another child by Chris and now even more by David, and this means I'll have to get rid of something I want to keep. I can't believe it, it's too cruel. Oh please let it not be true. Perhaps after I post this something will happen.

To make matters worse this is a lovely place and we could all be enjoying ourselves. Chris was right, there are still unspoilt bits though Robert Graves and Chopin haven't turned up yet. The hotel is super and we have a small beach nearly to ourselves and delicious food and lots of lovely walks. The kids are loving it and Helga's very good with them though I find her a strain after Inge who was so quiet — she's got a mad laugh and does everything too loudly. But it may be just my nerves. I expect I'd find anyone a trial just now.

Chris is being terribly sweet and considerate — well, he always is but more so — which is absolutely terrifying because it makes me think he suspects something. Whatever I want to do is okay with him and no matter how moody I am he's never cross with me.

I just can't believe it, every day I tell myself it can't be true but still nothing happens. Oh I want it so much and I can't have it, it's not fair. If I was at home I could have a test. I don't know how I'm going to last another week without knowing. But of course I won't have to, something's bound to happen before then.

Please not a word to David, there's no point in alarming him about nothing. If you can't pray can you cast a spell or cast entrails or whatever you do — *please*? See, I can make jokes so I must be quite rational only I wake up in the night, like a mad woman choking with terror and I have to tell Chris I've been dreaming — oh please let it not be true.

Love,

Gemma

P.S. Seriously— please pray for me— even if you don't believe — it might do some good — anything might — *please* try.'

The letter puzzled me, after my initial elation subsided. It seemed wonderful news to me: why was Gemma so distressed? I could only think that she was unsure who was the father of the child. Did she perhaps feel that she could not stay with Christopher and bear David's child, nor run away with David while pregnant by Christopher? Delicate scruples, it seemed to me, but who was I to question how women felt about these matters? Still, it annoyed me not to be able to rejoice wholeheartedly. I would have liked to revel in our triumph, whether it was due to Gemma's inefficiency, David's careless egotism or my own contrivance. We would never know, but for the first time in my life I felt I had a share in paternity.

When I was calmer, I put on the kettle and opened Gemma's letter to David.

(8)

'Darling my love,

I miss you so much. We seem to have found one of the few beautiful quiet places left on the island — if only you and I could be here together.

I think such a lot about our night together. Going to sleep with you, waking up with you. What luxury. If that's what a lifetime would be like— but would it? If I brought the children with me would you get sick of them? Would you be jealous if I had mine and you didn't have yours? If I left mine with Chris would I feel so guilty or miss them so much we couldn't be happy together?

I've been thinking about all this very seriously as you can see. We must get something settled soon. I know things are terribly difficult as they are but I don't want to exchange one sort of problem for another. There must be a solution — so many people are in our situation after all and they find ways out of it. Perhaps if we all lived near enough to each other

183

(though not too near of course) we could have the children Monday to Friday and Chris could have them at weekends. Then Cathy might let you have yours when mine were with Chris. It all sounds very complicated but I'm sure we could work something out.

The really awful bit I can't get over in my head is telling Chris. It wouldn't be so bad if he'd been a rotten husband — if I'd had a difficult marriage the way you have — but he's really done nothing wrong and it seems so unfair to leave him and take his children away from him when he doesn't deserve it. Still, perhaps he'll be better off without me. I can't have been making him very happy lately.

Darling I love you so much, I don't think I was really alive till I met you. We'll manage to be together somehow won't we? Only we must be very sure what we're doing. There are so many people involved. I think I'm a bit afraid of putting too much pressure on us and spoiling what we have. But I can't imagine living with Chris for the rest of my life — not even another year. It just isn't living. It's funny when you think how lightly we started, and now we're facing all this upheaval. We were so sure it would never come to this, weren't we? But now it has and of course you're right, we can't go on meeting in Uncle A.'s spare room for the rest of our lives. I don't actually hate it the way you do but I'd love us to have a place of our own — God how I'd love it. It only worries me that maybe we're being too greedy and if we try for too much we'll be punished and lose it all. Please be very sure you won't have regrets — I promise I won't have if you don't.

Remember how much I love you. Oh darling please hold me tight.

Your Gemma'

When I had resealed David's letter, I read mine again. They might have been written by two different people. How strange women are.

'Must be a big thing this time,' Catherine said lightly. 'He hasn't laid a finger on me all the time she's been away.'

184

They were sitting on either side of the table when I came in. Gemma looked tanned and fit and well, her brown face contrasting strangely with her expression of stricken misery. David looked pale and sick and angry.

'Well, go on, tell him,' he said, pointing at me with his thumb. 'He might as well know.'

Gemma barely lifted her head to acknowledge my presence, though I had not seen her for two weeks. 'He knows already,' she said in a low voice.

'Oh, great. Who else have you told? Maybe I'm the last to know.'

She muttered very low, 'No one else.'

'Apart from a few dozen friends and relations, I suppose.'

'I had to tell someone. I didn't want to worry you.'

I had never seen two people so savagely unhappy. I even suggested leaving them alone again, although as far as I knew they had already been alone for three hours, but they both demanded that I stay, so insistently that it occurred to me they were hoping I would arbitrate.

'She's going to kill my child,' he said to me. 'That's all. She's going to have it sucked out of her, all blood and bits, into a bottle. It doesn't take long, only about five minutes, and you don't feel a thing, well, maybe a bit of discomfort or the odd twinge or two, but nothing you could really call pain. Isn't that splendid? Her shit of a husband was explaining all about it on TV. It's the in-thing nowadays — did you know that? All the smart trendy people are having it done. Lunchtime abortion, it's called. Well, it saves so much time when you're out shopping.'

Gemma started to cry silently, big tears rolling down her cheeks like a child. I wanted to put my arm round her but I did not like to touch her in front of him.

'I suppose you think it's a good idea,' he said. 'You've been encouraging her, haven't you?'

'I don't know anything about it,' I said with dignity, 'but it's Gemma's decision.'

'And it's *my child*.' He banged his fist on my (rather valuable) table. I really wished he wouldn't.

'I haven't got a choice,' Gemma said, barely audible.

'Why don't you get your precious husband to do it for you since it's so easy and he's so keen on it?'

'Aren't you being a little hard on her?' I said, as it seemed my duty to intervene. 'I happen to know Gemma doesn't like abortion any more than you do, but if she thinks it's necessary——'

'It's murder,' he said flatly. My heart sank as I heard the no-argument tones of sheer irrationality. The fanatic on his soap-box.

'Would you feel so strongly,' I enquired, 'if it was Christopher's child?'

'She says it isn't.'

'But if it was. That wouldn't be murder, would it? You'd be glad to get rid of it. It's only *your* children that are sacred.' I was thinking of Catherine.

He didn't answer (which convinced me I was right), just kept looking at Gemma, who stared at the table, tears streaming down her face.

'Is it Christopher's child, Gemma?'

She shook her head.

'How can you be sure? You still have it off with him, I know you do.'

'If Gemma's not sure,' I said to pacify him because Gemma didn't seem able to help herself much, 'isn't that a good reason for having an abortion?' It annoyed me slightly to think that we were going through all these contortions when one good hefty lie from Gemma would settle the whole matter.

He turned to me. 'She says she loves me, she says she's going to leave him and come away with me — and now she's going to kill my child.' His voice cracked oddly; I wondered if he too was on the verge of tears. All this fuss, I thought, about an unborn child, a foetus, a clump of cells that may not even be there.

'Gemma,' I said with sudden hope (I had wanted them to suffer, yes, but this was ridiculously exaggerated), 'aren't we being a little premature? You weren't even sure you were pregnant when you wrote to me.'

'I had a test as soon as I got home.' I could hardly hear her.

'Oh yes, she moves fast all right,' he said bitterly. 'She's a real expert. Apparently you can only have the super new method if you catch it early — that's right, isn't it?'

Gemma blew her nose. His prolonged attack seemed to be making her pull herself together.

'Up to eight weeks,' she said.

'After that it gets a bit messy and old-fashioned. You might have to suffer and that wouldn't do, would it?'

'It's not that at all.' She began repairing her face. 'If you have vacuum extraction you can go home the same day. If they do a D and C they keep you in overnight. I can't explain that to Chris again.'

'You see?' He turned back to me; he seemed set on scoring points, checking with the umpire. 'It all comes back to bloody Chris. Mustn't tell him lies, must we? Can't be away overnight, he might get cold in bed. You're going to kill my child just to keep your fucking husband happy. Christ. And you said you loved me.'

In the middle of making up her face, Gemma started crying again. 'I do,' she said. 'I do. And I want your baby. But I can't have it. I can't tell Chris I'm having your baby while I'm still living with him. It's too cruel. Can't you see that?'

'Then leave him. Leave him right now. Just don't go home.'

I went away to make a cup of tea for us all and left them to it. From the kitchen I could hear them shouting at each other. It was strange to have so much sudden noise in my home, where voices were seldom raised. Was I perhaps getting a little too much reality? I was not altogether sure now how to proceed: I had envisaged Gemma staying with Christopher and bringing up David's child; I had imagined her rejecting David at a later stage, not running away with him. I had never considered abortion, and while in a sense I welcomed the drama of it, it would, might one say, be short-lived. Not to be compared with the long-term interest of a cuckoo in the nest. Besides, it might make Gemma depressed, and while unhappiness can be colourful, depression is dreary for all concerned.

By the time I went back with the tea there was a terrible silence. I poured three cups. The sound of the liquid flowing from the pot and into the china seemed unnaturally loud. The spoons chimed against the saucers. It was eerie, unnerving.

187

'You don't love me,' he said as if I was not there.

'I do. I *do* love you.'

'If you loved me you couldn't kill my child.'

They did not seem to have made much progress. I handed round cups of tea.

'Look,' Gemma said. 'Between us we've got four children already. We don't even know what we're going to do about *them* yet. How *can* I have another baby when——'

He cut in. 'The others belong to Chris and Cathy.' He made them sound like a couple. 'This baby's ours. We can make a fresh start.'

'And leave them *all*? Is that what you mean?'

'Why not? Don't you see, it's our big chance. It's fate. You once said you wanted more kids.'

'Not like this.'

'Then you should have been more careful.'

'So should you.'

'Children, children.' I was embarrassed: I reverted to cliché. 'What's done is done. It won't help to quarrel about whose fault it is.' Although in fact nothing could have interested me more, given my own involvement in the matter. But I did not feel it was a safe topic. 'You've got to decide what to do.'

'What the hell d'you think we're doing?'

Anxiety was making him ruder than usual.

'She never meant to leave him,' he went on in a contemptuous tone.

'I never believed you really wanted me to,' Gemma said defensively.

'She's too fond of home comforts — afraid she might have to rough it for a change. She wants the best of both worlds. A rich husband and a bit on the side.'

My ears ached with his abuse. But there was something familiar — an echo — about the way he talked about her as if she were not there. Yes. He reminded me of Beatrice. For both of them Gemma was a child, a toy, an animal. A beautiful object to have about the house, to be abused or shown off at will. I resented the essential vulgarity he shared with Beatrice. They were coarse clay, both of them.

'Gemma,' I said soothingly. 'What would you really like to do?'

She said again, 'I haven't any choice.'

'Oh, for God's sake.' He banged the table again, making my precious china jump and tinkle. I winced. 'Be honest. You mean you want to kill it.'

He seemed to have only one thought in his head.

'Look.' I tried to be fair. 'All this haste, isn't it putting you both under pressure? If you want the baby, Gemma, why don't you have it? Stay with Chris till after it's born. Let him think it's his and decide what you're going to do later when you're not so upset. Would you agree to that, David?'

To my surprise he said humbly, 'I'd agree to anything to keep the baby. And make Gemma happy.'

She put out a hand to him across the table and he took it. They hung on to each other tightly. Gemma started to cry again, just when I thought I was getting somewhere. Lovers are very unpredictable.

'Chris would know,' she said.

'How would he know?' I was baffled. 'He hasn't guessed so far.'

'He'd know it wasn't his.'

I had never seen anyone cry so much.

'How? He can't be sure, even if you are.'

'He can.'

'Why? I don't understand.' Now we were both attacking her. She said with extreme reluctance, 'He's had a vasectomy.'

I would really prefer not to remember the next week. They did not make love at all: I felt a fool locked in my bedroom while they were in the kitchen crying and arguing, or while they lay on the spare-room bed and talked endlessly round in circles in the hopeless way that people do when there is no solution but they cannot bear to leave the subject alone. Between meetings they each insisted on trying to indoctrinate me with their separate points of view, David in person, Gemma on the telephone, as if once convinced, I might persuade the recalcitrant other. I was exhausted.

Gemma appeared to consider a vasectomy a badge of

189

shame, which was why it had taken her so long to tell us about it. She felt she was betraying Christopher by admitting something so humiliating. David, on the other hand, viewed it as comic (which for some reason enraged Gemma). To me it seemed eminently sensible of Christopher, given his views on family size and his knowledge of Gemma's fecklessness, and her current predicament only served to prove how right he was.

'He said he ought to practise what he preached,' she said wretchedly. 'Whatever method we used I was always forgetting or doing it wrong, I don't know why, because I wanted another baby, I suppose, although I didn't *think* it was on purpose. But Chris said as he was the one who didn't want any more and it was such a simple operation for him, he should have it done. He said it wasn't fair to keep recommending it to others if he wasn't prepared to have it himself.'

The inescapable puritan logic of that sounded so exactly like Christopher that I almost laughed. He was the sort of man who would have become a vegetarian if he felt himself unable to kill a sheep, despite the fact that the world is full of slaughterers. It was ironic and embarrassing that his good sense had rebounded on him — on all of us. But laughter would have distressed Gemma, who saw nothing even faintly amusing in the situation. So I tried to comfort her instead, but she would not be comforted.

I asked if she had seen her own doctor yet. I had no idea how one set about getting an abortion these days but it seemed the logical place to start. She said no, he was too close to Chris and she was afraid. I invoked the Hippocratic oath and she said of course he wouldn't tell but he'd be carrying the burden of her secret (as she was carrying the child, I thought) and seeing Chris every day, he might let something slip. And even if he didn't, the idea that someone so near home knew all about it threw her into a panic; it seemed to be tempting fate. She had thought about going to one of the charity places for anonymity but they were full of Christopher's friends doing part-time work and they didn't do the method she wanted yet. The National Health Service, yes, they would be cheaper still, but she doubted if they could move fast enough for her, they were so overworked. She made so many objections that I wondered briefly if she was trying to talk herself out of the whole thing. (But in the end it turned out that she was trying to talk herself into spending money. Mine.)

Beatrice rang up and I felt a pang of guilty terror. Gemma wasn't looking well, she remarked conversationally, as if I should know why. Yes, she'd had a lovely holiday and yes, she was very brown, but the fact remained that she didn't look at all well. Wasn't that odd? I took a deep breath and said I had noticed the very same thing and I couldn't understand it. In fact I had been going to mention it to her myself.

Every time I spoke to Gemma I felt we were sitting on a time-bomb ticking relentlessly away. If only I could persuade David, she said. She hated to do it without his approval; well, she hated to do it at all but it seemed much worse that way. Besides, she needed his support, his comfort. She had already wasted a week trying to persuade him: couldn't I try?

I had already tried; I tried again. David proved inflexible, using the word 'murder' as if he had invented it. If Gemma was prepared to kill his child, it meant she did not love him. There was nothing to discuss. I tried to argue that it was the immediacy of the decision that presented the problem, rather than intrinsic morality. Gemma within another week or two must either abort and stay with Christopher, or remain pregnant and run away with David. I winced a little at the words 'run away'; they sounded so melodramatic. I pictured Gemma with a suitcase scuttling down the garden path while David waited in a car with the engine running. But he saw nothing incongruous. To him it was the ideal opportunity: a reason to do sooner what they had planned to do later. Unless of course Gemma had never intended to do it at all, he added accusingly. For my own satisfaction I tried to get out of him if he had ever really wanted her to, since she obviously didn't believe him and it seemed to me a most unlikely plan (why on earth couldn't they simply go on as they were?), but he insisted it was what he had always meant.

'Well, of course he's lying,' Catherine said, 'if you mean not telling the truth. But he probably does believe what he says, for what it's worth.'

I was still amazed to find myself in her living-room. But the children were sick and she could not find a sitter. I looked round greedily, sure that this was my first and last visit to such intimate territory, anxious to absorb as much as I could. The flat was incredibly cluttered, toys and books and bits of suede and leather all over the place. A cottage industry, David had called it sneeringly in those far-off days before we began. Now, when I looked at Catherine, I felt I had known her all my life.

She didn't apologise for the mess, merely sat down in it and began stitching something.

I said, 'I'm flattered to be here. I didn't think you'd risk it.'

She smiled. 'Why, in case one of the children said to David, Mummy had a funny man here? Don't worry, they're used to Mummy's funny men. They wouldn't think it worth mentioning.'

Not quite the answer I wanted but I had to make the best of it. I sat down opposite her and studied her pale angular face. I felt I wanted to save her from something but I was not sure what it was.

I said inadequately, 'I'm so glad to see you.'

She smiled and went on stitching. Presently she said, 'If she has an abortion, he'll leave her. If that's what she's afraid of, she's absolutely right.'

I said, 'But you had one and he didn't leave you.'

'I had two, but he doesn't know about the second. Of course he didn't leave me, I'm his wife.' A look of extraordinary self-satisfaction passed across her face.

I wanted to question her but I did not dare. Why did she seem so pleased? Not for the first time I wondered what I had blundered into; what went on between them; was nothing as it seemed?

She said in an amused, artificial tone of voice, as if she knew my thoughts, 'He's stuck with me, you see. But girlfriends have to prove themselves. Very keen on grand gestures, David is. Self-sacrifice and the world well lost for love. All that. I lost track of it years ago but I think that's what he wants. To him,

192

you see, getting rid of his child is a personal insult. He's very insecure. But I told you all that, didn't I? He wants people to prove they love him, all the time. It gets very exhausting.'

I said, 'But I don't see what Gemma can do. She's obviously afraid to leave her husband for him.'

Catherine said gently, 'She's right to be afraid. It wouldn't last.'

'But she can't stay with her husband if she's pregnant. He's had a vasectomy. And if she has an abortion you say David will leave her.'

'That's right.' Her tone was utterly calm.

'I think she knows that.'

'She'd be a fool if she didn't.'

The minutes ticked by. She put aside her stitching and poured us two drinks. She resumed her seat and told me that presently we could eat a salad lunch and some home-made soup.

I said with a touch of desperation, 'So she doesn't know what to do for the best.'

'No. She's really in a mess.'

Her cool rational callousness was beyond anything I had ever encountered. I was thrilled and disgusted. I did not know how to deal with her. I wanted to run away and yet I felt I had a lot to learn.

I said, 'You don't seem very upset.'

She shrugged. 'No. If you remember, I did try to stop all this happening, right at the beginning. But you wouldn't help me.' She said it very gently, logically. Without reproach. She was stating a fact. 'So there's no point in my getting upset now. It's not my problem any more.'

Gemma said, 'I want to see Peter. He's the only person I trust.'

'Peter?' For a mad moment I imagined she meant Peter Hughes; that she must be having a fit of nostalgia for her first love. I pictured him ineptly trying to abort her with a bicycle pump borrowed from his father's shop.

'Peter Grayson. My baby doctor.'

It was suddenly clear. 'A first-rate chap,' I said, my total-recall memory bringing Christopher's words back to me.

She didn't notice the allusion. 'He's marvellous. He'll understand.' I felt she was casting me out along with David. 'And if he doesn't want to do it himself, he'll refer me to someone he knows.'

'Gemma,' I said uneasily, 'are you sure all this is legal?'

'Of course it is.' She sounded quite cross.

'But do you really have grounds for abortion?'

'*Yes*. Don't be stupid.' She quoted something about the risk to the physical and mental health of the pregnant woman and her children being greater if the pregnancy continued than if it was terminated, but she quoted it so fast I lost track of her. When I remarked that she was very well-informed she shrieked at me that I was just like David, and how could she help knowing all about it, being married to Christopher? After that there was a long silence and I felt I had failed her.

'All I want from you is money,' she said hurtfully. 'Can you lend me some money? Chris will notice if I'm overdrawn and Peter isn't cheap but he's the best. I'll be safe with him.'

I was reminded of Beatrice's words on Gemma's wedding day and I was close to tears.

'Of course I'll lend you money,' I said. 'As much as you like. I'll do anything you want, you know that.'

'That's all I want,' she said, started to cry and hung up. I hovered, but she didn't ring back.

Something was bothering me; I spent the rest of the evening in a kind of daze. I had a problem to solve. If Catherine had been there, I could have worked it out sooner. But hours later, in bed, it came to me; I saw where I had blundered. I had got the roles confused; I had cast the wrong actors. None of this trouble would have arisen if I had realised fully what I was about. I was even surprised that Catherine had not pointed out my mistake; it was so simple. Christopher wasn't Criseyde's dead husband after all: he was Troilus, in all his fidelity and tears. So David wasn't Troilus, as I had fantasised: he was the glamorous, the unreliable, the threat: he was Diomedes. I had got it all wrong, from the very beginning.

Book 5

'What should I say to you? I hate Criseyde;
God knows that I shall hate her evermore!'

You are going to blame me: I can feel it. Despite the fact that I only gave them what they wanted. That it also happened to be what I wanted is incidental. Thanks to me, they have lived more fully than I, but nevertheless you are going to blame me, because it turned out badly. As if endings were all that mattered.

On the day of Gemma's abortion, David abandoned all pretence of working and sat about my flat consuming martinis by the pint. I envied him for being able to find such an easy relief for tension, and at someone else's expense. We were both very anxious and reproached one another like parents.

'Why aren't you with her?'

'She wouldn't have me. It was you she wanted.'

'I couldn't face it.'

'She shouldn't be there alone.'

'She shouldn't be there at all.'

Deadlock. I had to admit he was consistent, at least. I wondered how much guilt he actually felt: had he rationalised it all or was he now busy swamping it all in drink? I studied him: it was strange to consider what fevered emotions he had aroused — in me, in Gemma, once upon a time (presumably) in Catherine. It was not one of his good days: he was looking ordinary.

'We could have been happy,' he said. 'You should have left us alone.'

I began to protest my innocence but he cut me short.

'We didn't stand a chance with you breathing down our necks, poisoning everything. You never wanted me to have her, did you, not for myself. Only for you. I had to do it for you.'

197

He helped himself liberally to martini. I said nothing. Time passed slowly. I wondered what stage Gemma had reached by now. Was it all over?

'You never meant us to be happy,' he went on at last; he seemed to need this alcoholic monologue. 'You're not interested in happiness, are you? You can't be happy so why should anyone else? If she'd gone away with me you'd have lost her, wouldn't you?'

Well, it was one way of looking at it. He was obviously hell-bent on blaming me for everything. I decided to maintain a dignified silence. Never argue with a drunk.

'She did love me,' he said presently, emphatically, as though I had denied it. 'You don't believe me but she did.'

He seemed in considerable distress, but I had to remember he was an actor. It was easy to forget that, since he was not a very good one and worked so seldom, but it remained a fact and could mean that he was acting now. He was also consider-ably drunk.

I sat and watched him as one might an invalid: warily, with concerned detachment, alert for signs of recovery or deteriora-tion.

'She must love him very much,' he said suddenly, 'to do this for him. I don't think I can bear it.' And he started to cry. I gazed at him with fascinated horror. I could not comfort him because the same thought had occurred to me; I felt he was right.

He sobbed for a while as though his heart would break, as though he had a heart to break. Then he seized the telephone.

'I've got to talk to her,' he said in a frenzy.

'You can't ring up somebody at a hospital,' I said, wonder-ing if he was entirely sane.

He ignored me, dialling. And looked at me through his angry tears as if I were the one who was mad.

Then all became clear. He said, 'Cathy, I can't bear it, you've got to forgive me, we can try again, it'll be different this time, I promise, Cathy, please listen, don't leave me, Cathy.'

He went on and on. There was far more that I don't recall precisely because it was so repetitive. I listened in amazement: it was like having Heathcliff in my living-room during one of

198

his bad patches. Catherine's answers must have been brief and to the point, or else he would not let her speak at all, for his monologue seemed almost uninterrupted. It was all begging and pleading and sobbing, all wild promises and unlikely resolutions, a dreadful exhibition totally lacking in dignity and punctuated by her name, incessantly repeated like a church bell tolling or a dog howling in the distance. On one level it seemed impossible that Gemma should be having an abortion while he behaved like this, yet on another it made perfect sense. I longed to go and listen to Catherine's answers, however mono-syllabic, on the bedroom extension, but reckoned that while David in his present state would probably not notice, my chances of picking up the receiver undetected by Catherine were nil. So I remained where I was and surveyed the wreck before my eyes. Crying had made him very ugly.

Eventually Catherine must have said something final or he must have run out of energy, for he suddenly put down the receiver in mid-sentence, buried his head in his hands for a moment, then jumped up, looking green in the face, and went off to be sick in my bathroom. I could hear the dreadful retching sounds from where I sat. When he came back he looked at me with loathing, said he hoped I was satisfied, and slammed out of the flat.

I stayed where I was for some time after he had gone. The silence was miraculous. I wondered if I might even be losing my taste for drama, but decided it was the extreme vulgarity of the scene which had distressed me. I did not realise how well off I was at that moment. Later, when I went casually into the bathroom, I found myself obliged to clear up vomit.

Gemma, who had some excuse for melodrama, was totally silent. She sat in the car like a little ghost, not saying a word; hugging herself and rocking gently to and fro. She alarmed me. If I spoke to her she would answer, but that was all.

'Are you all right?'
'Yes.'
'Was it awful?'
'No. They were all very kind.'

199

The hospital and my flat were not far apart, but it seemed the longest, slowest drive I had ever undertaken. The traffic was dense and all the lights were against us. Every time we stopped, crowds of people in summer clothes crossed the road in front of us; it was a hot day. But Gemma, I noticed, was shivering. Her silence created appalling tension in the car: it was like a cold thick fog through which I had to slice in order to breathe. I would have preferred tears, anger, hysteria. Anything.

'Soon be home,' I said cheerily.

'Yes.'

'I expect you'd like to rest and have some tea.'

'Thank you.'

She was so remote from me it did not seem possible I had known her all her life. I could not think what to say to her; I searched my mind like a phrase book, finding only stilted formalities, all irrelevant to the situation.

'Try not to worry. You'll feel better soon.'

'Yes.'

I gave up and concentrated on driving. Unused to Gemma's car, I found the gears a little awkward. Gemma spoke only once of her own accord. As we drew up outside the flat she said with an obvious effort:

'Is he here?'

I said, embarrassed, 'No, he left early.'

I felt I had failed her utterly. The one thing she wanted I could not provide. She got out of the car in silence, but her disappointment was heavy in the air and she moved stiffly, like an old woman. I felt I ought to be careful of her, apart from wanting to touch and comfort her; I put my arm round her shoulders, very tentatively, but she shrugged it away.

Inside, she lay on the sofa like an obedient child, sick on a summer's day. I wrapped her up in blankets and she shivered, while outside the sun shone. I made tea for her and began explaining it was just as well David had gone; it would have been too emotional for them to meet today, too exhausting. I tried to make it sound as if David had been considerate, thinking only of her welfare, while we both knew that he had deprived her of the one thing she needed: his presence. She listened till I ran out of insincere, well-meant words, then she said politely:

'Could you leave me alone, please.'

I went and sat in my study like an outcast. I thought how far we had come, looking back like a traveller at the bumpy, dusty road behind. I could not see the path ahead. I felt very old. I felt I had run out of ingenuity.

At four she came and tapped on the door and said she was leaving. She had made up her face with care, for Christopher and the children, I supposed; she looked nearly normal. I tried to get over my feeling of exclusion; I asked if she was fit to drive and should I come with her. She said she was supposed to have someone with her but she preferred to be alone. I said I was worried about her and asked her to ring me as soon as she got home.

'They'll think it odd,' she said.

'You can pretend you've forgotten something.'

'I'm tired of telling lies. Anyway, if I don't turn up, they'll ring you.' She gathered up her things. 'But I'll be all right. You needn't worry.'

I could not reach her: she had passed beyond my control. It was very disturbing.

She said like a polite guest going home from a party, 'Thank you for everything. I'll pay back the loan as soon as I can.'

'Please forget it.' I felt suddenly desperate. 'Let me come with you.'

'No. Really not.'

I saw her out reluctantly. At the door she paused and said abruptly, 'D'you think he'll ever forgive me? Because if he doesn't, I'll have nothing to live for.'

'I shouldn't expect him back if I were you.' Catherine's voice was crisp on the phone and she had perversely chosen the early morning to ring: a time when I scarcely knew who I was, so how could I be expected to recognise her and make sense of what she said.

'What? Why not?' I tugged off my mask and blinked at the daylight.

'He's gone to Birmingham. He thinks they're going to write

him into that serial, the one he did a week in. They've built up his part or something. God knows. Anyway, it's work. I think you'd better find yourself another cleaner.'

'But he can't . . .' I heard myself spluttering with indignation. 'He can't just disappear like that.'

'You must be joking.' There was a certain grim satisfaction in her voice. 'He's renowned for it.'

'But what about you and the children?'

'Oh, he'll be down at weekends, I expect.' She sounded as if the pattern was boringly familiar.

'But the other day — when he rang you from here — he was so upset.'

'Oh, that.' A long pause. 'Yes. He always is.'

I tried to gather my wits. 'Look, I don't think you understand my position. What do I tell Gemma?'

'Tell her it's over. She probably knows anyway.'

I was shocked. 'I can't do that.'

'Why not? It's the truth.'

'Then he's got to tell her himself.'

'Why? He'll only make it worse. I'm sure you could do it much better.'

'But she's had the abortion, she's very upset, all she wants is to see him, she rings me up every day to ask if he's here——'

'Mr Kyle, I'm sorry, but that's not my problem. I told you what would happen and it has. You wouldn't stop it when you had the chance. There's really nothing I can do.'

'Can't you make him write to her?'

'I can't *make* him do anything. Besides, he's very bad at letters.'

'But if you ask him. If you explain. He listens to you.'

'He hangs on to me. It's not the same thing. Look, I'll have to go. My little girl's being sick.'

It was a bizarre time for me. Everything had happened quickly but most of it behind my back. Off-stage. From being the producer, I was no longer even a member of the audience. Gemma's telephone calls afflicted me like a hair shirt. Every day: 'Is he there? Have you seen him? Are you expecting him?' She sounded like a wraith; I found myself picturing Giselle. I could not manage to deliver the *coup de grâce*; I could not quite believe it was necessary. At any moment I expected David to materialise. Love affairs did not end like this — did they? So abruptly, so haphazardly? No one could leave his mistress on the day of an abortion and disappear to Birmingham. People telephoned; they wrote letters. So I temporised: I said no, he was not here, I had not seen him, but I was expecting him — he was bound to turn up sooner or later. Meanwhile, my life seemed to have come to a standstill: from seeing all three of them, I saw no one.

Gemma apologised each time she rang up, which made me feel worse. She was so polite. 'I'm sorry to keep doing this but I *must* speak to David.' I longed to magic him out of thin air. After a week or ten days she became hysterical, sobbing down the phone, 'I can't bear it, you've got to find him, you've *got* to.' She was like an addict demanding a fix. Naked embarrassing pain like a raw bleeding wound was on the other end of my phone. I could not bear to tell her he had gone to Birmingham; it seemed so callous. I said perhaps he was ill.

'Look,' Catherine said briskly at eight a. m. to my horror and disbelief, 'you've got to stop this. She's outside my flat every day.'

The telephone calls had ceased; I had gratefully assumed resignation. I said faintly, out of the bowels of sleep, 'What do you mean?'

The voice was irritable. 'Oh God, surely you know. She drives here every day. She sits outside in her car. She walks up and down. She cries.'

'Gemma?' I was stupid with sleep.

'Who else? She's small and dark and pretty, right? And she drives a Renault. Well, she's been here every day for a week. I can't stand it. You've got to stop her.'

I began to wake up. 'How can I stop her?'

'Tell her it's over, for God's sake. Get her off my back. I can't stand these bloody women and their emotions on my doorstep.'

I had never heard her express so much feeling before.

'Get your wretched husband to tell her,' I said. 'That's all she wants.'

'He's in Birmingham. Haven't you told her that?'

'No,' I said. 'It's not my job. And it's not your job either. Does David always get you to do his dirty work for him?'

'Usually. When something's over he wants to forget it ever happened so he just cuts out. Anyway, I think he's got a girl in Birmingham.'

I was silent, trying to force my brain into some sort of working order.

'Are you still there?' she demanded sharply.

'If she went to Birmingham,' I said, 'would he see her?'

'I suppose she could picket the studio. But he won't be pleasant if she does see him, believe me. When he's finished with someone he turns very nasty. I don't think he likes being reminded of the mess he's made. She's really much better off not seeing him, honestly. It'll only make an even worse ending.'

I was still thinking. I wanted to gratify Gemma's wish, even wrongly; I needed to be powerful enough to do that. I also could not quite believe that a meeting would not melt David's heart, if he had one. Surely he could not look at Gemma and feel nothing?

'What about weekends?' I said. 'You told me he'd be home at weekends.'

Catherine said quickly, 'But she can't get away at weekends, can she?'

'No, not easily. But if she could— would you get him to see her? And that would be the end of it.' Or a new start?

Catherine sighed. 'No, he's in Brighton at weekends.'

'Are you protecting him?'

'Why should I?' She sounded weary.

'Is he hiding in Brighton?'

'No, he's visiting his mother.' She had put on a patient voice as if talking to an idiot. 'The children are staying with her.'

'In Brighton?'

'That's where she lives.'

'But I thought she was dead.'

'I told you he has fantasies.'

.   .   .

Gemma came to see me. She went and shut herself in the spare room for a long time like a pilgrim; she came out pale and distressed but somehow uplifted.

'Thank you,' she said. 'I was afraid to come but it *does* help— it *does* make me feel a little nearer him. Where is he? You know, don't you? You must tell me. Please. I can't bear it. Please tell me.'

'His wife rang up,' I said gently, 'to say he's giving up his job here. He's in Birmingham, he's got a TV part. He's going to be there for months and he's not home at weekends.'

She was silent.

I said, 'My love, you've got to stop going to his flat. You won't see him there and you're only upsetting his wife.'

To my surprise she said, 'Perhaps if I upset her enough she'll let me see him. I wrote him a letter but I don't think she sent it on. I know he'd have answered if he got it. I'll have to write to the studio. You see, he's afraid. He thinks I'm going to be bitter and make a scene. But I won't. I just want him to forgive me. Then we can start again.'

She settled herself on the sofa and stared at me with large, imploring eyes, begging me to agree with her.

'I know he loves Cathy and I love Chris. But that's all right. It doesn't affect how we feel about each other. We just got too greedy, that's all. We thought we could have everything. But we couldn't.' She paused. 'Well, we've paid for that.'

'You mean *you* have.'

'No, both of us. He was terribly upset. You saw him.'

I did not know what to say.

'Look,' she said, 'you haven't always seen him at his best. But when we're alone together he's lovely to me. Really.'

I remembered when she had said much the same thing about Christopher.

'Then why hasn't he been in touch?' I felt callous in the extreme but I could not bear to let her go on constructing false hopes.

'He's hurt and angry. He feels guilty. Look, I understand all that. I can make it all right. And he's working. It's only two weeks and a bit.'

Silence. I marvelled at the generosity of women. But the self-deception was alarming.

'If you saw him,' I said, 'and you found it was over . . . Could you face that?'

Her face changed. 'But it isn't over.'

'But if it was.'

'No, really.' There was absolute terror in her eyes. 'You don't understand. He really does love me. That's *why* he was so upset. What I did — it was like his mother rejecting him all over again. That's why I've got to see him — to tell him I understand.'

'His mother's alive and well,' I said, hating myself, 'and living in Brighton.'

She frowned as if I were talking a foreign language.

'He lied to you,' I said.

She said calmly, 'I expect he felt as if she was dead when she rejected him. It's the same thing.'

I gave up. Now I was reminded of Madam Butterfly finding excuses for Pinkerton.

'I've got to see him,' she said, with almost religious fervour. 'I can make everything all right again. I know I can.'

Perhaps she too was clinging to a belief in the magic powers of sight and touch. For myself, I felt as the newspapers say in times of disaster at sea or down a mine or on a mountain: hopes were fading. There would be no survivors. I smiled at Gemma and poured her a large drink. It was all I could do at present. Too soon for talk of getting over it, of meeting someone else, of forgetting. The only real cure, but she did not yet want to be cured.

She said, 'I'm sorry I can't finish the typing. But it's such a sad story. I can't face it.'

David wrote:

'Dear Professor,

Sorry I won't be coming back but I'm going to be up here for six months at least and I've really had cleaning people's flats anyway.

Could you tell her I won't be back. I got her letter. Cathy sent it on with the rest of my mail. I won't have Cathy hounded like this, it really is intolerable, you've got to stop her going round there and making a nuisance of herself. Tell her she's better off without me or something — you're supposed to be clever, you should know what to say. I could never feel the same about her anyway after what she did so there'd be no point in meeting. Tell her that if you like. Just get her to stop annoying Cathy.

I'll send your keys back as soon as I can. I put them in a safe place when I packed and now I can't find them.

Yours,

David

P.S. I've never worked so hard in my life before. The series goes out three times a week. It's like being back in rep.'

A sombre piece of work, I thought: as heartless as Catherine had predicted. How well she knew him. So that was what marriage did for people: made them experts on each other. Two details interested me: his use of the word 'intolerable' in defence of Catherine, and his avoidance of Gemma's name. Neither gave me hope for the future.

It's easy to be wise after the event; we all know that. I can feel you preparing to condemn me because I made the wrong decision. But at the time I gave it careful thought and I could not see what else to do. I wanted Gemma to have her heart's desire and I wanted Catherine to stop ringing me at eight a.m. All right, I could take the telephone off the hook, a detail, but I did not want to be rejected by Catherine, and I needed Gemma and David to meet again. Life was in danger of becoming both empty and unpleasant. Even Christopher had taken to ringing up to ask if it was really necessary for Gemma to come up to town every day to do my typing, it meant the au pair didn't get enough free time, and would the poem be finished soon?

What would you have done? Not now, with hindsight, but then? What would you have done in my position? Having got this far, I felt I had to see the matter through.

I telephoned David. He was always out or busy. I left messages. He didn't ring back. Finally I telephoned and said I was his agent. He came on the line instantly.

'I want you to see Gemma,' I said. No point in preamble: he might hang up.

'Oh, Christ, it's you.' He sounded furious but also, to my surprise, exhausted. 'They said it was my agent. Look, I'm rehearsing, for God's sake.'

I sensed I did not have much time.

'I'll give you fifty pounds to see her,' I said swiftly. Bribery always seemed to me a better bet than threats, particularly when time is limited. Appeal to his baser nature as quickly as possible.

'You must be joking,' he said, exactly like Catherine.

I had had qualms about fixing Gemma's price: it seemed a little crude. But haggling would be cruder still and now was not a time to waver.

'All right, a hundred.'

'Christ.' There was an exhalation of breath and a long silence. 'You do realise I don't want to see her at all.'

'Why else do you think I'm offering you money?'

Another long silence. 'Look, it won't do any good. It's over.'

'She wants to see you,' I said. 'It's up to you what you say. At least it will stop her bothering your wife and bothering me and bothering you — she won't believe it's over unless you tell her yourself.'

'I could write her a letter,' he said craftily. 'Aren't you wasting your money?'

'No, because I don't believe you'd write. And anyway, she doesn't want a letter, she wants to see you.'

'God, women are crazy.' More silence. 'A hundred, you said.'

'Yes.' I paused, then added quickly, 'And don't try to push me up, that's all I can afford.'

I heard him lighting a cigarette. 'Oh, the hell with it. Tell her I'll see her on Friday. About lunchtime. And remember it was your idea. Cash, of course.'

'Of course,' I said.

Well, it may not seem very romantic to you, and indeed it wasn't, but it cheered Gemma up; she became positively radiant, in fact, and said there, now did I see, it was going to be all right, he had only needed time. Time is money, I might have said, nastily, but of course I didn't.

Catherine too cheered up; she was so relieved not to see Gemma's car like a sentry outside her front door every morning. I was the hero of the hour and allowed to sleep late, as befits a hero: the sleep of the just.

Friday of course loomed large in my calculations now. It might be the beginning of a Brave New World; it might on the other hand be Custer's Last Stand. There was a lot at stake and I ought to be prepared, whether for victory or defeat. I got a hundred pounds out of the bank, in twenties, so as not to make a bulky envelope, addressed it to David and left it prominently on the hall table. I gave Gemma keys and told her I was going away for the weekend. Then I settled down to wait.

The week dragged its feet; then Friday was upon me suddenly, nastily, at an early hour. Even I could not sleep through its implications. I scuttled through my bath and breakfast routine for, who could tell, Gemma might arrive early. I was back in my room, locked in, shored up with coffee, the papers, biscuits, fruit, cheese, wine, the tape recorder, the camera, all that was necessary for a fateful meeting, by eleven o'clock. And just as well: at eleven thirty she arrived.

The compromises that life forces upon us. I would have given . . . well, not anything, but a great deal to be with her in those moments, to share her anticipation, to comfort and encourage her. But I could not do that and be in my bedroom, away for the weekend, at the same time. No wonder the theme of the *doppelgänger* is so popular. Obviously we all long for a dual personality. To be in two places at once: the summit of human ambition.

Looking back now, with your censure at my shoulder, however well you disguise it, I cannot easily describe that day. A lot of it was plainly boring, though it seems insensitive to say so. Gemma arrived and I could only guess at what she was doing. She made coffee. She played records. She certainly spent a great deal of time in the kitchen and the living-room. This is the disadvantage of conspiracy on the grand scale: it

209

does not permit you to engage in trivia simultaneously. I should have liked to be with Gemma, drinking coffee and choosing records, reassuring her. I think I sensed the chance might not come again. Life is not rich with such opportunities.

I am not sure when I began to worry. Let alone when *she* began to worry. One o'clock, a reasonable hour for lunch, came and went. I had no way of knowing if she had brought food to prepare or ready cooked; equally I could not tell what David considered to be 'about lunchtime'. She was in and out of the spare room, turning back the bedspread, brushing her hair, spraying herself with scent; she looked lovely but anxious. Extremely anxious, now that I think about it. I nibbled at my refreshments and got my equipment ready. The time dragged.

About two I began to think in terms of delayed trains and broken-down cars. Of accidents and sudden death. Gemma must have thought so too, for she made two telephone calls. I did not dare pick up the extension but I assumed she was ringing the studio to check and ringing her home to say she would be late. The time crawled by. I longed to go out and comfort her but I had imprisoned myself as surely as if I were chained to the bed. I read a little. I longed for a cigar to calm my nerves but of course dared not risk the smell of smoke. She came back into the spare room and sat on a corner of the bed, rocking to and fro. She did not cry. She picked up a corner of the bedspread, put it between her teeth and bit on it. I wanted to hug her. Then she lay down on the bed, her face turned away from me. After about ten minutes she got up again, smoothed the place she had lain in, and went out of the room.

I waited. It was all I could do. But I did it fearfully. I ate and drank a little, but without enjoyment. Fear began to drip into my soul like water from a faulty tap, slowly at first, and then with gathering momentum. I could not formulate the fear for some time, or rather I could but I dared not, in case I made it come to pass. There was a very precise corner in my mind which I avoided turning for a long time and yet when I finally rounded it, I seemed to have got there abruptly.

David was not coming. It was after three o'clock. He had found something more amusing to do — he had got drunk and

210

passed out — he had been drugged or killed or arrested — was lying dead or injured in a ditch — he was out of reach of the telephone. Or he had simply never intended to come at all, in the first place. Perhaps a hundred pounds was not enough. I had sealed Gemma's fate by being thrifty. Or else he felt that this was the simplest, cruellest and most absolute way of expressing rejection that he could devise, involving no effort on his part and ensuring maximum impact on Gemma.

Now more than ever I longed to break from my prison of a room to share her agony, but there was no way I could do so without exposing the entire deception. What happened next still shames me a little, though I maintain it was human and understandable. Fear is very tiring. Waiting and hoping and finally giving in to despair consumes a lot of energy. I fell asleep.

It was dark when I woke. Darkness in August meant it was quite late. I lay on the bed straining my ears for sounds. But Gemma must have gone home; she could not explain such a protracted absence. I was in a dreadful dilemma. If she should still be there, by some mischance, all would, as they say, be revealed. But she could not be. Surely it was impossible. I longed to believe she had gone, her ordeal over; even more I longed to urinate, and I really preferred to do so in the bathroom: chamber pots are so sordid. This pressing need helped to convince me that Gemma had gone, but trying still to be cautious, I eased my way out of the room with the minimum of sound and crept to the front door. After all, she too might have slept, though her state of anxiety made it unlikely. The entire flat was in darkness; I peered at my watch, but it had stopped. In the hall I scooped up David's envelope (it was an ill wind, etc.) and put it in my pocket, then I opened and slammed the door as if, abandoning my weekend plans, I had just come home. Filled with anticipatory delight at the prospect of relieving myself, I advanced to the bathroom and switched on the light. There was blood everywhere.

Afterwards, when I had time to calm down and think, I did allow myself some small congratulation on not losing my head. The temptation to panic, as I took in the shock of all that sticky red like spilt paint on the white bathroom fittings, was very great. It was so extremely vivid and so copiously distributed: my bathroom looked like a slaughterhouse. Tracing the flow, after I had absorbed the initial shock and realised what it meant, and finding Gemma in the sitting-room nearly made me keel over. But I am proud to say I did not waste time examining or trying to revive her; I picked up the phone instantly and demanded an ambulance. Even while I was doing that, I found myself thinking that this was a nightmare that could not possibly be happening to me.

Waiting for the ambulance was the next worst part. It did not take long but it seemed forever. I did not want to stay in the room with her — and yet I could not leave her alone. It seemed so discourteous. Similarly, I did not want to look at her but I could not look away.

She looked very dead. I felt myself beginning to cry as I watched her; I felt I was keeping vigil beside a corpse. I told myself there was a chance, she was young and strong and healthy. But she felt so cold when I touched her cheek. And there was no question of investigating her wrists: I was not prepared to probe for a pulse amongst all that wet redness.

After being alone with her for a few minutes it occurred to me I would have to ring Christopher. It seemed an intrusion, reminding me that her life belonged to him. Till then I had been alone with my love.

On the way to the hospital, beside her in the ambulance while the experts did what they had been trained to do, I reflected soberly that I had killed her, as surely as if I had aimed a gun at her head or her heart. And yet — and yet who could have expected her to take it all so seriously? Criseyde had not committed suicide, as far as we knew. I had only been trying to let her live more fully — all right, as well as exploiting my own desires, all *right*. Have it your own way. Whatever I say, you will no doubt malign me. But I had truly intended to expand her life as well as enrich my own. She had no right to opt out of the scheme: it was well-intentioned. I had never imagined she could be so dramatic.

212

The ambulance man was distressed by my tears; he patted my shoulder. Perhaps he thought we were lovers. I hoped so.

At the hospital, impelled by a sense of urgency and the savage parting from Gemma, in which everyone around me seemed to consider I was superfluous, I gathered up my flimsy courage and telephoned Christopher. I had not done so before partly out of cowardice, partly because I did not know which hospital the ambulance would take us to. Now I had no excuse left. As I walked down the corridor it seemed odd to me that people with less urgent tasks could pass me casually, as if the world had not just ended.

Christopher took it well. He did not question me. I had been dreading what to say, but in the end it was simple; in fact I had no choice. I told him there had been an accident at my flat; I told him which hospital Gemma and I were in. Then I forced myself to say:

'She cut her wrists.' I had to prepare him. 'I found her when I came in.'

I could hear his shock in the silence, but when he spoke he was very much the doctor, all emotion under control.

'How bad is she?'

I said honestly, 'I don't know.'

He said, 'I'll be there right away.'

Now you might think, once we all knew she was going to be all right, that they would be grateful to me. I hope it has not escaped your notice that if I had not been concealed in my room (for my own purposes, all right, I grant you that) Gemma would have bled to death. My being there saved her life. A superbly ironic justification of my behaviour, in my opinion. Well, Christopher could not know all that, of course, but even with the facts as he saw them, that I had come home unexpectedly to find Gemma in the *process* of bleeding to death . . . even that should have been enough to evoke a little gratitude. Instead, I found myself banned from the hospital: doctors and nurses ranged against me, Christopher using his

213

professional influence, no doubt; they say these people always stick together. I was not allowed in.

I simply could not believe it and went time and time again with flowers and gifts but I was turned away. Finally I came face to face with Christopher and Beatrice outside the building, just getting out of a car: at the sight of me Christopher turned white and Beatrice purple. (Well, you know what I mean: they both changed colour dramatically in opposite directions). In clipped tones like the hero of a wartime morale-raising film about the RAF, Christopher at his most pompous informed me that Gemma had told him 'everything', that he regarded it all as my fault and he had forgiven her on condition she never saw or spoke to me again. I was too outraged to speak: grief and rage and disbelief all chased round inside me. My silence gave him strength: he went on about my being a pernicious influence (his exact words) on Gemma all her life and that statement (perhaps because of its suggestion of associated blame by implication) set Beatrice off. She started to cry, there in the hospital courtyard, uncontrollable tears, as if they had been welling up for centuries, while Christopher and I stood and watched her in helpless amazement.

'You're evil,' she sobbed, pointing at me like a pantomime witch, 'evil,' and tears streamed down her ugly face. 'You're thoroughly evil.'

I found her ugliness more offensive than her words but I could not accuse her of that at this late date, so I said, reasonably enough, that she was not only monotonous but inaccurate. There was an element of evil in all of us. Myself, perhaps I had a more developed gift: an evil streak, you might say. But I am a modest man; I would not claim more than that.

I thought, for a moment, that Christopher was going to hit me. But physical violence was against his code of ethics. Instead he fell back on the respectable violence of words. 'Stay away from Gemma,' he said, for all the world like a Western hero now, 'or I'll kill you.'

I began to laugh at the idea, but Beatrice played her master stroke. Still howling, and indescribably ugly, she took a step towards me and shrieked (oh God how I remember these words): 'Your mind's as deformed as your body.'

I felt myself pale and step back from her. No one in the family ever refers to my appearance: it is an unwritten rule. The specialists did their best, it was not enough, and there is an end of the matter. I have had to learn to live with it, and most people I meet pretend not to notice. But Beatrice, with her bitch-instinct, had struck home. I was dumb with shock. I turned away.

And where should I turn for comfort but to Catherine? But she was elusive, not answering the telephone. Finally, I presented myself at the flat; God knows I had nowhere else to go. She seemed surprised to see me, saying, 'Oh, it's you,' in a tone so neutral as to be positively unwelcoming. She let me in, though, into the tiny cluttered room; her children, both girls, were playing on the floor with bits of material. They looked up incuriously. It was the first time I had seen them. They were dark and pretty like David but with an air of detachment like Catherine, far beyond their years. They looked away and went on playing; I could not charm them.

Catherine sat down in a rocking-chair and resumed stitching some pale suede that looked like a pouch.

'What made you come?' she asked, as if I were acting under some compulsion.

I said, 'You weren't answering the telephone.'

'No. I didn't feel sociable. I've never understood why people feel compelled to answer a phone just because it's ringing. If I don't want to talk I don't pick it up.'

'I'm sorry,' I said humbly. 'I shouldn't have come.'

She looked up at me like one of her children and smiled politely. 'Well, you're here now,' she said.

I began to tell her what had happened; I was inhibited by the presence of the two little girls on the floor, although they did not look up again. They reminded me of Asian children, quiet and self-absorbed, with adult gravity and composure that were both attractive and unnerving.

She said, sensing my inhibition, 'It's all right, they're not listening. Grown-up talk bores them.'

215

I finished telling her about Gemma. She said, 'I shouldn't tell him all that, if I were you. He hates being blamed for anything. It always has to be someone else's fault.'

'But it's entirely *his* fault. She only did it because he didn't turn up. And she'd have died if I hadn't come home early. I saved her life and now her wretched husband won't even let me see her.'

She smiled faintly. 'Yes. It's an unfair world.'

'Don't you even *care*?'

She put down her stitching. 'I don't feel anything. I thought I explained that to you months ago. I simply don't have feelings any more.'

I said, 'What did David *do* to you?' and the younger child said 'Daddy,' without looking up or pausing in her game.

Catherine said, 'Yes, darling,' to the child, and to me: 'Nothing. Why do you think he's so powerful? I did it all myself. I let him hurt me for a while and then I decided to stop.' She paused and added thoughtfully, 'It's an awe-inspiring sight when you take away the magic from someone and watch them crumble. You'd better do that with your niece if you really can't get her back.'

I heard myself saying, 'She was all I had.'

'Yes, I know, it's awful. But you'll get used to it. I was like Gemma once, can you imagine? All that emotion. Oh, come on, cheer up. Let me give you a drink. It's gin for you, isn't it?'

She got up and fetched ice from the kitchen; she poured me an enormous gin and tonic, and half a tumbler of neat whisky for herself. She went to a lot of trouble cutting up lemons for me.

'It's been very interesting this time,' she went on brightly. 'All that stuff about Troilus and Criseyde, and you master-minding everything. Quite a change from all those heart-broken husbands and fathers I usually get, begging me to call him off as if he was a dog I could put on a lead.'

'It's a game, isn't it?' I said. 'You're both playing some kind of game.'

She shrugged. 'It's the way we live. I wouldn't call it a game myself, but you can if you like. Anyway, what were *you* up to?'

I said with dignity, 'I was trying to be creative.'

'Oh yes, of course.' She smiled. 'That makes all the difference. You know, it used to worry me, I thought maybe I'd end up like you, wanting other people to have the feelings I can't have, wanting them to do all the loving and suffering for me. I was afraid it was the next stage. But I don't think it is. I think I can stay numb for ever. I'm like a fly in amber. Or a specimen in a bottle.' She giggled. 'I'm preserved in formaldehyde.'

I said, 'But *he's* doing it all for you, isn't he?'

She frowned. 'Oh no, not you too. Don't you start analysing me. I get enough of that from my doctor. It's very boring, let me tell you. People don't realise how boring it is.'

I said quickly, to make amends, 'Have lunch with me next week.'

'How can I?'

I thought she meant the children. 'Next month then. When they're back at school. To show you've forgiven me.'

She took a large draught of scotch and stared at me, very straight, with a look of surprise.

'But it's over. There's no point in our meeting now it's over.'

Panic. Panic and terror, like the end of the world and nowhere to hide.

'Why not?' Such a normal voice. So calm. Where did I learn to dissemble as well as that?

'Because they were our only link. Surely you see that?'

I shook my head. I was suddenly afraid my composure would slip. I might be going to cry and I did not trust my voice.

'It's always the same,' she said patiently. 'I get to know whoever it is — it completes the circle — and I like intrigue. But once the affair is over . . . what's the point? What would we talk about?'

I cleared my throat and said, 'Ourselves. Each other.'

She shook her head. 'It wouldn't work. You can't have me just because you've lost her. Besides, I'll be too busy. This girl in Birmingham, she's bound to have a husband or a father. Sooner or later I'll be hearing from him. And I don't have that much spare time, not with the children and my doctor and a part-time job.'

217

She looked at me, perfectly serious and pleasant. Everything about her was beige today — her hair, her clothes, and her smooth unlined face with the good bones that would last her a lifetime. My eyes clouded over, blurring what I saw.

'I hate to hurry you,' she said gently, 'but David will be home soon.'

'Daddy,' said the child again.

'Yes, Susie, Daddy's coming home for the weekend.' She smiled at me. 'And he'd hate to find you here. He doesn't like bits of his life overlapping. He really has a thing about it.'

I finished my drink; I needed it badly. I could not believe I would never see her again, yet that was clearly what she was telling me. I could not explain why she had become so important, but it must have been written all over my face that she had.

'Come on,' she said. 'It's not as bad as that. We're non-players, both of us. We'd be no good to each other, we've opted out.'

I followed her blindly into the hall. At the door she paused and said sympathetically, as if I had an illness, 'Did you want to make love to me — is that why you're upset?'

I shook my head.

'If the children weren't here you could have done. I wouldn't mind. Just to say goodbye. It doesn't mean anything.'

I said, 'I only wish I could.'

'If I was a boy?'

'No. It's all over. All of it.'

'I'm sorry,' she said gravely. 'It was obviously important to you.'

I got home to find David systematically smashing up the spare room, as if trying to erase a memory. I could not think what the noise was when I entered the flat, and the shock when I saw him was considerable. He was breaking ornaments, ripping sheets and overturning furniture. When he saw me he said with a kind of snarl like the villain in a bad melodrama, 'Stay away from my wife, you cunt,' and went on destroying things, but in a very methodical way, very much as he had cleaned the flat, as if following a system. The destruction was punctuated with more snarling remarks. 'You've been to the flat, haven't you?' A vase crashed. 'I saw your car.' A lamp overturned. 'You've got a fucking nerve. Well, I'm going to teach you a lesson.' A stool went flying. 'You don't go near my home and my wife, is that clear?'

I feared for the mirror (both the discovery and the expense) so I put myself between him and it and said, 'Gemma cut her wrists for you, you bastard,' more to distract him than anything else. 'She tried to kill herself and I saved her life.' I think he must have known already (perhaps she had contacted him) or else he simply didn't care, because his face didn't change. He tried to push me aside but I stood my ground, thinking of Gemma's wrists and Christopher's revenge and what the mirror had cost, and I said, 'You bastard, if you'd turned up she wouldn't have done it, where the hell *were* you?' and he hit me in the mouth.

It wasn't a hard blow but it shifted my plate uncomfortably and it frightened me. I ran into the bedroom to pick up the phone, but he was after me at once and I only got as far as the first nine. He hit me again and this time he got my glasses: they tugged at my ears as they came off and I heard the scrunch of glass. I shut my eyes tight in case of splinters and hoped they were lodged painfully in his fist, but he hit me again, in the stomach this time, and it hurt very much. I doubled up and I couldn't get my breath. He said, 'God, you're pathetic. You're just a worn-out queer with a limp prick, aren't you? So get out of people's lives.' He struck me a light sharp blow to the chin, almost playful, as if to straighten me up. 'Answer me. You're a closet queen . . . and you can't get it up . . . that's right isn't it?' He was playing with me now, hitting me often but without force, just enough to knock me off balance while he abused and humiliated me. I had seen boxers behave like this in the ring; I knew what to expect.

He was enjoying himself and there was nothing I could do: if I hit him back he might become really angry and kill me. Besides, I had a sense of sacrifice, of expiation. If I suffered a little, it might make up for everything; they might all come back and love each other again and I wouldn't be alone forever.

219

But without my glasses I couldn't see very well and we were all over the room as he went on hitting me and insulting me and I went on moving away. I dodged one blow and that made him angry so he hit me much harder next time and I stumbled. Losing my balance, I reached out blindly, clutching at anything to save myself from falling, and realised too late I had got hold of the tapestry. It gave, and we fell to the floor together.

I shall never understand. There was a moment's total silence while I lay under the tapestry gasping for breath and picturing David looking through the mirror into the other room. In a moment he would begin to kill me. He would beat or kick me to death; there was no way of saving myself. No one would hear if I shouted; these old flats were solidly built and sound-proof. That had been a selling-point when I bought mine. I was so frightened and so sure of imminent death I am ashamed to say I actually wet myself. Terror flooded my entire body and overflowed.

What I heard next I can still hardly believe. Laughter. After a full minute's total silence, he began to laugh. It was an explosion. Exaggerated, theatrical laughter—but genuine. He sounded as if he was releasing the tension of years. He laughed and laughed, while I lay disbelieving my ears.

'Well, you crafty bugger.' He laughed some more. 'You cunning old sod.' More laughter. 'Christ, that explains everything. Oh, for God's sake, get up. Don't lie there cowering. I'm not going to hit you again. You're an old man. Yes, I'm ashamed of myself. What more d'you want me to say?'

But I did not move. I was embarrassed to face him, rumpled and bruised with all dignity gone, my glasses smashed and my teeth askew, and I did not think there was anything we could usefully say to each other. Besides, I felt safer where I lay, under the protective shroud of tapestry.

After a while, when he realised I was not going to get up, he said, 'Oh, all right, have it your own way,' and he flung my keys down; I heard them tinkle as they hit the carpet alongside my ear. He didn't stay to chat or persuade me to come out of hiding, he left; really left, striding along the corridor and slamming the front door behind him. I waited a minutes to recover, playing it safe, and then I emerged like a mole, blinking in the sunlight. I made my way cautiously down the hall, but he was not there, not lurking to spring out, pounce on me or punch me; nor to laugh again and perhaps put his arm round me. I was alone.

Afterwards I could only think it was his vanity that had made him laugh. Like a true actor, he was flattered that I had gone to so much trouble to see him perform.

Gemma wrote:

'Dearest Uncle Alex,

Chris doesn't know I'm writing because I promised I wouldn't, but I have to say a proper goodbye to you. If I keep my promise not to see you or speak to you or write to you ever again, I think it's all right to send you one letter, just to say goodbye.

I am so sorry. *I love you*. I can't make Chris understand and I have to put him first, after what's happened and all the terrible things I've done, but I *know* you did your best for me, the way you saw it, and I let you, so that must have been the way I saw it too. I can't be really sorry it happened. There were awful bits of course but if I had to choose and have none of it or all of it, then I'd have to choose all of it.

I still love David but I know he doesn't love me any more and I also know I'll get over him one day although it seems ages away, like being grown up when you're a child. Chris has been wonderful, so understanding and forgiving. He doesn't know about the abortion — although sometimes I think he does because of the way he looks at me or things he says. He goes on about me making sacrifices for him and him being privileged and funny things like that, and the other day he said would I like us to adopt a baby. But I don't know, it doesn't prove anything. He may just be trying to take my mind off it all. All I told him was I had an affair with someone I met, in your flat, and when it was over I wanted to die.

Of course I know you *were* sort of the bad influence he says you were, but then I always knew that, right from way back when you used to keep me up late when Mummy was out. That's what made you fun and made me specially want to see you. Everyone doesn't have a wicked uncle and it *did* annoy Mummy so. I don't know how I'm going to manage without you but I'll have to. It makes me cry just to think about it but I don't want to write you a crying sort of letter. I seem to have done a lot of crying lately but I expect I'll stop soon, Chris says it's my hormones. Does that mean he knows about the abortion?

I don't know how to stop this letter. How can I say thank you to you for making me — helping me — what's the word? — have an affair with someone who always loved his wife more than me, and have an abortion when I really wanted a baby? And yet that *is* what I'm saying. I knew what you were doing and I knew your motives weren't *all* good but whose are? I don't feel Chris understands at all but I can't talk to him about it he feels so injured and of course he's right. I *have* injured him.

I am so upset I can't see you again. It's like being walled up alive. Chris is so sure you'd get me into bad ways again. Right now I feel too exhausted to think of it but I know what he means. At the same time it's rather unflattering to think that he doesn't imagine I could get into bad ways without help.

I feel very old. As if I'd been on a long journey or in prison or studying a foreign language. I feel I've learnt something because of you and now I can't use it, the rest of my life will just be marking time. But I can't do anything else because of the children, and Chris being so marvellous. I've got to keep my promise.

Please Uncle Alex remember I love you however wicked you are, I can't bear to think of you lonely and miserable without me, the way I'm going to be without you. It's something about childhood, isn't it, that you and I remember, I don't know what but they didn't share it and that's why they're jealous.

David's wife wrote me an awfully nice letter. I was so surprised. I can see why he loves her so much. She's lucky. If only she'd love him back and then he might be happy again.

Please take care of yourself and *remember me* even though